The Half-Life of Everything

Deborah Carol Gang

bancroft press

Interior design: Tracy Copes
Cover: J.L. Herchenroeder
Author Photo: Mary Whalen

978-1-61088-233-0 (cloth)
978-1-61088-234-7 (paper)
978-1-61088-235-4 (kindle)
978-1-61088-236-1 (ebook)
978-1-61088-237-8 (audiobook)

Published by Bancroft Press "Books that Enlighten"
410-358-0658
P.O. Box 65360, Baltimore, MD 21209 410-764-1967 (fax)
www.bancroftpress.com

Printed in the United States of America

For families everywhere that have been forgotten by someone they love

PART I
BEFORE

Kate had read or heard somewhere that normal forgetfulness is misplacing your keys, while Alzheimer's is not knowing what keys are used for. Surely, she thought, there was a middle ground between the two—like when you locate your keys but, for the briefest part of a second, you think, *Are these really mine? They look familiar … and yet they don't.*

Like anyone who was fifty-one, Kate worried about her memory, though her true specialty was dreading disease. In temperament, she wasn't particularly neurotic, but breast cancer had a hold on her. The disease was so common she had begun to think of it as a normal stage of life, like acne or menopause. And for as long as she could remember, she had paid attention to the risk factors. She had barely adjusted to the trauma of getting her period too young when she learned it was associated with breast cancer. Jewish grandparents from Eastern Europe—also very bad. Delayed childbearing—sensible but also very bad.

"Moist ear wax," she told her disbelieving husband. "I don't know if it's on the current list, but it was mentioned once when I was a teenager."

"And you remembered it," David said.

"Hey, as we used to say: 'It's not paranoia if they really are after you.'"

He didn't dismiss her fears. He too assumed himself to be one swollen gland away from death, though he could largely avoid the topic of his own diagnosis. But the thought of losing Kate brought on a feeling of helpless dread. They had been married for longer than their friends, but when people teased them for being high school sweethearts, David would remind them that he and Kate actually met in their mid-twenties.

In their first half-hour together, they learned that they had graduated the same year from the same urban high school, but professed to have no memory of each other. Every subsequent attempt to find an association from then drew a blank. She thought she remembered him having a small part in "Bye Bye Birdie," but no, he wasn't in it. He described a scandalously short prom dress, but she said, "Not me. I wore a borrowed dress in an odd shade of yellow that had looked good on my cousin."

When they told their story to new acquaintances who had attended smaller high schools, they would embellish the routine. "I remember when you left the lox and bagels in your locker just before we had two snow days," she would insist.

"Never happened," he'd say, "but *I* remember the Farrah Fawcett haircut you wore for exactly one day."

In their early years, he sometimes said that he had been in love with her for three years, yet she never noticed him. She would dismiss the idea. Still, sometimes it surprised him that she didn't have an old image of him filed away in her mind. She had a great memory, cluttered though it was by lists of birthdays, books to buy when available in paperback, and movies missed and now to be rented.

Computers didn't relieve her of many of those tasks, but Kate liked how easy it was now to send articles, photos, and links. "We are all linked now," she'd say, "for better or worse." For short-term needs, though, she was loyal to Post-it notes in a range of sizes, shapes, colors, and degrees of stickiness.

Occasionally, he'd try an actual event on her, as he did late on the evening of their twenty-fourth wedding anniversary. They were celebrating quietly at home, knowing that next year Kate's parents would plan something loving but excessive. "You *must* have seen me at the senior talent show," he said. "You know, my Bob Dylan act. I may have been invisible before then and after then, but surely I wasn't that day."

"Oh, I was probably in the grove selling pot to sophomores," Kate said. A well-behaved student despite the anarchy of the times, she had created an alternate persona for his amusement. He laughed and pulled her to him.

"Yes, I can see how you would have been too busy with your crimes to notice me. Perhaps you can make it up to me one more time."

Later that night, after David was asleep, Kate went downstairs. She had a nagging thought that she wasn't ready for the morning. She looked for her list of things to do but didn't see it. Now she'd have to reconstruct everything before she'd be able to sleep. She found a stray Post-it note, but what could "Find used labels and Book #3" possibly mean? She started to rewrite the list, wondering if earlier she had organized the tasks only in her mind and not on paper. She would probably forget some item and could picture David teasing her. "So the Memory Queen is human after all." Then she noticed her car keys—not in their proper spot, but still reassuringly familiar.

CHAPTER ONE

In the beginning, he visited her every day, month after month and, if Dylan and Jack were home from school, he'd take one to visit on Saturday and the other on Sunday. It seemed to embarrass the boys less if they went separately. Smaller numbers of visitors were easier on Kate, too, because she still tried to feign recognition. If a larger group came for a birthday or holiday, she'd become anxious, as if she knew that her genial but generic welcome would be found out, as of course it was. David hated to think that somewhere in her mind lurked an awareness of what had happened to her—that, with her remaining pride or competitive nature, she could still observe herself and suffer at the sight.

She was now in her second year of living at the facility after being cared for at home for three years. David always thought of Kate as having "left" him and the boys, although not in the literal sense of the word." On this particular Wednesday, he tried to take stock: Early onset, quickly deteriorating—not a good thing. Maintaining most of her good nature—a very good thing. It was her still-pleasant demeanor that had made him believe they could manage her at home indefinitely. It wasn't a likely outcome, but it wasn't unheard of either.

He and the boys came up with systems and schedules and

sought out advice. When the occupational therapist suggested Post-it notes as a possible improvement, they burst out laughing. The problem wasn't a lack of memory aids, and the problem wasn't Kate's temperament. The problem was that Kate had always liked to walk, especially in pleasant weather. If it was mild, she would plan picnics, discover unlikely restaurants that served outdoors on three rickety tables, or think up errands. *If we take the longer route to buy the Times, then we can get bananas and milk too.* No hiker, Kate preferred destination walking: ice cream cones, window-shopping, used bookstores.

David would tease her. "You are the world's most expensive walking partner. I have to take fifty dollars to even leave the house with you."

"I was meant to live in New York."

"Fifty dollars might not last a block there."

As her memory left her, she'd slip away to find gardens or snowmen. From what David and the boys had heard from neighbors in surrounding blocks, she'd engage anyone in pleasant conversation, sounding coherent enough that the stranger wouldn't realize she had no idea where she was. David desperately wanted her at home and had tried to stay ahead of her with deadbolts, then door alarms, and finally the graduate student twins, Theresa and Tracy.

Kate seemed to like them, though no one was sure if she knew there were two of them. David and the boys had their own problems sorting out identical twins who had cruelly similar names and worked ever-changing shifts. The twins covered Monday through Friday, alternating their hours so they could get to their college classes.

Tracy (or maybe both of them) would push him. ""Mr. D, you should call us more for weekends. Don't pay us. We'll just come study and you can go do something." He would agree to call but almost never did. On weekends, it felt like hiring a baby sitter, or being unfaithful.

Dylan was away at college by then, so Jack and David and whichever twin was on duty would do their best, but every few weeks they'd find that Kate had disappeared. Or worse, they'd get a call before they noticed she was missing. One moment he was watching her nap in their room, and the next she was at Starbucks, and not the close one—the one you walk through traffic to get to.

David guessed that some of their friends thought stepping in front of a car would be a kind and even natural way for things to end. Maybe he was the one who thought it. He wondered if he would then feel free and relieved. Sometimes he'd glimpse her absence for a moment, but right behind the freedom was a sadness so bleak, so lonely and frightening, that he could never see past it.

Then the time came to look for an "assisted-living" place for Kate. He liked the name—no jargon, truthful. He had expected to be caught between a barrage of "how can you do this to her?" and "we thought you should have done it long ago." But it turned out that no one outside the family really cared. People have a sadness quotient. They had tired of the drama and the pain and she didn't really exist for them anymore.

Kate had one friend, their neighbor Martha, who stayed in contact, helped her buy new clothes and visited regularly. Kate and Martha would look through old photo albums together or Martha would make cookies and give Kate easy assignments so she could help. Kate seemed to enjoy it and to feel safe around her. David and Martha rarely talked or spent time with one another. They had barely mastered the skill of not crying around the other. He was worried that he was seen, not by Martha but by others, as a pathetic figure, a man determinedly married to a woman who wasn't there—like the Japanese boys and their pillow girlfriends.

———————

The incident they couldn't ignore happened when Theresa and Jack were home and each thought the other was with Kate. David was the one to track her down after frantic multiple phone calls from both Jack and Theresa. He found her farther from home than any previous ramble had taken her, sitting on a bench in a tiny triangular park at the intersection of three streets. Shivering a little, she said, "You're so late, David. I thought you had forgotten me."

That night Jack came to him. "I know you've been waiting for me to admit that we can't take care of her anymore. We don't even know if Dylan's coming back after college, and I'm supposed to leave in the fall. Dylan's kind of useless anyway—he mostly goes to his room and cries."

It was true that Dylan, no longer hardened against the grief, would cry during his visits home. And crying upset Kate. She'd try to comfort whoever was sad, and if it didn't work, she'd cry too—or get agitated. To avoid such outward displays of sadness, David and the boys used the Lamaze breathing she had taught them for undergoing dental work, or they would look towards the ceiling—a suggestion one of them heard on NPR. If things were really tense, one of them would say, "Well, you can't have everything." No one remembered who had said this first, but the mildly dark humor proved to be a reliable weapon.

"Dad, please let's wait until I leave for college. It's less than four months. Sports will be over soon, and I'll help more."

David stared at this boy, who until recently wouldn't shut the microwave door after removing food, who had to be reminded ten times to write a thank-you note, and who left cereal bowls with aging milk for others to find and dispose of. Jack had been adult-sized for several years—he hardly recalled Jack even going through puberty. The kid had just morphed without awkwardness. He and his brother had Kate's complexion, the kind that tanned easily and made you expect brown, not blond hair with pleasing stripes of darker blond. They used to tease David that he was a different species, the only one with dark hair and curls that emerged if he skipped a single haircut. He had skipped many haircuts at Kate's request.

David had once been the tall one, but both boys surpassed him by early high school. For the last year or so, Dylan would hide behind Jack, copying his stance but obscured by Jack's thicker silhouette. They enjoyed scaring David and he always seemed to fall for it. He didn't mind. He would rather see them silly than unhappy. Now, looking at Jack, who was studiously not crying, he realized that the narcissism of adolescence was over.

"I know Mom is gone," Jack said. "She's just someone who looks like Mom. But I *like* having someone around who looks like Mom. It helps a little. I mean—" He found a tattered Kleenex in his pocket and blew his nose. "Since we can't have everything." He gave a half smile. "I don't want her to leave before I do. I'll take her driving and on more walks. We'll buy stuff for the dorm. I'll just have to be around more."

And he was, but he was leaving for college in late August, and that was non-negotiable as far as David was concerned.

━━━>◦◦◦◦<━━━

Eventually, August came and the four of them found themselves parked in the surprisingly small lot of the Caring Glenn Residence. The day after July Fourth, they had begun working their way down a list from the local Alzheimer's group. This was only their fourth place (unlike the names of plumbers, those of assisted-living facilities clustered towards the middle and end of the alphabet).

Dylan hadn't seemed surprised or angry when, shortly after he arrived home for the three weeks between graduation and a summer internship, his dad told him that the time had arrived. He showed no sign of claiming, as absent relatives sometimes do, that things could be managed better.

Perhaps he saw David's exhaustion and watched as his little brother managed to look simultaneously eighteen and thirty. Perhaps, like David, he was determined that Jack go away to college as he had.

Only the twins had pleaded for more time. "We can keep this going until we graduate," one of them said. "My boyfriend will cover if we need him to." But David just smiled, puzzled that they seemed to genuinely love Kate when they had never really met her.

He and the boys had debated whether they should bring Kate along for the tours. David remembered similar discussions about whether to bring their young sons to a concert or a funeral. They often guessed wrong and found themselves saying, "The kids would have loved this" or "I'll take him to the car." They didn't want to frighten her, but they thought she'd make a good impression, and they also hoped to detect signs of a preference, though so far she just seemed uniformly puzzled. Yesterday, when they toured a small garden belonging to a facility none of them liked,

Kate praised the garden and surprised them by saying, "Did they want our advice on something?" But that was all she said.

"I don't like this—the parking lot. It means hardly any relatives visit," Dylan now complained as they looked around the very small lot and saw that the employee area was the only one with cars. Despite the limited parking, the building itself turned out to be large and expensive-looking. They entered through an over-perfumed and over-decorated lobby that led to activity rooms with fabric flower arrangements on every surface and homilies hung in tiers of two or three. He and the boys studied them while their guide left to take a call.

One said "Every Ending Leads to a New Beginning," seemingly more cruel than wise. Another read "Live Out Loud," which the boys decided was bad advice. They were puzzling over "Life Itself Is the Proper Binge" when Kate spoke up to say maybe they shouldn't worry about it. Jack then pointed to one on the far wall, "Life is Short, Fill it Up," and said, "That's something you would say, Mom," and she said, "Why, thank you." David reminded himself she could sometimes be less vacant than she seemed, though only for long enough to hurt.

"I envy these families," Jack said quietly. "Their people probably didn't get sick until seventy or eighty." Dylan put his arm on Jack's shoulder. David reminded himself that when Dylan graduated from high school, his mom had been a vague but credible presence. For Jack, she was a stranger looking at the wrong kid.

They finished their tour and were standing at the main entrance where David was preparing to thank the guide and politely convey their lack of interest. Kate interrupted his first sentence to say, "Is everybody warm enough?"

"We're good, Mom," Dylan said.

"Because it may get cold."

Kate had always worried about others being cold—she couldn't believe the boys' youthful furnaces could rev so efficiently.

David stood closer to her. "Everything is fine. There's nothing to worry about."

"Excellent," she said, sounding completely reassured, and the tour guide nodded approvingly.

CHAPTER TWO

Mrs. Nowicki touched Kate's arm lightly and said, "It's your husband, David. He's here to see you."

David thought he saw a slight moment of recognition, but it was so brief he could have imagined it, and now Kate wore her empty, polite expression as she said, "It's good to meet you." He wanted to bolt. Instead, he sat near her and they listened to music while he showed her photos from their front garden, which he had kept up for the sake of the neighbors, leaving the back on its own except for the mowing.

Each year it became a little less like the house that she'd lived in. Nothing was actually torn or broken, just worn past the point where she normally would have brought home samples of carpet, paint, or fabric and then steered him to her choice. There were no fresh flowers in the house now.

"Kate, do you want to go outside for a while?" he asked, and she blinked a few times, then stood and followed him through the back porch to the large lawn, where they found an empty bench and watched two of the house cats play. After a while, she stood and walked towards the wooden fence at the back of the lawn, stopping at the first row of viburnum to finger the leaves. She looked with unusual concentration at the man-made pond just beyond the fence.

"We can't go to the water now, but I'll take you this Saturday through the park entrance," David offered as he walked towards her. She appraised him, which moved him—it was so much like when he would ask her to watch hockey with him and she'd say, "I believe I'll clean grout instead." Odd, how opposition carried a certain charm for him now.

He guided her back to the bench and they sat for what seemed like a very long time, though he wouldn't let himself look at his watch. Finally, he walked her back to her room. As he turned to shut the door behind them, she did too and they bumped hard against each other. She drew him to her and kissed him. Her tongue parted his teeth briefly, but then she stepped back. "I don't want my husband to see us."

"Katie, Katie," he whispered, and then in a louder voice, "I understand. I'll leave."

Though he didn't. He took a chair and opened an old *Sports Illustrated*, though he wouldn't remember any of it when he later tried to talk sports. Kate took a seat too and seemed to forget he was there—or at least didn't seem to mind—and after a few minutes, an aide arrived. He considered this aide to be Kate's favorite, though he had nothing to base it on except that he liked how she spoke to Kate. All of the aides seemed kind and professional, but Tyiesha had a way of working with Kate while seeming oblivious to her decay.

"I'll help her get ready for bed unless you want to, Mr. Sanders." Young people seemed incapable of calling him by his first name. Couldn't she see he was young too?

He pointed to his briefcase and said, "I need to tackle the insurance. I'll be in one of the visitor rooms."

She steered Kate towards the bathroom. "Sounds like I've definitely got the better job tonight. Good luck."

"Thanks," he said. He stood and surveyed the small alien room. Leaving without her was always a mixture of loneliness and relief. He walked down the hall towards one of the small rooms, part-parlor, part-office, where visitors could take a break, meet with staff, or do paperwork at the half-size desk. He passed Mrs. Nowicki, who stopped for a moment as he waved his briefcase at her.

"Oh, good, David. I didn't want to ask how it was going, but I see you're on it."

"Yes, a double Scotch, please." Her mouth twitched a little as they parted, and he gave himself extra points for getting the sweet but serious woman to laugh.

He laid out his paperwork that now had a new pile labeled "dispute." After paying efficiently for almost two years, the insurance company for the good policy had decided that his skimpy, almost-nothing policy, like something advertised on TV by a badly faded movie star, might be primary after all. Who would think that the words "primary," "secondary," and "recalculate" could cause such dread and fear and problems? Before this, his worries had been about car accidents, illness, and money, even though it had been years since he and Kate were poor.

There was a list of other items to fret about in descending order, but he kept them pretty well at bay. Still, here he was: illness and money—and, always, car accidents. And now, *recalculations*. He sorted his piles and looked for the log. He had followed Martha's warning to keep a record of every phone call, email, and contact with an insurance company or any other players. "You'll think you won't need it because the first couple of people you talk to will make you believe it's easily fixed. They'll be lying. Keep that in mind—almost everyone you talk with is either lying or mistaken." She had managed the medical bills for her parents' final years as well as for her husband's heart surgery, an operation that was a success, though the billing mistakes almost killed *her*.

He couldn't find his log or the to-do list he'd attached to it. He sorted through files and loose papers a second time; without them, there was no way he could reconstruct all of his work. He knew he had become intolerant of the sensation of losing things, and he felt like a young child overwhelmed by unfairness. The log wasn't there, nor the bills he'd been working on, and he remembered nothing of the contents. *Fuck this*, he thought. He swept his arm across the papers just as a voice behind him said, "Hello, I'm Jane, one of the social workers."

He turned to see a woman in her late forties—or maybe a young fifty—assessing the papers on the desk. "I'm David Sanders," he said. "I haven't seen you here before."

"I've consulted with the L for two or three months, but very part-time and not usually at night."

She used the same abbreviation he and the boys had come up with for the Loon Lake Ladies Retirement Home. "Mom would have loved the name," Dylan had decided. "She'd say, 'My brain has retired. I must join it.'" They all liked doing Kate impersonations.

Jane wrinkled her forehead. "Your name is so familiar to me. I've heard of you from outside of here."

"I teach in the history department at the university."

She shook her head slightly, as if that wasn't it.

"And what do you do, Jane, besides walking the halls listening for the sounds of a relative's meltdown?"

"For starters, I give out a lot of Kleenex. And I help people in despair over their paperwork. Yours looks worse than usual. Did you throw it in the air or just shuffle it?"

"Kind of both. Just so you know, I'm usually more cheerful

than this."

"No one expects you to be cheerful."

"Are you sure? I feel like Kate and I are on perpetual probation."

"If Kate deteriorates and can't be managed here—and there are no signs of that—it has nothing to do with how you act. You're not graded. And she's not exactly graded—either we can take care of her safely, or we can't."

He thought of figure-skating pairs and how a healthy marriage is like that, minus the grace and the horrible costumes. Such mutual dependence—your scores might be high or low, but you were getting the same score. Not for him and Kate. Apparently they weren't in the pairs' event anymore.

"I can help you sort through the insurance stuff," Jane said. "The business office can only go so far trying to untangle things."

He sighed. "You're willing to look at this mess?"

"I like the challenge. I don't get mad or panicked like relatives do. Well, sometimes I do. Being human and all."

"I can see why you'd want to establish that before agreeing to take this on."

She smiled. "That's for another day. You'll have to sort out these piles first. Show me everything in order and then I'll start." She gave him her card. "I'll leave you to it," and left the room in her quiet, sensible shoes.

David let himself watch her walk the first hall length until she turned a corner, then he worked a while longer, putting things in their proper folders. He found the log, which was not hiding or missing after all, and he felt cheerful—or maybe something more than cheerful. It was an unfamiliar feeling.

CHAPTER THREE

David had two remaining good friends. Several others had drifted—whether it was when he became chair of the department or when Kate got ill, he wasn't sure. The timing had been so close. One who remained, Tucker, was an associate history professor who had liked being in the orbit of David's family life. "Soon I'll be too old to have kids without looking ridiculous, so I may have to appropriate yours," he had said more than once. They still got along well at work, but Tucker, recently and traumatically divorced, didn't want to be around the sad person that David was outside of the university borders. They'd begun to confine their time to work, just after work, and the occasional movie where little was expected of them.

David loved his job. He knew he was lucky to have it and, early into Kate's illness, understood he had to keep himself together at school. He was careful not to be distracted or visibly miserable, but he couldn't keep that up outside of work hours. His other friend, Ian, didn't mind morose.

"It's not catching, what you have," he said when David commented on Ian's imperviousness to his moods. "And it must be exhausting for you—all those hours on the job making sure no one pities you. Well, I pity you plenty, so don't bother being fake with me. Besides, you're still funny. You're a dark, pathetic, funny bastard, and my brothers are four thousand miles away, so you'll have to do."

Ian ran the university's international programs and had emigrated from northern England for the job. Stocky, with the ruddy skin and imperfect un-American teeth that could give away his nationality even before the working class remnants of his accent did, Ian was so happy to have a tenure-track job, and now tenure, that he never complained—or at least not about anything personal or job related—as if he feared it could all be taken from him on grounds of ingratitude. And he never complained about the weather. "The lot of you are spoiled," he'd say. His accent strengthened with each beer.

So Ian was now the only person David confided in. Others changed the subject with practiced speed, but with Ian, he could give his brief but terrible update and Ian would listen and then say "That is so fucked," and no matter how long before they next met, he would remember everything David had said.

They never parted with anything more emotional than "later, man." Neither initiated awkward hugs or bumps. Once last year, David had cried in the privacy of a rear restaurant booth, Ian his only witness. Ian waited and then said, "I don't see how it is you don't do that all day long. Tough as titanium you are—nice guy but tough as titanium."

Once, noticing a waitress flirt with David, Ian said, "You must get horny. I mean, Christ, you had a wife who basically never turned you down." David was pretty sure he had never said such a thing—it was an exaggeration—but maybe Ian had just picked up on what he hadn't said.

"Listen, the next time Daphne goes to England, let's you and me go to Vegas." Ian's wife returned home three or four times a year, about three trips to every one that Ian could make. Ian missed her, but they had made a deal when he took the job. He never strayed, at least as far as David knew. "I like the reunions when she comes home," Ian said once, mildly.

"Vegas? You call it Vegas?"

"We can see the Crazy Horse show. It's classy, they say. They're real ballet dancers, naked, in toe shoes and everything. And then afterwards, you can call one of those numbers you see everywhere and have a date. No one will get arrested. I won't be calling anyone, of course. I'll be in my room wanking off."

"You know I'm not doing any of that."

"But you could."

"You've done it? *Dated?*"

"I've done everything." Ian had grown up poor and tough. He added, quietly, "I'm just saying, there's everything to play for."

———

As he drove to the L, David's attention was flagged by the words "baby boomers" and he turned the radio up. He was always interested in what his cohort was up to, even if the baby part sounded sillier and sillier as they either aged or died. He listened to a scientist say that people born between 1959 and 1969 can expect to live until the age of—pause—70. Seventy! Shit, you mean he only has a dozen or so more years to live? David knew that like most of the *babies*, he planned to die at 92, still fit. Lonely though he was, he didn't want life to end. Anyone who knew even a little history knew that despite his bad luck with Kate, he was still an extraordinarily lucky guy.

The topic of the radio show turned out to be the paltry retirement savings his age group had managed to put aside. Not him. He sometimes thought he'd done nothing *but* save for retirement.

He turned off the radio and parked. *Give me a show about married widowers,* he lectured the silent radio, *and then I'll listen.*

He signed in and found an empty office. It was a Friday, not his normal day, but he decided to see Kate afterwards anyway. Kate wouldn't know it was an extra visit, but he couldn't picture being here and not spending time with her. Or he could picture it, but he couldn't do it. He had developed a sort of tic of imagining himself being watched when he was at the facility, or when he was anywhere except work and home, as if he were on a reality show being judged for his skill and style as the husband of a sick wife.

He was fishing files from his briefcase when Jane came in saying, "Don't throw them out! I beg of you!"

They both laughed and he didn't feel embarrassed.

"You'll like my records," he said. "I got out Kate's arsenal of Post-its and highlighters."

"She was the organized one?"

He nodded. "I didn't even know what an Explanation of Benefits was until this happened. She handled the insurance and the tax returns. She was good at math—everything except time zones. She always knew how many hours difference but did the arithmetic wrong."

"Did she work? Outside the home, I mean."

"When we met, she was an accountant. I was in grad school. Then we moved here for my job and she joined a big-deal accounting firm. But after she had the first baby, she lost interest in accounting."

"She didn't work after that?"

"She went back to school. She is—was—a nurse-midwife. Turned out that was her real calling."

Jane glanced down before meeting his eyes again. "It must have been horrible for her when she had to stop working."

"Yes," was all he said, and when the pause felt too long, he added, "Horrible is the right word."

"She sounds gifted—and except for setting watches—very efficient and capable."

"That wasn't who she was, though. It was a means to an end—she'd say that all the organizing was just so we could get to the fun part of living. I can hear her now: 'We can't enjoy life if our kids don't learn to spell, or we miss the T-Ball sign-up, or someone has a toothache because they don't floss. Come on, boys, let's get those dishes done so we can get to the fun part!' Sometimes, she'd—" David stopped abruptly and looked at the ceiling.

"David."

"I need a glass of water."

Jane brought him water, judging skillfully, he noticed, how much time he needed to collect himself.

Then she asked, "How is it that you have not one but two long-term care policies? Do you have any idea how unusually prepared that is?"

"When Kate turned forty-nine, not even fifty, mind you, her mom and dad gave us each long-term care policies. They said they'd pay for five years and after that, split it with us."

"Wow, that's generous."

"I know. At the time it just seemed nutty, money down the drain. I tried to argue with them. I had a little teaser policy through work, an almost worthless thing, and I had actually looked into the idea of getting better policies, but it was so expensive and I just didn't see us as such pessimistic gamblers."

"What did Kate think?"

"You know, I had forgotten about this part, but later that night on her birthday, I tried to get her to laugh with me about this truly bizarre gift and to talk about how we could get them to change their minds. She acted like she agreed with me, but I could tell she didn't." He added something he had never thought of before. "I wonder if she knew something already."

They sat quietly for a moment. Finally, Jane said, "This is going to be solvable, but it may take a while. One of these companies is obviously wrong about who has to pay first, and the fees are high enough that they both have to pay, so I don't know why they're acting like eight year olds." She shrugged. "I'm going to offer you a few books to read. If you haven't seen them before, you're welcome to borrow them, and hey, they're *not* about insurance."

He laughed a little and thanked her, then signed a paper allowing her to talk to the warring companies as well as his HR department. He watched her make her first call, eventually leaving a message.

"I see you are human," he said. "You get stuck in voice mail too."

"Flesh, bones, and a beating heart. The whole package."

Jane turned aside to tidy up the desk and he took the chance to study her. At the sound of her vibrating cell, she took a complicated call about rescheduling a meeting involving many extremely busy people. He closed his eyes and tried to figure out why she seemed so familiar to him. She was as dark as Kate was fair, though they were about the same (average) height, and both were still slim. Kate looked like a young woman from the back and, in crowded settings, he used to catch himself feeling guilty for admiring a *girl*—he used the word in his mind only—who proved to be his wife when she turned around. He wondered again how old Jane was. He suspected she had the olive skin that Kate had once pointed out to him. "Mediterranean women's faces don't age," she'd said wistfully.

As Jane talked softly, he realized that it was her voice that got him. It had been years since he had heard Kate's normal cadence, but here it was, the slightly fast pace, not because she was in a hurry but, in case you were, the slenderest of an East Coast accent now layered with Midwest, and slightly formal vocabulary. He listened to Jane patiently offering new dates and times and didn't open his eyes until she ended her call.

He cut off her apology with effusive thanks for her help. They made plans to talk in a week and then he left, first stopping by Kate's room, where she was napping. He watched her for a moment. The blond prettiness that often faded so early had stay-ing power in her case. Her skin was sturdy for a blond. Of course, now that she was ill, she did fade to something close to plain. Beauty depends so much on alertness. She was sweating lightly from the sun, which was striping the bed through the half-open blinds. He shut the shades quietly, then left for home.

CHAPTER FOUR

The next time he went to see Kate, he went straight from work without taking a walk first because he didn't want to use up the daylight. When he found her in the library, he took her hand and said, "Let's go out back for a while. It's plenty warm." She didn't speak and braced herself in her chair, an unpredictable resistance that had appeared recently. He sat with her for a few minutes. *Christ, I've been inside all day on a perfect day and I do not want to sit in here.* He waved in the direction of the closed circuit camera and mouthed "outside," kissed the top of Kate's head, and went out back to one of the benches they liked. "They" liked. He didn't know what Kate liked anymore.

It was a bench *he* liked, yet his sensibility about benches came from Kate, who would point out what made a bench welcoming, which materials felt nice to the touch, how benches in a corner or at an angle felt more inviting. When the kids were little, the four of them could make an adventure out of a walk to one of Kate's favorite benches. Kids are happy with so little. He positioned the paper he'd brought, a day-old *Times* that he was determined to get through, but then put it down after the first article, preferring to watch the birds torment the squirrels.

Soon, the cats would wander by to be harassed by the squirrels, plot lines not unlike the article he had finished. A shadow fell over him. "Hi, David, I thought I recognized the back of your head."

He jumped up to greet Jane just as she sat down. They both started to move and he said, "Stop. I will slowly sit down and stay there." They laughed and settled in. Jane was wearing a not very sensible skirt, a "going-out skirt" as Kate would say, meaning not for school conferences or jury duty. Instead of her usual blazer, she was wearing a sweater that wrapped and tied and maybe dipped lower than she realized. He imagined she had a date after work with a husband or someone newer—the jewelry on her left hand was ambiguous. He had a thought of envy, a now common emotion for him that he was skillful at setting aside. It wasn't anyone else's fault. She arched her back slightly to pull her cell out of her pocket, glance at it, and put it away. He looked and then looked away.

"I'm making progress on the insurance situation," Jane said, "despite the fact that yesterday one clerk said the problem was that Kate had moved to another facility."

David laughed. "Well, that sounds like progress, all right."

"Oh, if I get an idiot, I just thank them and hang up and call back. You never get the same person twice. The next person straightened that part out. You can be sure your wife still resides here. "

"Thank you," David quietly said, thinking how strange his life had become that someone taking care of him, just a little, could almost make him cry.

Jane continued, "I don't know if it helps you to know that this is one of my favorite assisted-living centers. I know a lot of that is about money—that it's so well endowed and doesn't have to be fully self-supporting, at least not for the building and the grounds and all that. You're lucky."

"Yes, I'm very lucky."

She turned to him and said, "I'm sorry. That was so stupid. I don't usually say dense things like that."

"It's okay. I am definitely grateful. And there is some luck twisted inside that. Please, let's talk about something else. Do you know how to talk about movies?"

She did, though she was one of those people who wait and watch movies at home, so first they discussed the virtues of Netflix versus Redbox versus On Demand, and now streaming (which he didn't understand at all and understood no better after her explanation), while he put in his plug for seeing movies in big theaters. She made him concede that sitting next to a two-pound box of popcorn is not a good smell. And people talk too much. They came up with enough titles they had both seen to keep things going for a while.

He found he missed his sons more than he missed Kate. The memory of Kate's fast, smart mind was too faded, but the boys would enjoy this. They talked until sunset, though not only about movies. "Tell me more about your work. Tell me about someone you helped today," he suggested.

She told him in a general way, of course, about the man who thought his wife's dementia was willful—a punishment for undisclosed things he had done which hurt her.

"And how do you help him?"

"I don't argue with him. I say, 'You wish you could go back and change things,' and then he cries. We do that every week. He says it's the only peace he has."

They let a silence sit between them and then Jane said, "Teach me some history." He suggested she pick an era. "All of the above," she said, seriously. "None of it ever took in school." He thought how odd to meet another smart woman who, like

Kate, had only the vaguest sense of the past.

"Try World War I," she suggested. "It still seems like a silly reason for a war."

"All wars are silly," he countered and then began to lay out the background, which nearly everyone seemed to have missed in high school.

She listened carefully and, when he found a good stopping place for the first installment, she said, "Why do you like history so much? I know it's endlessly interesting, but why did you choose it?"

"The usual reason—I had a phenomenal teacher in tenth grade—but also because it's over. You're not waiting for the other shoe to drop like you are in life. And, theoretically you can learn from it, although almost no one ever does."

She smiled at that and said, "Maybe too few people even remember what happened. Like Watergate—I know it was a huge event, but I don't really understand it."

"You realize that you *lived* through Watergate, right?"

"Be nice. I was like ten when Nixon resigned."

He was well practiced at being kind about people's ignorance—it was the only way to teach. He wasn't sure if Kate would have known anything about the Korean War if not for M*A*S*H, but he had always answered her questions without betraying his amazement.

Jane looked at her watch. "I need to sprint to my next meeting, but I'll remember what you've told me—unlike high school. I'm really a much better listener now." She stood and walked backwards a few steps before saying, "We can cover Watergate next time."

Dylan pulled up in front of Jack's off-campus house. It was a dump, the kind you could enjoy if you were sure you'd never live that way again. As he climbed the stairs, Dylan mentally counted four couches, plus one standing on its side. Jack came through the front door fast and they almost slammed into each other, then turned it into one of those body bumps that pass for hugs. Anyone would recognize them as brothers, with Jack slightly broader and slightly taller, with hair a shade more blond. Two guys leaving the house looked at Dylan and jumped a little when they saw Jack just off to the side. One of them said, "I'm seeing double," and they all laughed.

"What do you think, Dylan? A little different from the freshman dorm?"

"Definitely. You gotta live this way once." He peered past the screen door into the living room with yet more derelict couches and three TVs of various sizes, all huge. They went inside and sat, moving pizza boxes and game controllers aside.

"You always had those grownup apartments with one roommate—or no roommates. What was that about?"

"With what was going on with Mom," Dylan said, "there was no way I wanted any more chaos. Plus, I knew I had to study. Can you imagine leaving Dad like that to go to school and then screwing up? Like things weren't bad enough already." He cracked a knuckle, a habit he thought he'd lost. "Mom was together enough then, at least through my second year, that she came along a few times to visit. So this kind of scene wouldn't have been good."

"Kind of embarrassing too—with a lot of roommates around and their girlfriends, judging her and all."

Dylan admired how Jack just *said* things. He'd admit to petty, unflattering feelings and then you'd realize, well okay, the world didn't collapse. "Yeah, I hate people thinking that's who she is."

"You know, if you'd had a place like this back then, the shock could have snapped her back to her real self, like in that movie, the really old one on TCM."

"*Snake Pit*," Dylan said, pleased that Jack remembered. "You know, our real mother would have come here once to see the place and, after that, called you from the car."

"Or redecorated."

Jack took him on a tour of the seven bedrooms, one illegal. The larger rooms had yet another couch opposite a bed or futon. There were fans and space heaters—the largest bedroom had one of each going. The bathrooms sported layers of soap scum, dried shaving cream, and black deposits around the sink. Dylan almost asked Jack how he kept his contact lenses uncontaminated.

Along the tour, he was introduced to various groggy housemates. At least three had the same first name—he would wait to hear the distinguishing nicknames, which he knew could be as benign as Jersey Dan or as suspect as Tether Mike.

In the kitchen, which was surprisingly close to clean, he decided that he'd ask Jack if people stripped the batteries from the alarms and, if so, whether he and Jack should go to the hardware for more. There'd been a fire at an off-campus house where his dad taught.

Later, while they were seated in a restaurant waiting for their competitively large breakfasts to arrive, Jack testified that the smoke alarms were all operating—the landlord had switched to hardwired, so it wasn't even a temptation. He didn't ridicule Dylan for asking. One of the boys who had burned to death had been a year ahead of Jack—also a soccer player. They sat not saying anything for a moment.

"How do you think Dad's doing?" Jack asked.

Dylan shrugged and said, "Think he'll ever remarry?"

"He never seems happy or unhappy. Just blah." Jack opened and shut the menu. "But I don't see him much now. Why do you say that? About remarrying."

"Can you really see the guy living the rest of his life like this? Taking care of someone who doesn't know him? I don't think I'm going out on a limb to guess that they haven't had sex—who knows for how many years." He thought he saw Jack blush.

"Well, do you have a plan or something?"

Dylan laughed. "No, little brother, I don't have a plan. I'm just asking."

What Dylan really wanted to ask was why Jack never seemed to have an actual girlfriend—someone the family could meet. He used to think that Jack was just doing what good-looking, confident guys do: revel in seduction and excess and ... delay the routine of a relationship. Or maybe Jack, like him, was afraid of being in love. Besides, love leads to loss—not always, but a lot. Well, he sure wasn't about to bring the topic up now.

It wasn't like he had any of it figured out.

CHAPTER FIVE

"I don't consider myself a paranoid person," Jane said, "but I really think that some people are staring at me. At us. Do you know everyone here?"

"No more than thirty percent," David said. "I know they're staring. I want them to because I have to ask you something—and staring will be part of it." He didn't doubt the affinity he detected between Jane and him. Despite his many years of fidelity—or maybe because of them—he knew that attraction traveled mysteriously through space, no matter how camouflaged by politeness or rudeness. There were just too many tells.

He saw an earlier, braver version of himself at not quite twenty-five, as he entered a noisy smoky party and saw Kate across the room, backed against the wall by a large, loud drunk standing too close. She was trying to sidle away towards open space, but the drunk moved too, talking, almost yelling about how his father wanted him to join the family business but he wanted to prove himself first. As David approached, the drunk punched her arm too hard, saying, "You get my meaning, don't you, Kate," and David interrupted him with, "If you're Kate, you're wanted out on the porch."

As the drunk turned, David got between him and Kate and she moved quickly. The outraged drunk said "hey," but was too slow to react as David followed her, weaving through the crowd to a corner of the porch. She caught her breath for a moment, and then told him she was drunk too, and she was going to kiss him one time, but then they'd have to be properly introduced. And she did kiss him, and he could tell she wasn't drunk at all. Or just enough to kiss a stranger and sing, "Yes, I'm certain that it happens all the time" and he surprised himself by whistling, almost perfectly, the preceding line.

And now he was in a coffee shop with a woman named Jane because talking to Jane was the only time he felt like himself—the only time he could get enough air into his lungs. If he was married, then what he was about to do was wrong. But *was* he married? Married in a way that bound him beyond finances and caretaking? It's called *ambiguous loss*, he'd learned, but really it just felt like loss—the regular kind. He and Kate had lived together without being married—no small thing at the time. Now they were married without living together, and he was sitting here with a woman he didn't know. He might be about to ruin what he had, but he was closing in on fifty-seven and his life was a twisted fairy tale, like Sleeping Beauty without the good ending. In a flash, he'd be old.

"Okay," Jane said, giving away nothing. "Ask."

"Do you want to go out sometime? And I don't mean to discuss insurance."

"You mean like a date?"

"I mean do you wanna hang out sometime?" He hoped he sounded like a man who knew how to flirt, despite decades of avoiding it.

She laughed. "You can really tell which of us works with young people."

"I promise never to say 'dude,' and I have no tattoos. But

people *will* stare. I am that car wreck on the side of the road."

"Good to know all of this, especially the tattoos, but those aren't the things I'm worried about." She glanced around. "For today, let's just go over the insurance like we planned, and then I'll think and you'll think."

"I'm okay with that." He'd said his piece and that was enough for now. He thought about his notoriously terrible Monopoly skills—terrible because he always wanted everyone he loved to come out equal. He would encourage the kids or Kate to buy certain properties to protect themselves and it never worked—one or more of them, including him, always lost big. He wanted everybody safe, and they wanted to have fun. He might be about to ruin what he had, but he had learned that nothing was safe.

Jane reached into her briefcase and brought out papers and her summary, written in "plain English for the normal middle-aged brain," as she put it.

"The L has agreed for now to stop billing you for the balance," she explained. "You need to sign this request to appeal the decision of the company that quit paying. I think they know they're primary and should be paying first, but the lower-level staff doesn't have the authority to reverse the mistake."

She managed to sound lawyer-like but flustered, too. She gestured at one point, knocking over the remains of her latté. He helped her clean up and their hands touched. After the third touch, he put his hands in his lap. "I know you didn't have to help, and I would have slogged through it somehow, but thank you."

He looked up to see a neighbor and the chair of the Poli Sci department watching him. He smiled and waved as they glanced away.

———◆———

"I know I've missed a couple of visits." David apologized to Kate's unreadable face and immediately felt ridiculous for it. He went on. "I was at the annual trophy hunt in Chicago." A small contingent went each year to recruit grad students, preferably a few from the Ivies. He started to describe his favorite prospect and then stopped. He always felt he had to say *something* to her, and the list of things that weren't ridiculous was very short, but still, what was the point? Recently, he had begun reading when he was with her and she didn't seem to mind. She was more remote and blank than ever, but at least he could get caught up on his newspaper. After reading for an hour, he said goodbye and went to find Jane. If she wasn't alone, he'd say he needed to show her the most recent letter from his insurance company, the one that completely contradicted the letter that came before.

While he waited by the antique double desk that served as a workstation, he studied the three monitors, imagining as usual that a panel of judges was rating his performance as loyal, care-taker husband.

He saw a figure down the hall leave a resident's room and jumped away from the desk. A staff member he didn't know approached him.

She knew him. "What can I do for you, Mr. Sanders?" and when he told her, there was the slightest hesitation before she said, "Jane's not assigned here any more."

The words didn't sound like English to him. He understood each word, but the meaning didn't seem possible. Why would she leave without telling him? She ran her own business—no one could *make* her leave.

He strained to read the clerk's badge—Delores or Delia or something. He remembered to properly introduce himself and asked, "Do you know how I could find her? Wait, I have her card." He took it from his wallet as he spoke. "No, the only number on this is for here."

He tried to keep the edge of panic from his voice. Delilah—it *was* Delilah—appraised him. "Is anything wrong? Does your wife need something?"

Had she put the slightest stress on the word *wife*? Yes, he thought. My *wife* needs everything.

"Kate's fine. I just left her."

He knew he should mention his insurance claims and the facility's botched billings, but he didn't. He just stood there trying to look less crazy than he felt. The desk phone rang. She let it ring for just the amount of time it took her to take the business card from his fingers and write seven numbers on the back.

CHAPTER SIX

David waited in the lobby of Jane's office building until he saw her approach the entrance. She pushed instead of pulling the outer door and then rolled her eyes and smiled to herself. He wondered what had preoccupied her, though in her line of work, there would always be plenty. He met her just as she came through the second door.

"I wanted to return these books to you."

Jane didn't say anything.

"You lent them to me a while back," he said.

"I didn't forget. Is that why you're here?"

"You know that's not why."

"I don't know what I know."

How like Kate. Six quiet words to let him know he was acting like a jerk.

"You're right," he said. "I guess I was thinking you'd consider me merely as an insurance problem."

She almost smiled as she said, "Very romantic."

"I'm playing hooky today," he said. "Can you come with me? I promise I'll act like an adult and talk about my situation."

She shook her head. "I absolutely cannot miss the first hour of the meeting. Maybe I can get away after that and meet you here." She looked surprised, as if she had just said the opposite of what she had planned. She turned and walked to the elevator.

"Jane, you forgot your books."

"You'll need something to read while you wait."

"I've read every one of them."

The elevator door closed. He took out his phone, prepared to look at email, but instead spent the time just waiting, with an almost forgotten feeling of expectancy, as if he was fifteen again and the world of love and sex was about to begin.

——>•<——

Jane walked out of the elevator right on schedule, signed out at the desk, and sat next to him.

"So you really read these books?" she said, drumming her fingers on her portfolio.

"I read the two by spouses of people who became ill early on. The other one I had to stop. I kept thinking he was seventy-eight when he got sick—not bad enough for me to really care, comparatively. Crass, huh?"

"Yes, crass is the word." Her hands were still now and she gave him a complete smile.

"You're very flattering, Jane. Of course, you hardly know me." He needed to close this deal. "Anyway, I was thinking we could walk on that land the university owns. Have you been out there to see whose side you agree with? Developers versus preservationists?"

She glanced down at her shoes.

"Or maybe not," he said.

"I read all the letters in the paper, but I don't trust either side," she said. "I'd actually like to see what's in dispute. We just have to stop by my house first—I can change in ninety seconds—if you don't mind waiting in the car."

"I can manage ninety seconds."

They took his car. He put on the radio and they chuckled at an interview with an irreverent comedian. "I hardly ever get to hear NPR during the day," he said, "and I haven't mastered podcasts yet."

"Can't your boys show you?"

"Oh, they have. I guess I need to ask again. There's a humiliation factor."

"I could probably show you," she said.

They were in one of the older neighborhoods, similar to his but with smaller houses on smaller lots. She directed him to park in front of an impressively maintained bungalow, painted shades of green and dark orange that should have been too bold but weren't, with vintage furniture on a roomy front porch. He drew a breath in sharply.

"Kate loved bungalows. She subscribed to that magazine, *Cottages and Bungalows*. There are back issues still around the house." He thought he must be going on too much about Kate, and yet he had the impression Jane found it reassuring.

She gathered her belongings and got out of the car. "I'll be quick."

And she was. As they drove to the contested land, she described the morning's debate over whether to move the social work practice to a bigger office. She hated disruption, she explained, and would probably vote no until they had to use the bathrooms for counseling sessions. There were only two cars in the lot next to the hiking trails, which surprised him until he remembered it was a weekday. They headed out, beginning at the section that would remain parkland. He started to explain the controversy between the university and the preservationists, but the issue seemed so unimportant he let his voice drift. The day was now warmer, the sky a more convincing blue.

They hiked mostly in silence, each pointing out hawks and pheasants until they reached the road that led to the other parcel. They returned to his car and he retrieved the water bottle he kept there. He wished he'd thought to stop for fresher water.

"Let's sit for a while," Jane said. "It's such a gift to be outside on a day like this."

It was good to have her take the lead in any small way. Pursuit had its limits, he thought. They found a substantial log under a large tree and sat.

"I apologize for only one water bottle."

"It's fine. Anyway, I finally mastered how you're supposed to squirt this type into your mouth from above." She did this, soaking a wide strip of her shirt. "Well, maybe not mastered." He made himself not look at her breasts. Someone in the distance called to a dog.

"Do you have any pets?"

"We agreed that taking care of our two Labs was more trouble than raising the boys. We loved the dogs and they were wonderful, but they always wanted *something*."

She laughed. "I know enough people with large dogs that I believe you."

"Now cats? They're easier, but we never replaced them when they died either. I think our every need to take care of something was satisfied by the kids."

They sat quietly until David said, "There must be some questions you have for me about everything."

Jane said, "Yes," and nothing more.

He guessed she could let the silence lengthen to thirty minutes without stepping in. He sat up a little straighter and made eye contact. "I think you would want to know if I still consider myself married."

"Thank you. I know that was hard to put out there."

"I consider myself a widower." His voice caught on the last word. "Going to see Kate is like going to a grave site. Except weirder." He put his face in his hands for a moment. "I've never put that into words before."

"I'm sorry," Jane said. Her voice had a quiver. "It must be hard for you to see the older spouses visiting, some of them content that their partner is simply alive. But you're young, and it's not at all the same."

"I get way too much credit for being loyal to Kate. Wouldn't anyone do that?"

"Just be glad you're not a wife. In the Alzheimer's world, somebody started calling them 'sheroes' and it caught on."

He looked at her in mock horror. "I do appreciate you for restricting yourself to words that are in the dictionary." He needed to figure out what to say next since she wasn't going to lead him. And she shouldn't. "I'm guessing you'd also like to know more about my ties to Kate's family," he said. "Like are we close and do *they* think of me as a widower."

"I had wondered if they were horrible. You don't talk about them except when it comes to the insurance."

"They're not horrible at all. *My* parents were like self-centered roommates, but Bill and Eve are great—happy and busy and always collecting new people. Smart, very smart. Her mom is fun to be around—as long as no one is sick or in danger. We saw them pretty often for being six hours away."

"So what was it like when Kate got sick?"

"Okay at first. It was good to have help with all the appointments and lab tests. For all her worrying, Eve thought they'd find some way to fix her. But Bill never did. He'd seen it before with his uncle and his dad, though not so young. When Kate got bad, the boys and I wondered if they would want her to move in with them, and they did bring it up once. They felt guilty but didn't think they could keep her as safe as we could. They didn't want to give up everything. Who could blame them?"

"What's it like now? I mean, since the families were so close."

"Eve's an aging, still beautiful version of Kate. The same inflections—they gesture the same. They make some of the same pronouncements, like 'When you start to measure things, you realize how complicated life is.' Bill used to call them Old Twin and Young Twin." David spat out the next words: "I can't stand to be around her. She still does fucking Sudoku puzzles."

"Does it hurt her that you avoid her?"

"She can't stand to be around me either."

She sighed so quietly he barely heard it.

"I keep thinking they'll call me and say, 'David, we love you too and we wouldn't criticize you for...'" He waved a fly away. "Needless to say, no one has said that. And I'm not ready to talk to the boys yet. Kate was very clear on what parents decide and what kids decide. Once, in middle school, Dylan tried to make a case for flossing as a personal choice, and she worked him through his arguments until he surrendered with 'Okay, I will floss my goddamned teeth until I am one hundred percent self-supporting.'"

"She didn't mind the swearing?"

"Not as much as bad gums. It was hypocrisy and illogic that she couldn't take. She probably taught them what a false syllogism was when they were in sixth grade." He felt he'd gotten off the topic and worked his thoughts back to what he was trying to say. "I've decided to talk to our lawyer about what's involved with divorcing Kate and whether a divorce is good or bad for her. I don't even know if he'll talk to me—maybe he's half Kate's lawyer, and I'll have to get my own."

"Big decision."

"In some ways, it doesn't seem big. There've been no arguments, and there hasn't been any infidelity. It's just that one of us is missing in action. Maybe I'll change my mind, but it feels more like getting a death certificate."

He thought he was done but then heard himself say, "I would never have divorced Kate." He watched Jane nervously, wondering if he'd said too much.

"Don't look so alarmed," she said. "I know we wouldn't be sitting here if she was well, and that's why I'm okay with being here. People who are capable of fidelity are very appealing. That's why women prefer widowers to divorced guys."

"I didn't know that."

"Widowers are presumed blameless. And faithful."

The sun was less direct now. She shivered once and then stood and said, "Let's go get my car."

They drove in near silence, the radio murmuring softly, until they arrived at the lot near her office. David walked her to her car and said, "I just want you to know that if I weren't picking up a guest lecturer at the airport and showing him the town and then dinner, and calming his nerves before his performance tomorrow, I would definitely try to disrupt your schedule even more than I have."

"I have two evening appointments and a dinner thing. That's nice to know, though."

"Can I call you tonight and schedule something—but at your convenience this time? I'll send my visitor off to bed before ten."

She started her car, which was snazzy and European and not

what he expected. He said, "You need a new muffler."

She answered, "Ten is fine," followed by, "I know." They both spoke loudly over the rumble.

———————⇒●⇐———————

David had just enough time to do dishes and sort newspapers before leaving for the airport. As he pulled up, he saw Martha on her way to get the mail. Stocky but fit, she always moved purposefully. Based on how much Kate told him about Don, he'd always worried Martha knew too much about him too. He understood that men were criticized for not talking with each other about personal things, but secretly he believed that women confided too much, and it irritated him that this was the presumed gold standard for friendship

He'd always been puzzled by Kate's close friendship with Martha. It's natural to be more lenient with friendships among neighbors and co-workers, but still, it seemed a big gulf. Once, he'd asked Kate about it and she said, "Martha never preaches at me. Have you noticed she never invites us to church things? And she doesn't mind my sarcastic comments about religion. After 9/11, when she admitted that her faith in a useful God was really tested and I said, 'You mean the Holocaust didn't do that for you?' she laughed a real laugh and said she would definitely make that point at bible study because they all just agree with each other and that's why she likes to hang out with me. How can you beat that?"

"And what do you learn from her," he had asked, and she said, "I learn to be nicer."

He walked past the few houses that separated them and called out to Martha. Her eyes widened in surprise and then she smiled. They had lately avoided each other beyond a wave or a hello.

"I feel terrible that I don't thank you enough for visiting Kate," he said. "I see your name in the log and I always mean to call or come over."

"Oh, that's okay. You don't have to thank me. She was such a close friend." She took a half step towards him and said, "It's probably not right to say *was*. I'm sorry."

"Hey, I understand. You're just being realistic. You still love her, but she's not the same friend anymore."

"I know, but *why?* David, I've prayed for her so much. My bible group prays for her. How can there be no way to help?"

Somehow, the failure of her religion to restore Kate made *him* feel guilty, as if he and Kate had let her down. He decided a hug was in order, and though hugging was another thing he thought women overdid, he experienced a surprising comfort as they embraced and then parted.

———>●<———

The home phone rang a little before ten. The caller ID showed "Bob," an occasional family nickname for Dylan. He was tempted not to answer because any conversation would take him past ten o'clock, but Dylan didn't call often.

"Hey, Dad, I'm glad you're home. I know you usually call on Thursdays, but I'll be tied up all day and evening in the lab, and the reception is terrible there. It's like a fallout shelter."

David smiled. *Fallout shelter?* He always forgot how much vintage culture Dylan had learned watching old movies. And *The Simpsons.*

"Anyway, I thought I'd call tonight to say hello."

"I'm glad you did," David said, lying and not lying. "How are you? Is this the start of the big depression research grant?"

"Yes, I'll be living and breathing rats for the foreseeable future."

"To try to figure out why medications work with too few people."

"Pretty much."

"Your mom would be proud."

A familiar silence settled in—they were used to paying brief respect to Kate.

"So what's going on, Dad?"

David eyed the clock. "No news," he said, now certainly lying, "though I should probably get myself organized for tomorrow."

"Christ! I had no idea it was so late. I'll let you go. And I haven't forgotten about coming home—we just need to figure out how to rotate the weekend shifts. I'll let you know, and maybe I can grab Jack on the way."

"I would love to see you both," David said, honest again, and then they said their goodbyes.

He pulled out Jane's business card, on which she had added her home number—a landline. He reached her voice mail, described the timing of Dylan's call, and said he would try the next day. He went to bed with the idea that he'd sleep well, though that had become unusual.

———————⋊•⋉———————

Today, Dr. Ratha was going on longer than usual. It was quarterly-review time, required by licensing and insurance, which meant that David stopped first at the consulting room of the doctor on contract with the L. Kate used to attend these meetings, but it was just him and the doctor this time. Ratha, with his impeccable, slightly British speech and beautiful suits that made David think he should go shopping, always took the time to be kind and would ask, heartfelt, "How are you, David?" and David would want to respond, *You need to tell me how long do I do this*, but of course he would only answer, "It's hard. We miss her."

Once the doctor had said, "I'm so sorry this happened to you," and David, taken by surprise, cried. After that, they stuck to the script. As usual, David let his mind wander since Kate's good blood pressure and cholesterol numbers didn't really seem like good news anymore. He reined in his attention in time to hear something about a clinical drug trial for which, if nothing changed in her condition, Kate would be eligible.

"I know that you're cynical about these trials." Ratha went silent. He moved his glasses first higher and then lower on his nose.

David didn't think of himself as cynical exactly. Kate had been considered for seven trials and had participated in three. If she had furthered the cause of science, he'd not been told of it, and there had been no benefit to her, only an ugly rash that took six weeks to clear. In sunlight, he could still faintly see it.

"I understand your lack of enthusiasm, but this is how we learn. Are you willing to sign the consent?"

"She did will her body to science," David said. "It's just…"

"Just what?"

"Earlier."

"Of course."

"We did the paperwork years ago, but I thought I would be dead and she would be eighty-nine and I'd never have to hear the phrase *donated her body to science*."

They both jumped at the sound of a food tray crashing on a

tile floor and then Dr. Ratha gave a deep sigh. David recognized the familiar inflection of resignation and sorrow, and he sighed too as he took a pen out of his jacket.

CHAPTER SEVEN

David's specialty was U.S. history, but he had also fashioned a niche—*history and society*—and found it a useful way to lure students to his classes and sneak some actual history into their minds. Along the way to tenure, he'd published two books, one on the history of divorce and one on the impact of air conditioning. Both sold far more copies than he had relatives—a big success in academia.

Bizarrely, the book on air-conditioning was adapted into a play by an avante garde Chicago playwright, and the play did nicely. No one made money, but his status within the university was elevated. A few of his colleagues resented his ten minutes of fame, though when Kate got sick, he was mostly forgiven.

He had turned down the first offer of department chair but accepted the second when he found he could no longer face so many hours in the classroom, with the concentration of youth, health, and egotism. The history department was one of the few where being chair wasn't a dreaded rotation but a respected promotion. Sometimes there was even competition.

Now the department secretary, Greta, was looking at him curiously. "Are you okay?"

He realized he'd been standing in front of her but hadn't said anything.

"I'm fine. Just daydreaming."

"Did you hear me say the internet's down? System wide."

He stared at her. "Has that ever happened?"

"People are acting like they're on a disabled plane that lost compression. Four to twelve hours is the estimate. Let me know if you need CPR."

"If it's still down at noon, I'll take you to lunch." He always meant to be friendlier to Greta. If she left, he would suffer. It would take three tries to get the right replacement.

He went to his office and realized that, for the first time in longer than he could recall, he felt like writing. You don't need the internet to write, he thought, feeling a bit triumphant as he returned to his third book, of which there were eleven pages, all written years before.

———⟫●⟪———

When David pulled up Friday evening, Jane was sitting on her porch. She motioned him over. "You were so complimentary about the house and the porch, I thought you might like to sit and have a drink." She held up a small bottle of beer. "I have red wine or these seven-ounce lady-beers. You can have two and still drive. And they're really cold."

"I didn't know they made those," he said and thought of Kate, who had never once finished a beer. He took one.

They sat with their drinks and watched a trio of skateboarders working their boards down the street. "Watching them makes me so nervous," Jane said. Did your kids do that?"

"No. They were heavily into rollerblading for a few years, but that was it." He took a large sip. It wasn't bad beer. "You know, Jane, I've never asked if *you* have kids."

"I don't. It wasn't because I don't like them. No big story there—we just didn't."

He studied her doubtfully, but she didn't elaborate. When they finished their drinks, she took the bottles inside and then locked the house. They paused by his car to watch one of the kids jump and pivot and somehow land securely.

Jane eased into the passenger seat, laughed at the several feet of legroom, and then moved the seat forward. David said, "A large son must have been the last person to ride with me." They drove to the restaurant, listening to a CD mix one of the boys had made. His sons were determined to push his musical knowledge past 1980. He liked most of their picks, and he liked being able to occasionally name an artist when at a bar with grad students.

Kick Push was playing and he explained to Jane that it was about two teen lovers trying to find a place to skateboard without cops hassling them, and she said, "Nice synchronicity," and he said, "Well, I did choose the disc."

<hr/>

A bottle of wine arrived and, as they talked about the restaurant and the neighborhood, he noticed they were both taking barely perceptible sips, perhaps equally determined to keep their wits. Finally, David took a large swallow and said, "You know, Jane, you're here tonight, and I know that means something. I know you're not—"

"Were you ever unfaithful?"

He cleared his throat. "No."

"Even when you were just dating?"

"No."

"Even when you had bad fights?"

"No."

"You work at a university around beautiful young women."

"Still no." She was watching his face closely. "I learned to admire without wanting."

"Not even when she got sick?"

"No."

"When she got sicker? When she moved to the L?"

"No. Not then either." The waiter passed close by the table but didn't stop.

"You don't believe me," he said, careful to sound kind.

"I believe you. I just don't believe I've ever met a man like you."

He sipped wine, then water, then rearranged his place-setting and said, "I know I'm supposed to be the one providing the information, but it feels like I should ask you about your ex."

She gave the slightest shudder. "Not yet. But let me ask you: How were you able to do that? I mean, to feel that one person was enough."

He couldn't think what to say, other than the truth. "I don't know exactly. Part of it had to be that Kate enjoyed sex, even after we got married and after the kids. She was fun and uncomplicated. She'd apologize for coming too many times. She'd say, 'It must be a nuisance for you to watch me or help when you're done and relaxed,' and I'd say, 'Kate, you just have to believe me. This is not boring.'"

He checked out Jane's expression to see if she seemed threatened or competitive, but she looked charmed—that was the unlikely word that came to mind.

"And yes," he said, "my job was dangerous in that way. But I saw some ugly female conquests of married profs and vice versa. Aside from the ethics, I was determined not to be ridiculous or to demolish my family. If a student comes into my office leading with cleavage and midriff, I say, in a fatherly voice, that they are not properly dressed for a professional academic environment, and I'll be happy to loan them my wife's cardigan for the duration of our meeting."

Jane laughed and said, "Do they learn?"

"After that they dress like novitiates." He refilled his glass and hers.

"Then what happened?" she said.

"You mean after she got sick?" She nodded.

"The first couple of years, it was still good. Well, sad too, but mostly okay. She was still able to enjoy sex and have an orgasm, not like before, but there was pleasure. Later, there were times I wasn't sure she knew it was me, which was perversely exciting, which I know makes me sound like a freak. That was a pretty brief phase."

"How did it end?"

He took a sip of water and gulped as he swallowed a small ice cube. He took two breaths while he waited for it to melt. "She couldn't respond any more. I knew she wasn't enjoying it. That much I could tell. I mean she never resisted, but there was no one there. So I made the decision to stop. That's an experience I don't wish on anyone—to know you've just had sex for the last time with a wife you love."

She murmured in the softest voice possible, "I am so sorry."

He opened his menu. "Now we're going to order and eat and talk about sports or something. Or you, Jane. Maybe we can talk about you."

"Ha!" she said, smiling. "Not a chance. But let's order."

"All right, we'll eat and make small talk."

"Lovely phrase, *small talk*," she said. "A poem in two words."

During the drive back to her house, Jane said, "I can't believe how good this is. What are we listening to?"

"They never label the mix tapes beyond 'Jack's Mix' or 'Dylan's Mix.' This is Jack Johnson. I happen to know that one—you hear him everywhere now, but it's good. Pleasant and not annoying."

"See what I've been missing all these years."

He turned to look at her, but she had her eyes closed. When he pulled up in front of her house, he turned to her.

"It's still warm out," he said. "Do you want to go for a walk?"

She nodded, but when they reached the sidewalk and he asked which direction, she cocked her head slightly and climbed the steps to her house, slowly, key in hand. He followed, stopping when she did at a table in the living room, where she gestured towards the remainder of the bottle of wine from earlier. "Do you want something?"

He studied her. "I don't know."

She motioned for him to follow her and began to walk down a wide hallway to a large bedroom. He took a moment to absorb the peacefulness of the room before he stepped inside and walked over to her. They kissed, then broke away to undress. It was the first time they had touched, aside from accidentally. He lay down too.

"It's too dark in here. I want to see you," he said. She got up and went to a window to adjust the shade to let in some streetlight. She turned, visible now, and walked towards him, not quickly, seemingly comfortable with being watched. He understood why. She was beautiful, still lithe and pleased with her body. Her breasts, which he'd guessed at from the tee shirt she'd spilled water on, were almost familiar, solely by imagination. He wasn't at all disappointed. He felt nineteen again—except for wishing he'd gone to the gym more.

She slid into bed and under him. He raised himself onto his forearms. "It helps that I can see you now," he said. "Because I sort of thought I might be dreaming."

"Yes, it's very strange. But I'm here." She kissed him, then broke away. "I'm quite sure of that."

"Looking back," he said, "I think I wanted you from the minute we met. Or maybe ten minutes after we met. When they said you didn't come to the L anymore, I—"

She put one finger on his lips and moved out from under him. They lay on their sides and he ran his palm along her body, down as far as he could, then back up along the inside of her leg and thigh, stopping when he felt how wet she was. "Okay, that's enough foreplay for now," he said.

She laughed and said, "Yes, we've already had plenty of that."

"How long have I been sleeping?" Jane asked as she sat up and looked at the bedside clock.

"Not long. Does it matter?"

"No, I'm just surprised."

He raised an eyebrow.

"I don't usually fall asleep that easily. I'm usually more..."

"Wary?" he said. "Does this mean you're starting to trust me a bit?"

She met his gaze for a moment, then sat up and tucked the sheet in more securely.

"Okay, Jane, you know way too much about me. It is definitely your turn." He settled into the pillow, raised one arm and, after a brief hesitation, she put her head on his chest and began to talk.

"It began in high school," she said. "We went to high school together—Charlie and I."

David jumped slightly. This wasn't what he'd expected.

"His family moved to town just before tenth grade, so when I started school that fall, there was this gorgeous, confident, smart new guy. More like a man—not your usual tenth grader. I think we were all in love by seventh period. But like I said, he was smart. He got himself established first. Football, advanced classes—made the right guy-friends. By Homecoming, the pretty girls were in a frenzy. Well, probably the not-so-pretty girls were too, but they had more dignity or something."

"Or no hope," David said.

"Yes, that was probably it. Anyway, he asked someone to the homecoming dance—Annie Slater—I still remember her name—and they went out for a few months, and then he broke her heart. He was already seeing Glenda. She's the last name I remember because, after that, he just kept going down the list. He would fall for someone—I really think that part was genuine—and they'd have six weeks or so, and then the next."

"Probably didn't hurt his social standing."

"It might have for someone else. But he had this power—he was the kind of person who made you feel more alive. When he turned his attention to you, the day was more vivid. *You* were more vivid."

He rearranged his arm to shift her weight, then pulled her closer. "So, where did you fit into this?"

"I was determined not to take my turn. I had a good friend who felt the same way, and we formed a sort of Charlie Anonymous group. I mean, we were in love with him too, but just not willing. Of course that intrigued him, and he and I became something like friends. Eventually, he accepted that's how it was with me, so we'd talk sometimes, or work on a school project together. My girlfriend succumbed senior year for a one-week stand."

"So were all of these conquests sexual?"

"Maybe not in tenth grade, but after that, probably. But, really, we weren't sure because Charlie never told his guy friends. And girls were much more circumspect back then." She stopped and brushed hair away from her eyes. "I don't know if I'm explaining him right. Have you ever been around someone and you just felt more…everything? He could do that. He could just make people fall in love with him *at will*."

"Yet you resisted."

"Well, he didn't make me a full-time project. And I had a few boyfriends. But, yes, I basically treated him like heroin."

He smiled at the analogy. "Keep going."

"Then we went to the same university, and he tracked me down at the start of our second year. He said he was done with all that—he'd needed to get it out of his system, and he had. He wanted to marry young and not regret it. And have four kids—he wanted four. I was twenty. It seemed plausible. Anyway, we fell in love, or I *think* he did. I think he always did. That first semester I could hardly breathe, I was so infatuated, intoxicated—what's another 'I' word?"

"Imperiled?"

Jane laughed and said, "I know this is weird, but can we take a break here?" She moved from alongside him and laid the length of her body on top of his. "Tell me if I'm too heavy."

He moved his hands along her gently. "I think I can handle it."

She slid down his body, then looked up at him. "I was prepared to help you, but clearly I'm not needed. We're not in Viagraland, are we?"

"Deprivation will do that. I don't think I've been this hard since I was thirty." He felt a twinge of disloyalty as he said it. She seemed to know that he didn't mean "stop."

"Jesus," he said silently, at the almost forgotten sensation. Nothing else feels like this. Though after a while, good as it was, he wanted her under him or on him and gently lifted her. She sat up and bent her knees to position herself, leaning forward so neither had to take their hands away, his on her breasts, she flitting her fingers through his hair—the sturdy loose curls that had embarrassed him for as long as he could remember.

"I've been waiting a long time to do that—these curls, I mean—well, all of it," she whispered.

He could admire her better now. He had expected her toned, fit body, remembering the references to being forced to watch Fox News at the gym, but to be here with her, to feel desire instead of grief, was beyond what he had imagined—and he had certainly let himself imagine this, though in images so vague and incomplete there seemed to be no overlap with the real thing.

He didn't compliment Jane's body or speak at all. In college, a girlfriend had praised him for not talking. "Why do men do a whole narration thing?" she'd said. "It's like they think we're making porn. It makes me feel self-conscious. I don't know if other women react the same way, but even if I'm really into it, the minute there's a comment, it's a turnoff." Certainly, Kate had never suggested he talk more. When friends complained about their wives losing momentum during sex, David would want to say, *Try not talking. Trust me, women want talking without sex and sex without talking,* but he worried he would sound smug—so he kept his mouth shut then, too.

Looking at Jane as she moved on top of him, he didn't last as long as the first time, but he could tell it was almost enough. "I'm sorry for my timing," he said, as soon as he caught his breath. "Let me help you."

"Just stay there," she said, almost sternly.

And he did what she asked.

———>•<———

The next day, Saturday, he woke to car horns, metal tables clanging, and loud conversations. Jane woke up too and groaned, "Oh no. It's the annual garage sale. I forgot to warn you." She put a pillow over her head, but he pulled it off.

"We should talk about today and our schedules," he said. "We should try to skip the awful part where he thinks she wants him to leave and she thinks he wants to leave."

"Do you want to leave?" She sat up and turned to face him. A voice from the street called out, "Hot coffee! Warm donuts for sale!"

"I want us both to leave and get away from this madness." He pulled on his boxer briefs (he was glad his sons had instructed him that these were necessary) and walked to the window and watched cars streaming into the neighborhood. "Though I wouldn't mind looking for a bike for Jack first. At college, bikes have maybe a three-week life-span."

She stood. "We better get out there soon if you want a bike. They go fast."

With that, they pulled on clothes and went into the kitchen, where he watched her make coffee. A mix of pale gray and white with a hardwood floor, the kitchen could be in one of the magazines Kate used to show him.

"I was going to make toast," Jane said, "but somehow I have a compulsion to get one of those donuts my neighbor is yelling about."

———◦———

David sat with his back against the tree while Jane lay perpendicular, her head on his thighs, a thick cotton blanket beneath them—a blanket he'd warned couldn't be very clean.

"It smells like sunshine. Sunshine and childhood picnics."

David smiled at that idea and then said, "You do know that you need to finish the story about your marriage, right?"

"I know. I'm not really trying to dodge you. I'm just out of practice talking about it. Thankfully. Where did I leave off?"

"Imperiled."

"Oh, yes. Twenty and stupid." She was speaking in a sort of detached voice. "So we fell in love and it was insane. Those first few months, I hardly slept. Couldn't eat. I did still study—he barely needed to study, but he always cooperated when I set limits." She grimaced. "We graduated and got married on the same day."

"Really?"

She shrugged. "Uh-huh."

"What did your parents think?"

"They didn't know anything about him from high school. I never confided in my parents. Did you?"

David smiled at the thought. "Never."

"And mine split up right after I left for college," she said. "They were completely wrapped up in themselves. It wasn't like they even knew enough to warn me about anything. After college,

Charlie and I were both working and, after about two years, I found out about two infidelities. Remember the old Star 69... before caller ID?"

David nodded.

"I was stunned and not stunned. Maybe I was most surprised at his carelessness. We went to therapy. He only vaguely blamed me. We got through it. People think they'll leave at the first whiff of an affair. But they don't. Maybe I understood who he was and expected to be tested. Then there were eight or nine years that seemed good—maybe he was even faithful. But technology intervened again. He was one of the first people I knew to get voice mail at work."

"Where did he work?"

"I know you can guess."

"Detail man for a pharmaceutical company?"

"Close. Keep going."

"Successful salesman of expensive cars."

"Close but not snazzy enough. He sold money. Or sold trust is more like it. He managed people's investments. You'd think he would be too young, but he was great at it—honest, intuitive, could practically predict the future. We lived well, or at least we weren't poor, and I was able to go to grad school."

"Until voice mail?"

She sat up now, cross-legged and facing him, her expression more dogged than emotional. "Yes, voice mail and then a cell phone. And the internet—he got a laptop and never brought it home. They provided the perfect anonymous, private world for him. He thought he had a way to amuse himself without losing me. He wasn't counting on the craziness of his women. Remember, everyone falls in love with him. Dumb narcissists keep all the attention on themselves. Smart ones turn the attention on you. Charlie is a very smart narcissist—and beautiful. He's aged like George Clooney, I hear."

David decided not to go out of his way to see photographs. "So, all this time, you're happy and you think you've passed some kind of test after getting through the first infidelities."

"It really sounds moronic, doesn't it?" Her voice became more animated. "One day a woman knocked on the door, all dressed up and holding out his briefcase. She tried to pretend she was flustered to see me, but somehow I knew she knew I existed. I just took the briefcase and said, 'You're welcome to my husband—he's available as of 11 p.m. tonight,' and I shut the door."

David thought he saw her blush and then she added, "I should probably tell you that after I found out the first time, I never had sex with him without a condom even though it made him really mad. I think somehow I never felt we were alone, just the two of us." She paused. "But condoms only work for certain things." She made full eye contact with him and gave him a smile. Maybe he had been wrong about her blushing.

"He was repentant—by that, I mean he was terrified, agonized. I was a 'great wife—the love of his life,' etc. etc. I got a list out of him, but I knew it was only partial. After a certain point, does the number matter? So back to therapy we went—but to a different therapist. I was worried a woman would fall for him like our first therapist did, though she hid it well. The new guy pretended to sympathize with me, but I could tell he envied Charlie."

"Shouldn't a therapist be able to not show it?"

"Go figure."

"So when did you know you were done?"

"At the third session—the *third* session—the therapist asked how I was going to be able to start moving past this, and I stood up and said, 'The only thing wrong with this marriage is that there aren't three more of me: a redhead, a blonde, and a lesbian'—and I left, slamming the door. I couldn't believe I had become one of those people that exits a therapy room slamming the door, but it did feel good. I knew a lawyer in the building and I found her office. They let me see her immediately, and I did that crying where you drench yourself, and between sobs, I told her what I knew, and she said, 'I think this is your time: no kids, you're not pregnant, do not let him near you, do not let him touch you.' And I looked at her and said 'I hate him—get me out fast and I want some money too.' We shook hands and she hugged me and I stopped crying and she said, 'Listen, no last fuck. Maybe he's never wanted kids before, but he'll want one now. And then you'll be married forever.'"

Jane shrugged. "It took a few months for him to go through his bag of tricks, but then he gathered his dignity and we had a good divorce." She gave a deep sigh. "Rookie mistake."

David couldn't think of anything to say. Her story was too beyond his experience.

"Then I moved here to join my friend Lucy and we started the business."

He pulled her to him, made space against the big tree for her, and they sat, her head against his shoulder. An ant walked by carrying a heroic burden. They studied it, like children, and David said, "I can't remember how they do that. I used to know."

They lay down and soon slept. At five o'clock, he woke, startled, and when he woke her, she again seemed surprised she had trusted him enough to sleep.

CHAPTER EIGHT

On their fourth date, he brought Jane to the house. While he fiddled with the front door key, he said, "Remember the old standard—sex on the third date?"

"Too late for that bit of etiquette."

"But for us, I think you coming to the house—that's our milestone." He unlocked the door. "It's just us. The guys would never drop in. They're hours away and they always call first."

They went inside and she began studying the art on the walls, then every photo and object. She stopped at a built-in bookcase and read titles. "It's lovely," she said. "I expected more of a dusty mausoleum."

"Kate told me early on, 'I don't need an oversized or expensive house. I just need to like everything—everywhere I look.' Plus, I cleaned."

"And bought flowers."

"I know this is weird for you, but let me you take you on the full tour. Let's get it over with and then you can run if you want."

"Do you truly not see that this is weird for you too? How can I ever know you if I don't know what you lost?"

"That's easy. Just circle the answer that says 'almost everything.'"

She paused at a row of albums, neatly labeled one through

fourteen. He pulled out the latest half-filled book. "Once I saw how much time the boys spent paging through them, I've tried to keep them up. There's two of you in this one."

He put the album back. "We can look at those later if you want. Let's finish the house." They continued through the now unused dining room and then the kitchen. She walked slowly, touching the fabrics.

"Is this where you lived when the kids were born?"

"Yes. Except for two years in our first ratty apartment, this was it." He took her hand. "I should probably show you the part that's not so great," and he opened the back door to lead her to what used to be the garden.

"Oh," Jane said.

"I've kept up the front for the neighbors' sake, but I lost heart for this."

"It *is* a little depressing."

"I know. It's weird what happens to a garden as soon as you turn your back."

"Maybe I can help you figure out a lower-maintenance plan," Jane said. "You might have to hire some jobs out. I've noticed you try to do everything yourself, but I realize that might be the result of the assisted-living and a son-in-college expenses."

"I also help Dylan a little bit with grad school, though he tries to refuse it. He's finishing his second year. Jack's almost done with sophomore year. But I'm doing okay as far as money goes. We pretty much banked Kate's paychecks, and she made decent money. Though I do have the need to have an ever-growing stash of emergency savings. I'm always waiting for emergencies."

"Well, they do happen."

They returned to the kitchen and each had a glass of wine. Afterward, as they climbed the stairs, she carefully looked at the framed photos. First he showed her the guest room and the boys' rooms, which were now neat and orderly but not redecorated. Kate would have done that by their first full week in college, he thought, but didn't say out loud. They went to his room. She walked around it slowly. He led her to an oversized, upholstered chair, pulled her onto his lap and kissed her.

"Are you sure? That this is where you want us to be?"

"I am. I want something good to happen here again."

"Well," she said. She stood and took off her clothes, then pressed herself against him. "Then this is what we'll do unless you tell me to stop," but he didn't say anything then, or later that night, and neither did she, save for the one time she asked why he was grinning.

"Because I can't believe you're here," he said, and then they were silent again.

In the morning, David woke to the sound of a barking dog and remembered it was Saturday. The dog probably barked every morning, but he only noticed it on weekends when he might have thought of sleeping in.

"What is that god-awful noise?" The question was muffled by the pillow Jane had placed over her head.

"It's a beagle." If she knew anything about dogs, that was explanation enough.

"You poor man. You really have been cursed, haven't you?"

"It's a sign we should get up."

"Do you want me to leave? I would understand if it's too strange for me to be here in the morning."

"No, I don't want you to leave. Don't be silly. I just want us to get away from that goddamned dog!" He bellowed the last three words, standing naked at the window, and surprising himself by not caring if he looked old or ridiculous in front of her. He felt a familiar feeling and searched for the right word. Then he realized what it was—*married*.

Soon the dog quieted and, though they had brushed their teeth and gathered up some clothes, they stopped, looked at each other questioningly, and went back to bed instead.

Afterwards, lying there companionably, she said, "You know, you made me tell you about my horrific marriage and my spartan sex life before Charlie, but your unmarried years are a total blank to me."

"Well, I was a guy. You get that part, don't you?" She kicked him lightly. "There was the usual number of women before Kate—usual for those post-revolution amoral times. All of it was fun—some of it was great."

"I missed most of that—connecting with Charlie so young—marrying so young. So it was fun, huh?"

"Oh, yes. But no sacrifice to give it up. The relationships weren't so great. If she wasn't nutty, then her ex-boyfriend was. Or her mom had moved in with her. It was always something. The few women that I thought were wonderful dumped me, of course. Anyway, all that variety is for the young and unattached."

"It sounds like you're fully prepared to get used to me—and then bored by me—but that it will be okay," Jane said, showing no signs of being offended. "That seems like a pretty healthy attitude."

He reached under the sheet and pulled her onto him. "It may take lots and lots of this to habituate to you, so I'm going to get to work on that now."

"You talk like a professor."

"Bad thing?"

She lowered herself to kiss him.

The dog barked twice and howled once. "Ignore, ignore,

ignore," Jane said as she ground her hips into him. He didn't have many moments when he wished he were young. He'd like to stop getting old, but he didn't long to be young. Still, right now he missed the young him. There was no way he could go again. Though he knew he could find some way to be useful to her.

———

David slept for a few minutes and woke to find Jane looking at him. He made a move to get up, but she touched his back and said, "No, wait. I want to ask you something. I'm not sure how to put it. Your marriage sounds so healthy, almost perfect. But you must have argued—everyone does. Well, except Charlie and me. We didn't have enough closeness to warrant an argument, and all his energy went into making me think everything was good. He was so agreeable and adoring, what was there to argue about? But you and Kate had a real marriage. It couldn't always be good."

He knew he lived in a state somewhere between divorced and widowed, so perhaps he could answer without feeling disloyal. He had the thought that she might not want to be involved with someone who viewed his former marriage as perfect, without conflict or even irritability. "We probably argued a normal amount," he said, "I mean normal for people who didn't have a lot to argue about. She thought I was too lenient with the boys, and I thought sometimes she was too bossy with them, though she was usually right. In any given conflict, she didn't care whether they liked her. I always wanted them to like me and wanted them to see my inherent, un-parent-like coolness."

"I can see you doing that."

"We only had one major fight. At a party, Kate drank too much, which normally never happened—it was a very boring university retirement party, so I understood. But she let this ass-hole flirt with her, and flirted back. And let him touch her. Not kiss her or anything but touch her the way aggressive guys find an excuse to do." He shifted his weight and checked out Jane's expression. She wanted to hear more. "I told her she should have known he was only doing it to get at me. He was the only one in my department who was openly resentful when my book got made into a play. I mean there was the most minor and fleeting flurry of attention on me, but he couldn't stand even that. He was chair at the time and terrible at it—talk about the inmates in charge of the asylum."

"Like what?"

"It's all too subtle to describe and it would just make me sound paranoid." He grimaced as he remembered how he had begun to think of uprooting the family to get away. "Eventually, he stepped down as chair. I always wondered if someone black-mailed him into it. They got an acting chair and added a little money and then I took it on. But that all came later. Back to this night. After I took the sitter home, I told Kate that she should have known he was only flirting with her to harass me. Using the word 'only' was a bad choice. You can't tell your drunk wife that some asshole didn't find her irresistible."

"Bad marital etiquette."

"She insisted I was jealous, which made me furious. I remem-ber yelling, 'I'm *not* jealous—I'm humiliated that you let yourself be used like that.' Then she was insulted that I *wasn't* jealous. All the yelling was very George and Martha. I threw a book. Can you imagine me defacing a book? The boys woke up and were scared, so we had to concoct a less awful explanation." Jane looked curi-ous. "Something about Dad thought someone was hurting Mom, so he was rude to the man and Mom got mad at Dad because, in fact, the man wasn't hurting her—just telling her a story."

"And they bought it?"

"They were so grateful for a way to believe their lives weren't coming apart."

"When you think about children who constantly live through worse battles..." Jane said.

"It scared all of us. I have to say, it was our only truly nasty fight. Really, we're both peacemakers."

"Thank you for telling me. It sounds awful, but also like a normal kind of fight—fought honestly. It's not the worst thing to show your sons that people can fight ugly on a rare occasion and still be really good together."

"I believe that about other couples and other children, but all I know about us is that we frightened our kids."

Jane kept silent.

"I like to think they don't remember."

<hr />

Picking up Jack made the trip longer, but Dylan didn't trust Jack's car. When he'd repeated Jack's description of the new rattle to their dad, he got only a vague response. *Vague* would be a good word to describe him lately. Better than *depressed*.

Jack was waiting for him on the porch or, "couch showroom," as he liked to call it. Dylan got out of the car thinking he might use the bathroom, but when he looked in through the screen door, he saw two bodies prone and another sitting upright but asleep.

"Let's leave now before any ambulances get called," he said. "We'll stop on the way."

After they got on the highway, Jack nudged him and said,

"So, fully grown-up big brother, are you seeing anybody?"

Dylan opened his mouth to answer but then stopped. This wasn't a typical Jack question. He didn't know why he didn't want to tell Jack. Maybe it was too soon. The only girlfriend he'd introduced Jack to had left him not long after. He thought she had sort of flirted with Jack, who didn't take the bait. And then it was over—though that was just after they'd had sex. Two weekends. Three times. He'd held onto the fact that she'd at least stayed with him one more weekend after the first time. He had liked her enough to picture them being together through his last year of high school.

"You're kind of serious," she had said. "I know your mom is sick, but it's made you serious and kind of glum." He supposed he did seem kind of glum compared to Jack's sarcastic but appealing manner. At the time, he had been glad that his mother was too absent to notice his pain and embarrassment. Now, he felt guilty to think there was anything good about her being sick. Plus, it might have helped to talk to her.

"Not really," he lied. "I mean, I'm mostly in the lab. Why? Are you seeing someone?"

"Oh, I'm always seeing someone," Jack drawled. This described him from an early age. He'd been one of those thirteen year-olds that girls liked and then never stopped liking. Their mother, still there for the early days of his appeal, would warn them both: "Use that power carefully and be kind. Kindness isn't everything," she'd say, "but it's almost everything."

Dylan had known she was really talking about Jack because, unlike Jack, he wasn't noticeable enough to girls to be in any position to exploit them. After his heartbreak, he had laid low until midway through college. The interesting girls weren't interested in him, and he was wary of the ones whose taste for bad boys suddenly evaporated. They seemed like they might be the kind who wanted to leave college matched up with a boyfriend who was at least a marriage possibility. Or maybe somehow he just knew he should wait.

"But, hey, what about Dad?" Jack asked. "When did we see him last? Four weeks? Five? Does he seem at all weird to you? On the phone, I mean."

"You mean how you feel he isn't listening to anything you say? And he keeps talking about being really busy, like that's something new."

"Yeah, I was wondering if he'd say he was too *busy* for us to come this weekend. But he seemed happy about it. And dinner tomorrow at La Bonne Vie. Kind of surprised a visit from us is that big a deal for him."

"Well, when you look at his life—I hope we're a big deal. I mean, I hope that we help. In general."

They drove the rest of the way without talking much. Jack searched out the worst of AM talk radio so that they could quote some gems to their father, and then they played cuts of the CD's they'd each made for him. Switching their father to downloads or streaming was going slowly.

David waited on the front porch. A Jehovah's Witness tract slipped from the storm door as he opened it and he studied the new title. The first, some months ago, had been THIS WAS YOUR LIFE! The second read YOU ARE DEAD A LONG TIME. Now he was looking at LIFE IN A PEACEFUL NEW WORLD with a drawing of paradise with impossibly large blueberries that the Hispanic mother and daughter could pick without bending over. A brown bear at their side docilely allowed the child to feed him. David hoped it was an omen that he could be loved by Jane for some reasonable period of time before he was scheduled for his long, long death.

As he waited, the order of the pamphlets began to seem deliberate and he wondered if it was a muted cry from young missionaries. He decided that if he were ever home for their visit, he would talk to the pair—didn't they travel in pairs like Mormons? He would offer non-threatening sympathy and provide asylum. Dylan and Jack would advise him on the deprogramming, and he and Jane would shower love and education on the youths. "This is it," he would say. "This is your life. Spend it carefully. There is no more where this came from. Don't waste your time on stranger's porches."

He heard a loud honk. "That was Jack," Dylan said as he trotted up the steps. "He thought he could scare you."

"He did. I was daydreaming." David hugged him and then Jack.

They moved into the kitchen and made their way through a pile of tacos and some Mexican beer. Even Jack was nursing his, and Dylan finally said, "Come on, college boy, that's how you drink?"

"I've sort of lost my taste for drinking a lot. Talk about *Snake Pit*, I am cured of bingeing. And the girls, Jesus, if I have a daughter, I'm putting her up for adoption. There are just no boundaries among the female sex anymore."

David and Dylan gaped. Dylan said, "I think our work is done, Pa. He is all growed-up." He and David high-fived each other.

"They said it couldn't be done, but here I am, wiser every day," Jack said.

They went back to customizing their tacos and eating, though more slowly. Taking advantage of a lull, David said, "I need to talk about something serious."

Jack jumped in. "Is it Mom? Is she okay?"

"No, it isn't Mom. And, no, she's not okay, but nothing's worse." He moved his beer two inches to the right. "I need to tell you that I met someone—a woman. Her name is Jane. She's a social worker and she worked briefly at the L but doesn't anymore. She's been divorced for many years, no kids. I've invited her to dinner tomorrow so you can meet her. I like her and I have no idea how you'll feel about this."

Dylan felt like someone had died. He wanted to cry. He wanted to tell his father to wait longer, though for how long and for what purpose he couldn't say. He finally looked straight at his dad and started to speak, "I..." was as far as he got. He had talked to Jack as if he was ready for this—as if he was so mature that he could recognize his dad as a person. He tried again. "I'm picturing Mom as she used to be, and it feels like you're being unfaithful. I know she's not here. But she still *is*."

He looked at Jack for help.

"Why are you doing this?" Jack started in a quiet voice but spoke louder with each word. "*Why?* No, I don't want to know why. You could have sex and not tell us. This is...creepy." He reached for his beer. His voice got quiet again and he slumped in his chair. "I guess it's a good thing. For you."

——➤●◄——

Dylan asked, "Is that her?" and David looked up to see Jane walking tentatively towards them, managing to look beautiful, friendly, and afraid. Both boys stood when she reached the table, something he had no recollection of either Kate or him teaching them. David stood to introduce them, and Jane gave each a quick smile and a longer look. She seemed almost transfixed.

"I've never been to this restaurant," Jane said, as they all sat. "I don't know why. No occasion ever seemed special enough." She looked as if she'd just given something away. "It's so beautiful."

"We're really glad to meet you," Dylan said.

"Yes, and I want you to know that we don't plan on reenacting a bunch of movies about step-mothers: *Nanny McPhee*, *Parent Trap*, and of course, *Step-Mother*." Jack added this cheerfully and ignored his brother's pointed stare.

"Your dad told me about you guys and movies. And *The Simpsons*. Thank you for not making me a villainess. I really appreciate that."

"Well, we're a pretty reasonable family, you'll find." Jack smiled.

"More to the point, we want our dad to be happy," Dylan said.

Jack said, "I can't tell you how great it is that you're not a grad student or something."

Jane's smile broadened. "Thank you. I thought that was really clever of your dad, too."

They studied their menus, sometimes reading aloud and occasionally correcting each other's French, which none of them actually spoke. No one mentioned the birthdays and anniversaries celebrated here with Kate.

"I want to order last so I can change my mind," Jane announced.

"Change your mind a lot, do you?" David asked.

"Only about food."

It might have been his imagination, but David thought both

boys were now checking Jane out more carefully.

They ordered, and Jane did go last, though it flustered the elderly waiter and, like the boys, she chose the beef. David wondered at the fact of being here with his sons and a woman he'd known for only a few months. Where was Kate? Shouldn't she walk in right about now? And Jane would fade out—or Jane would be Kate's co-worker who he was finally to meet. And he would find her attractive and nothing more.

"I don't know a single person here," Jane said. "I always pictured it like a private club where all the special people went. This city's not that big, but I don't recognize a soul."

Jack said, "Well, I can guarantee you *I* don't know anyone here, except maybe in the kitchen. There's probably a few stoners from high school washing dishes."

"Are you happy with your choice of where to go to school?" Jane asked and then drew Jack out about college and then Dylan about grad school. David could tell Dylan enjoyed talking about his work without having to explain every term. She knew the basics of his research.

After they each told her their highlights, she watched the busboy refill her water and then said, "I didn't have a chance to get to know your mother. I would have liked to have known—"

"After Jane moved on to other assignments," David said, "I missed talking to her and we started spending some time together." He could finally understand how a person might give a false confession.

The boys were looking at him curiously, perhaps wondering how far he was prepared to explain himself.

"Sorry, I kind of changed the subject, didn't I? What were we talking about?"

"Mom," Dylan said. "But we were pretty much done."

David and Jane waited in the small front garden while Jack and Dylan went to get the cars.

"They're lovely young men," Jane said. "Smart, loving, funny, polite."

"I don't know. Jack seemed a little challenging—or provocative—or something. I can't quite put my finger on it."

"Jack was fine. Think about the situation—he was just fine. They want you to be happy, but that doesn't mean it will make *them* happy. Really, I have generously low expectations of your family."

"I appreciate that," David said, "and it will probably come in handy."

"Just hang out with them tonight. You don't need to call me—I don't want to fixate on what they think of me, though I changed my dress three times before leaving the house."

"Hey,' he said. He kissed her on the cheek. "They have no voting rights in this. Can we meet for breakfast at nine? They won't be up yet."

She nodded.

"Tomorrow unknown," he said, "but today we are lucky."

"You sound like a fortune cookie."

"I am more or less quoting my most recent cookie."

David woke to the unwelcome wide-awake state of having drunk too much wine. He had been nervous enough to go past his usual ration. Dehydrated, he walked toward the kitchen to find some juice and was surprised to see light from the kitchen spilling into the dark hallway. As he got closer, he heard the murmur of voices. He stood in the entrance and saw Jack and Dylan, their backs to him, sitting at the table, empty except for a bottle of whiskey and two glasses. He couldn't make out what they were saying and then realized the sounds were coming from the living room. The boys had put on the few hours of cobbled-together home movies that David had finally transferred from tape to DVD. Dylan was slumped in a chair, his arms folded. David saw him wipe his face on his sleeve. Jack sat with his head down, resting his forehead in his hands. He was crying quietly. David backed away unnoticed.

—————◦——————

Arriving early, David got their drinks—Jane's extra-hot to keep for her—and then he grabbed a table that would let him see her when she came into the café. The boys wanted to see Kate that afternoon before they left and he was debating about going along. He thought he wouldn't go. He was almost always with them when they spent time with her. Even thinking about the energy it took for him to try to make the time more pleasant exhausted him.

"You look so serious," she said. "Is everything okay?" He had missed Jane's arrival and she was already seated across from him.

"I think I just decided not to go today when the boys visit their mother."

"Oh." She made a small sound but then stopped.

"Stand up, Jane." She did and he hugged her, then kissed her on the mouth.

"That wasn't much of a welcome, so we're doing a second take."

Flushed, she knocked the Sunday paper off the table as she sat down.

"I notice you're still referring to us as *we*. I take it this means me meeting the boys went okay?"

"It went fine. They're sad guys right now, but not about you."

"None of you seem like sad people. You're funny. You're *enthusiastic*."

"We are that, too. And I'm in love. The boys can't find a new love to replace Kate. I'm in love. It really makes up for a lot of things."

Neither of them had so far used that word and Jane froze at the sound of it. He leaned forward and said, "Yes, Jane, I mean *you*. I am besotted, bowled over, and conquered. Also surrendered and vanquished. None of which I ever thought possible."

"You do have a vocabulary," she said, smiling.

"Did you notice it was alphabetical?"

"Yes. *Skillfully* alphabetized." She looked down long enough that he started to worry. Perhaps he had misread her. Then she looked up and said, "That is a very beautiful way to start the day. I'm sorry that I'm not good at saying it. Can I just say 'me too' for now?"

He nodded and grabbed her hand and held it. "Let's go pick out some food, and then you can tell me in more detail everything you like about my sons. I need to introduce you to some people on the way." He had noticed Martha and Don across the room. "Or maybe not today. You can meet the neighbors later."

She looked at him intently and said, "I think your kids are great. And I'm going to think that no matter what happens." She must have guessed he was about to make a wisecrack because she put her finger to his lips and added, "Just leave it at that."

They took their place in line. She struggled as usual with ordering food. He encouraged her to get both of her choices, and they made their way back to the table, balancing plates. She arranged her food but didn't eat.

"Do I have to come right out and ask you what else the boys said? Or are you actually trying to torment me?"

"I'm sorry. Of course you'd—but like I said before, they don't have that kind of power."

"You are so naive."

"They _like_ you. They liked your self-sufficiency. In some ways, you reminded them of their mother. And of course, they love it that you're so very, very old."

They both laughed. "Do you think they'd like me even better if I were seventy?"

"You will be someday. So maybe we'll find out."

Quickly, she began to eat.

———

Dylan and Jack stopped at the desk to sign in, and the unfamiliar clerk said, "How nice of you to visit." She directed them to try Kate's room first. Halfway down the hall, Jack said, "I hope she's there. I hate doing a whole tour of this place to find her."

They knocked on her slightly ajar door and walked in. She was sitting near the window, and when they greeted her, she turned her head, but her expression didn't change. "What do you want?" she said. They reminded her who they were and she brightened. They sat and began to tell her things, describing every possible event or accomplishment they could think of.

During one silence, she began to sing "Yankee Doodle," one

of the songs she'd sung hundreds of times for Jack. But that was the only song, and eventually they talked over her silence, with Jack asking Dylan directly what it was like to work in a windowless lab so much of the day.

"You actually forget about the weather, so it's kind of shocking to go outside. We call it 'the womb,' as in 'This street is freaking me out; I'm going back to the womb.'" Kate smiled a little when they laughed.

"What does Dad do when he comes here alone?" Jack said quietly.

"He says he talks to her for a while, then reads the paper. 'My whole life, I've never had time to get through a real newspaper, and here I am—lots of time for it—so lucky.'" Dylan's mimicry of their father's delivery got a second smile from Kate, and for a moment her expression was familiar.

"You boys," she said, and they both leaned forward for something more, but she inched back in her chair.

⸺✦⸺

When the boys pulled up at the house, David was waiting on the porch, nervous about whether seeing their mother had changed their acceptance of Jane. They sat on either side of him on the wide first step.

"She still looks really nice," Jack said.

"Martha buys her new clothes when she needs them."

There was nothing but the sound of an occasional car passing. "And Martha does her hair sometimes. And brings someone in from time to time. For color maybe?"

They went in the house and the brothers raced around packing. "Glasses, contact lens cases, phones, chargers, mail that shouldn't be coming here—take it all," David called out. "And *socks*. Especially socks."

"The staff at this hotel is so uppity!" one of them yelled. "Only the price keeps us coming back!"

They came thundering down the stairs and onto the porch. Dylan hugged David and said, "Let us know when you tell Grandma and Grandpa," and David knew this meant Kate's parents.

There was never any confusion about who the grandparents were. His parents were witty, educated, popular, and *charming*, which he had realized early on were terrible qualifications for being a parent. The last adjective was the one most often attached to them, and he had grown to hate the word. Sensibly, they had not wanted children. He was a birth control failure whom they were kind enough to take in, like dutiful foster parents. While they could be instructive and entertaining, he hadn't quite felt loved. The mere fact that he'd been told of his unwelcome conception had alienated Kate beyond the possibility of any genuine friendship with them.

Last week when he called, his mother said, as usual, "Oh, David, I'm so glad you called. We were just thinking about calling you." They never called, but there was no point in correcting her. He and his mother chatted, with David careful to speak in concise sentences. He could hold her attention for a very short paragraph before her willingness to listen evaporated. She asked how his book was coming and perhaps he was feeling reckless, because he risked a reply.

She let him start on his second sentence and then said, "Dad's been writing an essay that he thinks he can submit to JAMA. I think it's called 'The Wisdom of the Not-So-Old Doctor.'" She called into the distance, "Did I get that right?"

He heard his dad say, "Oh, David won't be interested in that," and he thought *of course* he was interested, but before he could say anything, she asked about the boys. He obediently reminded her where Dylan worked and the exact title of the degree he was going for, and then she said they were "lovely boys—just wonderful." Poor Jack didn't even get his own mention.

He took another risk and said, "They say they don't hear from you."

"Oh, I don't think that's true. When is Jack's birthday? He'll hear from us then."

"Two weeks ago."

"Oh, good." She had sounded pleased. "We're not too late."

———

Dylan and Jack rode in silence. After a while, Dylan said, "You want to talk about it?"

"I'm good. You?"

"Same. What's that horrible phrase that's going around? 'It is what it is.'"

"Yeah, really bad thing to say, but basically true. I had to explain to one of my roommates about Mom—Ricky, the one you've never seen when he's conscious—and that was his response. I wanted to say, 'Yes, I know it is what it is, but that doesn't mean I can't punch you in the face and then *that* will be what it is.'"

Dylan laughed. "Have you ever punched anyone in the face?"

"Besides you?"

"God! I forgot about that. What were you grounded for, five years?"

"Mom kept yelling, 'Do you know how expensive teeth are?'"

and I almost thought Dad was going to punch *me*. No one ever asked why I was so mad at you."

"Yeah, that worked out well for me." Dylan glanced at Jack and then back to the road again. "They never thought I could be the problem child. But anything is possible when two brothers fight over a girl."

"Maggie Mahoney," they said in unison.

"Sometimes I think I still love her," Jack said, in a not entirely insincere way.

"You know she's still married to that math teacher, right?" Dylan said. "She got her teaching certificate too. She went through all of college married."

"You've kind of followed her progress, dude."

"Yes, I have." Dylan said. "Not proud of it, but I have." They continued in silence until he dropped Jack off at the ramshackle house.

"No lights on," Jack observed. "Hope they haven't all OD'd."

———◦———

Dylan had once told Lily she was beautiful and she'd frowned, as if he'd made a gaffe. At work, she didn't tailor her lab coats like the other women did, and she wore them over baggy pants, which (he'd guessed correctly) were from Land's End. Now, as she turned her unmade-up face to him, he reached behind her to free her hair, brown or dark red, depending on the light, from a loose ponytail.

"You love to reenact that, don't you, movie guy?"

"If you cut your hair short, I'll leave you immediately."

"What if it's cancer? What then, Mr. Romance?"

"You and I will have cured cancer."

She stepped back so they could shut the door. "How did it go? Did you end up telling him about me?"

"Things got complicated. He's met someone. And now we've met her. That's what the weekend was about."

"Wow. I mean, *wow*. I know you weren't expecting that."

"I wasn't. But, you know, why should he have a life sentence too?"

She held his hands tightly.

"So anyway there didn't seem to be a good time to announce that I've met someone great. Plus, I didn't want it to seem like he and I are *double dating*."

She laughed, but he was sure she knew what he meant.

"And maybe he should have some time to just think about himself. He's happy. It was so strange to see him happy."

Dylan said this without crying. He was completely sick of crying.

"And Jane," he said. "I liked Jane. I didn't want to. I wanted her to be wrong, someone totally wrong for him. But I think he got it right. I think the idea of Jane is wrong, but she seems…"

Jane had already done him a favor. The fact of her had disrupted his careful but not very healthy arrangement of not thinking about his mother, or at least not discussing her. He and Lily were having the longest conversation they'd ever had about his family.

"Seems good for him?"

He nodded. "This is going to sound childish, but I really trust the guy. So I figure if he's doing it, it *must* be right, even if it doesn't feel right. I sound like I'm eight, don't I?"

"Or it's actually kind of scientific. You know him well, so you have a lot of data."

"Do you always know the right thing to say?"

"Get used to it, Mister." Then, more tentatively, she said, "Did he say anything about a divorce?"

Dylan lost the rhythm of his breathing. He inhaled deeply and said, "No. I didn't even think to ask about it. It didn't even occur to me."

"Anyway, he probably doesn't know what he's going to do," Lily said quickly. "And Jane might or might not care."

"More research is needed," he said as he lifted her silky hair and kissed her neck.

CHAPTER NINE

"I ran into Dylan and Jack at the gas station," Martha said. She had seen David on his front steps and waved him over. "And we had a nice chat. They're so handsome. So grown-up."

David walked the few yards to her sidewalk. He clutched at the mail in his hand. "It was good that they visited," he said. "It gave me the chance to tell them something that I need to tell you."

"What? Is Kate worse?"

Worse than what? he thought.

"No, no," he said. "She's the same. And she's healthy physically."

"What then?"

He told her. The sound *Jane* seemed to hover in the air. After a moment, Martha said softly, "I guess I pictured you would eventually start to date in some *platonic* way. I mean, for companionship."

He remembered Don's heart attack years ago. Kate had told him how frustrated Martha was at Don's fear of sex, even long after his surgery. Kate gave her a book for men who are phobic about sex after a heart attack.

"It's not that I think you deserve to be punished," she said. "I just don't want you to stop being Kate's husband. Or stop taking care of her." She closed her eyes. "Every time I see her, I lose a day crying. I don't go very often now. Weeks go by sometimes, and Don wants me to stop even that."

"You can stop."

She shook her head.

"Well, neither can I."

She brushed away a tear and then in a rush said, "Can I ask if you were ever unfaithful to Kate?"

"Never."

"She worried some, you know."

"That surprises me. She acted so oblivious. Which sometimes made me wonder if I should be insulted."

"Well, she was smart that way."

David took her hand. "We were okay. Very okay."

She tried to smile as they said goodbye. He knew she would cry as soon as she was in her house, and he was glad to be spared.

As he walked home, David noticed he had two texts from Kate's sister Claire. The first announced she was coming to town for twenty-six hours. The second said she hoped he could pick her up at the airport Tuesday morning. He texted her back that the timing was fine, though he made it sound more welcoming than that. He didn't know Claire well. Kate's only sibling, she was an unmarried journalist who traveled from one global assignment to another. He had looked for signs that Kate envied her sister's exotic life and never saw any. Perhaps he was the one who envied Claire.

During her few recent trips to visit Kate, she'd been gentle and imaginative, using music or books on their favorite artists—Hopper, Burchfield, and Vuillard—to keep Kate focused, sobbing only after she'd made it out to the parking lot.

————⇒•≪————

Kate was sitting on the bed petting a cat while Claire sat in a chair, watching. David walked over to Kate and, when she didn't startle at his greeting, he touched her shoulder. He sat next to her and petted the cat, who immediately stood and left. He and Claire shared a laugh. Kate got up and walked to the door and back a few times, on the last lap almost running into the aide who had come to walk with her to dinner.

"We can't stay," David said to the offer of dinner. He and Claire said their goodbyes and walked out to his car. She was quiet and pale and seemed too exhausted to speak. She'd spent eight hours at the L.

He asked her anyway, "Does she seem worse to you?"

"Yes."

They drove home, silent for the first five minutes until she asked him about his work and about the boys. He asked about her job and she described her last three assignments, which were overseas, except for her ongoing piece covering makeshift health-care centers for underinsured Americans "at fairgrounds, high school gyms, or wherever volunteer providers could cram into inadequate space and deliver whatever care they could to citizens of the once richest country in the world."

"Do I sound cynical?" She waited for his answer.

"A little."

"It's hard, reporting awful things and always having to sound unbiased when what you want to do is scream, 'What do you mean you don't believe in man-made climate change, you moron!'"

"And then you come here for your R&R. Not very healing, though I'm very glad you took the time."

He parked on the street so they could go in the front door.

Kate always wanted visitors to have a proper entrance through the front and not past shoes and umbrellas and jackets at the side door.

Claire stood on the steps admiring the porch. "She was so good at this kind of thing. Even the porch is a lovely room. 'It has to look a certain way to feel a certain way.' I can hear her now."

"Well, it isn't what it would be if she still lived here, but come in."

They walked through the front entryway into the living room. Claire said, "It looks fine. It's the same. I really think it looks the same."

She started to cry, and he walked towards her to offer a hug, but she said, "No. I'll be okay." She gave a small sob. "It's just the contrast."

Yes, David thought. The contrast is hard to take. And always there.

"Just let me walk around," Claire murmured. "I'll be okay."

<hr />

David parked in an unloading area and carried Claire's bag into the hotel lobby. They hugged once quickly, then again as if to make sure. "I couldn't fit Mom and Dad in on this trip," Claire said, "but in two weeks I'm going to. I'll call you before I go. You have to decide whether there's anything you don't want me to say. Like about divorce. I didn't ask you about it, but *they* will. You'll have to tell me what to say."

"I'll figure something out. Even if it's inconclusive, I'll have a statement."

She smiled. "I'm sort of happy for you, even if it doesn't seem that way. It will take some getting used to, but I already get the part that you being sad doesn't help anybody."

"I'll owe you. Breaking the news about Jane to them—I'm going to owe you big time."

"We're even. We've always been even." She started to pull up the handle on her rolling bag.

"Hey," he said, "I forgot to ask where you're going next."

"Tunisia." She said this with a big grin as she walked backwards to the elevators. "It'll be a breeze. Tell the boys I love them."

⟼⟻

"Whoa," Jane said after he hugged her too hard. "Are you okay? Did something bad happen with Kate's sister?"

They sat on the porch steps. He gathered himself enough to answer. "'She's finally missing,' is what Claire said. Always before, she felt she still saw Kate there." He stood and helped her up, and they went inside to sit on the couch together.

"At dinner, I told her about you. She was so sad already, but I don't think the idea of you made her any sadder. She offered to tell their parents."

Jane inhaled sharply.

"You'll like her."

"Definitely."

Most of the lights were off, he realized, and the shades were down. She was ready to go to bed.

"If I were twenty-five, I'd bully you into letting me stay the night even though it's late."

"If I were twenty-five, you wouldn't have to bully me, but then we've already established that I was kind of an idiot back then. Let's be twenty-five tomorrow."

CHAPTER TEN

Claire was kind enough to call David as soon as Bill and Eve dropped her at the airport.

"I think Dad was more shocked than Mom. He wasn't angry, but I could tell he hadn't let his imagination go there. Mom probably had. Maybe that's why she's been angry with you. She's been anticipating this. They were reasonable, though. 'It's like being caught in the rain,' Mom said. 'Once you're wet, you can't get more wet.' The next day they asked me about divorce and about money, and then I asked them, 'What do *you* think? Do you think David will treat Kate badly?' They were quiet and then Dad said, no, he knew you would take care of her."

David said, "You are a good friend and a good sister."

"When we said our goodbyes, Mom looked at me funny and said, 'Do you think Kate knows?'"

"And?"

"I said no."

"Thank you."

"But can I ask you a question?"

"Sure."

"Is this Jane your transitional relationship? Or rebound? Or practice? Or whatever? There's a word, I think. God, I can't remember the word. I probably have it now too."

"After forty-something, everyone forgets nouns," David said firmly, as if he didn't spend too much time thinking about his own brain and about whether he'd be around for the long haul to look after Kate. "You have to refuse to worry about it. Anyway, I don't think that Jane is transitional. I think Jane is the kind of thing that happens only twice in a lifetime."

He waited for her to say something, and when she didn't, he continued, "Have you had that happen?"

"Several times. And they were always, *always* married."

"Kate thought you disqualified single men because they *weren't* married."

"I probably did. Once I knew that a guy was married, I would instantly see everything good about him. I'm working on it, though. I have to snag someone before my neck turns on me. Or my eyes droop."

He laughed.

"Actually, there is someone." She sounded as if she were betraying a secret. "And when I'm in New York, I see a therapist, who's helping me not turn against him."

"Who—"

"No. I can't talk about it yet. It feels kind of too new and fragile. That sounds so stupid, but I can't talk casually about it yet."

"That's not stupid, more like respectful."

"I like that."

"What are the chances you could come here for Thanksgiving? The boys would like it. I'd like it. You wouldn't need to spend eight hours at a time with Kate.

"Do you see her anymore, David?"

"Of *course* I do. Not every day like at first, but regularly. I make unpredictable visits. Not that I don't trust the staff, but still."

"I don't know how you do it."

"It's what people do for each other."

"It's good to know. I think I knew, but it's still good to hear you say it."

———>●<———

"You could have stayed," Dylan said, as they pulled away from Jane's house.

"Or you can drop us off and go back," Jack offered.

"No, it's my birthday and I want to hang out with you guys."

'Okay, but we're going to the bars later," Dylan said. "Without you."

But they didn't go out. The three of them gathered in the kitchen and didn't leave for several hours. They each nursed a beer and the boys went through the cupboards, ridiculing his out-of-date food items.

"Jane's a really good cook but her portions are kind of..."

"Small," Dylan finished.

Jack found some dried mushrooms, limp scallions, and the remaining ten eggs for a late-night omelet.

———>●<———

After David left, Jane forced herself to just sit in the kitchen, not scurrying around, only thinking. She couldn't pretend to know what the right pace was for this odd romance with a man both married and not married. "Will you think about us living together?" David had asked while helping her with the dishes. She had yelped a little when he spoke—the question was that unexpected.

"I didn't mean to actually scare you," he said, but she could tell he was amused and not offended. Now, alone, she did feel frightened, along with an equal part thrilled, which did nothing to guide her towards a decision.

She reminded herself to think kindly about the fiasco that was her first marriage. She had stopped being a teenager only months before Charlie showed up to claim her, the conquest that had once been denied him. She would have been so much better off if she'd let him humiliate her and break her heart in high school, when nobody—nobody—got married. He was smart enough to wait until marriage was plausible. She should have played the field in high school instead of losing at the big-stakes game later. But mostly and finally, she needed to forgive herself for having once been twenty.

PART II
WAKING

David actually cringed when Mrs. Nowicki stopped him and asked that they meet. He hadn't seen Kate for more than two weeks because of travel and then the flu. Or was it three? He'd wanted to come sooner, but when the director heard him cough into the phone, he was forbidden. Was she now going to examine his throat? They walked to her office, where a solemn young man was waiting. She introduced him as "Dr. Tsang, the primary investigator for the study."

David felt a moment of panic. What could he possibly be investigated for? Then he heard her elaborate: "the primary investigator for the new drug trial your wife has been on"—and he remembered Dylan using the short form, "P.I." and his heart calmed a bit. Now they were shaking hands and Dr. Tsang said, "Please call me John, Dr. Sanders."

"What's going on? Is something wrong?"

"There have been some changes in your wife's condition. She began showing some small improvements, and she hasn't regressed as people tend to do. We think it's because of the trial medication. There are three groups, and it's too early to break the code, so we don't know yet which of the two drug combinations she's on. I'm reasonably confident that she wasn't placed in the third group, the placebo." He looked as if he expected David to say something here, but David couldn't form any words, and the young doctor continued. "We wanted you to know that if you decide to see her today, you will notice some changes."

David stared, dumbfounded.

"I can't stress enough that these improvements may not last, and all of this could be very painful for you. You certainly have the option of waiting to see her until we know more."

David wasn't sure he had ever been astonished before. He heard himself say, as if from a great distance, "What do you mean by 'improvements'?"

"We see more signs of alertness, more responsiveness. Please understand that we have no way of knowing how your presence will affect her or how temporary these changes could be."

"Of course I want to see her! Can I see her now? I don't see any reason to wait."

Mrs. Nowicki stood and said, "I'll take you to her. She's in the library."

"I hope it goes well," Dr. Tsang said, "and please stop in the consulting room before you're ready to leave. I'd like to hear your impressions."

Mrs. Nowicki said nothing as they walked in silence to the library. She left him at the door with, "I'll be close by."

Kate was sitting in a love seat, the Trout Quintet playing on a nearby radio. One cat was on her lap while another perched on the chair back, looking jealous. David approached and, without looking up, Kate said, "David, why did we stop keeping cats?"

David froze. He struggled to sound calm as he answered, "I don't know. The last cat died and Dylan arrived. We just never got back to cats, I guess."

"I love these cats," she said emphatically, looking up at him.

There was a crispness here, faint and missing for so long, but detectable. He didn't trust his legs and wanted to sit but couldn't imagine navigating his body even a few inches.

"But I could probably learn to love a new one."

He realized she had spoken as if it were a question for him to answer.

"Oh, Katie," he said. "I'm sure you could. "

He looked at the ceiling, hoping for control. Kate held out her arms and after he covered the short distance to sit beside her, he began to cry and then sob. She held him and, after a long while, she tried to dry his face with tissues. Then he reached for the box so he could dry where he'd drenched her.

They both blew their noses, the pile of wet tissues growing in their laps. Kate studied him and said, "Poor David."

He said, "Well, you haven't exactly been at your best either, you know," and they smiled at each other and then laughed, or perhaps he was crying again, he couldn't tell.

———

An aide brought two dinners into the library for them. Neither was hungry, though they urged each other to eat, and she did eat a few bites.

"You need energy," he said. "This must all be exhausting."

"The food here isn't really very good."

"I know." He didn't really mind the food and often paid extra to share a meal with Kate. Mostly, he had liked someone cooking a meal for him.

"I mean, it's not truly terrible, just not very inspiring."

"I'll bring you lunch and dinner tomorrow if it's not against the rules. Think about what you'd like."

She laid her fork down with a dreamy expression.

"You don't have to decide now. Take your time."

A quick thought of Jane flitted across his mind, but when he tried to picture her, it was like trying to think of a forgotten word—that elusive tickle—and he stopped trying.

"David," Kate said. "These last few nights, I've stopped feeling so…temporary. I really think I'll still be here tomorrow—maybe not next week necessarily, but tomorrow seems likely. But, still, I want to stay on here for a bit. I don't trust any of this."

He didn't think she meant him.

"Here's what you can do: tell me three good things about each boy," she said, and he did, even though it made her cry again. Then he told her about the dented cars and drowned cell phones, none of which was funny at the time, but it made her laugh. Finally, and only because she made him, he left to walk towards the exit. After six paces, he returned to the library to look at her and hold her one more time. The second time he left, he made it to the next hallway, where Dr. Tsang was on the lookout for him.

They sat, leaning forward almost knee to knee and talked for thirty minutes. No, the researcher couldn't guarantee how long the improvements would last, though he was hopeful. Yes, David could bring Kate nutritious food. And no, he wasn't to tell anyone except their sons, and not over the phone.

"This is what's called a Phase I clinical trial—the first group of people to ever be given this treatment—and there are only 63. Usually we never even get to Phase II, where we can test 100 to 300 people, but I'm hopeful—very hopeful."

David wasn't sure he was following all this and was suddenly too tired to pursue it. They stood and shook hands and then segued into a brief hug. One of them seemed to be quivering, or maybe it was both of them. He left and drove home, hoping some sleeping pills could still be found in the bowels of the medicine cabinet. He couldn't imagine quieting his mind any other way.

———————>✺<———————

Jane drove to work mulling over the fact that it was Wednesday and she hadn't heard from David since Sunday. On Sunday, they had talked a little more about living together, and she thought the conversation had gone well. She didn't think she had betrayed how frightening she found his suggestion. She understood that David had found married life safe and trustworthy, the opposite of her experience, and he was offering her at least some version of what he had known with Kate. Was she willing to join lives with someone she couldn't be married to? She was in a kind of Catch-22: if David divorced Kate to marry her, he wouldn't be quite the person she thought he was. She could only completely admire him if she couldn't completely have him.

If the time came, she would tell him they could live in his house if he wanted. It would be better for Dylan and Jack. "Sometimes young adults need a familiar place to come home to as much as younger kids do," she would tell him and he would tease her. "Sometimes I think you like those boys better than you like me." But she hadn't had a chance to make this hypothetical, sometime-in-the-future offer because her only text to him had gone unanswered, though he didn't always notice the alerts reaching his phone.

She arrived at the staff meeting a little early and, like many of her co-workers, also a little annoyed. The regular Tuesday meeting had been rescheduled on short notice because the primary investigator for the drug studies they were involved with couldn't make it that day. Everyone wondered why he couldn't just come to the next scheduled meeting, but instead they had been summoned on a Wednesday.

Dr. Tsang was first on the agenda, and he introduced himself again, looking young and nervous. People listened politely as he reminded them of the clinical studies in place. Then without any fanfare, he announced that it appeared that three of the local subjects were showing a positive response to one or more of the drug combinations being studied. Jane stopped breathing.

A young psychologist, Ethan, joked, "Yeah, so what else is new?" and everyone laughed.

"Yes, I know," Tsang said. "I know what you're saying. The effects could be gone tomorrow. But today it looks interesting. So we're going to talk about how to answer relatives' questions. The staff has been reminded of every rule in HIPPA, including not discussing patients even when omitting names." He took the time to make eye contact with everyone. "People will lose their jobs if they talk."

Jane was breathing again, but barely.

"We've also asked the relatives not to discuss this with anyone, and I think they understand why. If privacy is breached beyond a certain point, we cannot guarantee that their loved one will continue to be included in the trials. However, you may be asked questions either by a subject's family, or patients without dementia, and their relatives, or possibly by staff. I've printed out some sample questions and how we'd like you to answer them, but I need your help with things I may have overlooked. And I want to know if the answers are worded in a way that seems natural, and believable. I know I sound like a robot sometimes. At least that's what my friends tell me." A few people laughed, surprised at his informality.

"It is possible," he said cautiously, "that at some point, members of the media will arrive. No one may speak with them. Refer them to me, and ask that they email me. They will try to trick you. Assume everyone who isn't your relative or best friend is media. If we do our jobs right, they won't arrive. We don't want them. Hopefully, my warnings will prove unnecessary, but please, I beg of you, don't grab your fifteen seconds of fame on the backs of the subjects and their families. Did I get that saying right?"

"We get your meaning," Ethan said.

Then Tsang handed out pages of scripted answers for them to use if needed. On the third page, in large, bolded letters were his name and email address.

Jane sat motionless, staring at the papers. One of the three had to be Kate. There was no other reason David had stopped calling. Everything that had seemed right, or right enough, now seemed wrong—wrong and dangerous. She should have stayed clear. She should have treated it as a secret fling. Maybe she should have waited for him to divorce.

But how would that have changed anything? A divorce wouldn't have stopped what was about to happen. And even though she knew that whatever miraculous remission had occurred might be fragile and short-lived, she couldn't even begin to bring herself to root against Kate.

As the meeting wound down, she pretended to get a message on her phone and left the room murmuring apologies. She cancelled her next two appointments and drove home, shaken and lightheaded. Hardly anyone she knew had died, and yet this feeling was so familiar. She felt desperate to reach the safety of her house, but when she entered through the kitchen door and went to get a glass of chilled water—her throat felt dry and feverish—she was greeted by a photo of David, laughing, and another of the boys arm-wrestling in her kitchen.

She hung her coat next to the jackets he kept at her house, which hung above the extra work shoes he wore when, over her protests, he helped her with outdoor chores. She paced through the house, which felt dulled, as if a film had settled across everything.

———>●<———

His love for Jane was somewhere. It was as if there was now a folder—he could picture it on his cluttered screen—marked "Jane" that he couldn't open right now. He would call her tomorrow. He would call her house while she was at work and leave a vague message. He would text her, "Miss you. Things are crazy," with no abbreviations. Jane teased him about his text etiquette— "so proper, so refined." He would defend himself: "Do you really want to hear from someone who doesn't think he has time to spell 'you'?"

———>●<———

"Don't you hate it here?"

Kate reached for her hairbrush and worked it through her already tidy hair.

As he waited, she set the brush down and made eye contact.

"The first few times I went outside, it was so intense, sort of like LSD, but different and not fun. I felt assaulted by the birds, squirrels, flowers, noises, my thoughts—there was so much *life*. Everything was too much. It's safe and quiet here. My mind is racing all the time. I go through test after test with them, trying to remember what I remember and where it stops. I think I remember arguing about driving. I thought you were jealous and wanted to imprison me."

Yes, he had been relentless in criticizing her driving, determined to prevent whatever accident was on its way as she drove around lost and disoriented.

She gave him an apologetic smile that broke his heart. "After a series of days of consistently having my brain back, I felt ready—enough to see you—but I can't run right home. See it all again. Lose it all again."

Her voice got small and she said, "I'd be lost—what with all the changes. There must be new countries I know nothing about."

"Actually, there were a lot of old countries you knew nothing about."

She stuck her tongue out at him.

"We can catch up. We'll start with what you remember, and you can read one news magazine a week online. Or one a day—whatever you want."

"The doctors might not like it."

"I don't know. We'll listen to them, but you get to decide things. I'm just your medical power of attorney for when you're incapacitated. Like you are for me."

She stared at him, "Wait, am I *still* your medical power of attorney?"

It took him a moment to get her point. "It never occurred to me," he said, and he laughed and then laughed louder.

Kate was laughing so hard she struggled to spit out the words, "You may want to update that document sometime."

An aide walked by and peeked in, "Everything okay here?" They became quiet and he moved to sit closer. He raised his arm for Kate to slide under, fitting against him, as she had for most of her adult life.

⟶➤●◄⟵

Dylan left work as soon as he arranged for someone to cover his shift and walked the short block to Starbucks to wait for Lily. He and Jack had been summoned home: Their mother was improving on some experimental drug. Dylan couldn't imagine it. For the first few years, he would regularly delude himself that she was getting better and not worse, but nobody, including him, made that mistake anymore.

Lily found him at the out-of-the-way table he'd been lucky to grab. She'd slipped away from work to have coffee with him before he went to get Jack. Unusual for her, she tried to get him to talk about what it was like to go home. His family was a topic she had learned to avoid.

"There's no reason to describe it," he said now. "There's no reason for even one more person to experience this."

"I don't think that's how it works. You don't get to have this huge thing that I can only guess at." She gave him a sad smile he'd never seen before.

He grabbed her hand, swallowed his coffee in two gulps, and suggested they walk to a nearby park. Then he told her everything he could remember.

"One time, she asked me where my camp counselor was. This smart woman—this person who had helped me with my college admissions essay—thought I was at summer camp."

When he started to cry, he didn't stop talking. He talked on and she rummaged in her purse for tattered tissues that he quickly saturated.

"'Somewhere, she misses you.' My dad would say that some-times." His eyes were sore and he was exhausted in that way peculiar to crying, but he didn't regret telling her. Maybe it would make him feel better someday.

"Is this why you ignored me for so long? My friends thought I was nuts to keep hoping."

"Do you remember that stand-up comic we were watching, the guy with the initials instead of a last name—Louie CK? 'You'll meet the perfect person who you'll love infinitely and with whom you'll grow old together. And then she's going to die. That's the best outcome. The best thing that can happen is—she'll die.'" She moved closer to him on the bench and he opened his jacket to fit around her. "It's dangerous. It just seems dangerous. That's why I go back to my place sometimes. When I start to feel married."

She held onto his jacket as she turned to face him, then whispered, "Thank you."

———◦———

Kate's door was ajar, and David hung back as the boys knocked once before entering. Kate stood next to the small couch, watching both boys, who walked towards her. "Hi, boys," she said. She looked a little afraid. "I feel a lot better now."

She drew them into a tight circle and they hugged for a long time. Someone—probably both of them (David couldn't tell their voices apart)—said, "Mom," three or four times, but after that it was quiet. They broke apart and squeezed onto the love seat. It seemed to him that they hadn't settled in like this since elementary school. No one talked, and oddly, no one cried. The three of them had their eyes closed and almost seemed asleep.

When David got to the kitchen early the next morning, both boys were up, wet hair combed and dressed marginally better than usual.

"You're up early."

"We're going to see Mom now. Where's that little video camera we got you?" Dylan asked, looking through some drawers.

David found it in a drawer Dylan had just rifled and handed it over with a fresh battery. "There's a small tripod for it in the corner of the coat closet. You're going to record your mom?"

"Yes," Jack said.

"'Tell her I'll bring lunch… unless she's too tired."

Jack found the tripod and headed out the door, then turned and, not quite meeting David's eye, said, "You know, don't you, that we won't tell her anything? You do what you need to do."

"Unless she asks," Dylan clarified. "But I don't think she's going to ask. Us." He didn't want to think about the Jane situation. His dad took care of everything, and he would take care of this too. Had he and Jack been too welcoming of Jane? Maybe they should have been less sad and more angry and persuaded their dad he was giving up too soon. Hindsight. The concept of *too soon* had never entered his mind then. What other grounds for objection? That their dad was married? He could have easily gotten a divorce. What would a divorce have solved? No, the only honest argument was: *You should be alone.* And they hadn't used it.

When the sun was high enough to warm the garden, they found a bench they could all squeeze into. Dylan set the tripod in place and turned on the tiny video camera to see if he had his mother positioned correctly—or if she objected—but all she said was, "It's so small—it looks like a CIA gadget. Wherever did you get that?"

"We got it for Dad maybe three years ago. He used it at Jack's graduation. It's a little outdated. Most people use their phones now." Dylan watched her puzzle out that statement. "We didn't use it a lot, but I'll play what we have for you when we get to a computer." After a pause, he said, "I wish we had used it more."

Jack intoned for the camera, "It's a beautiful Saturday morning and we are at the Loon Lake Ladies Retirement Home—no apostrophes—and we are about to ask our mother, 'What's new, Mrs. Sanders?'"

Kate gave a big smile. "Oh, it's just another day hanging with my kids. They're going to fill me in on the last few years. I hope they'll just start talking, because I don't want to have to ask a bunch of questions. Plus, they do *not* like being questioned."

They tripped over their words trying to describe for her what she had missed.

"Some of it, you'll need to see the photos," Dylan said, "to get what we're talking about—like Jack's date for senior prom—her dress."

"In my defense, I did not know she was crazy when she asked me."

They caught her up on school—like their ACT scores, which were within one point of each other. "Don't tell me who scored higher! I don't want to lose respect for the other." She could still make them laugh. She asked about girlfriends and, surprised she'd never suspected, they finally confessed their adolescent rivalry over Maggie. "She was two years older than Jack," Dylan said. "I don't know why he even thought he had a chance."

"I can't believe either of you thought you had a chance. You were still boys and she was gorgeous. "

"We know that now, Mom," Dylan said. "But thanks."

"Yes, thanks."

"And mature too. I mean, I saw her flirt with your dad once at a block party."

"Really? What did he do?"

"I'm not sure he noticed. He was trying to help the younger kids get ready for the bike race."

They told her about Maggie's marriage to the math teacher, whom Kate remembered right away. "You both loved him. He was a great teacher. The mothers used to talk about him too. There was just something about him. You boys never had a chance. I will definitely have to get someone to tell me the luscious details on all of that."

She pulled a notebook out of her pocket and wrote something down.

"What are you doing?" Jack tried to read her writing.

"I've started a list of everything I need to catch up on."

"Well, Mom," Dylan asked, "is that item a list kind of thing or more of a Post-it kind of thing?

"Don't tease. You'll be needing lists and Post-its yourself someday."

They both pulled rumpled aging lists from their back pockets. Dylan's had a small sticky note attached.

Kate gave a delighted laugh. "You are wonderful young men and you make a mother proud. Now, onto the all-important topic: Are there any current girlfriends I should know about?"

Both of them looked at their laps, frozen.

She tilted her head towards Jack. "Are you seeing anyone?"

A small sound of relief escaped him. "I'm trying to make the most of my college years and the supply of beautiful girls."

"Women," she said.

"Yes, women."

"Well, it's probably good to do that for a while. Carefully, of course."

"I am careful and kind," Jack agreed. "Reasonably."

She turned to Dylan, who took a breath and said, "There is someone. I haven't told anybody about her, but I met someone."

Jack's mouth fell open. "Dawg, how long ago? Why didn't you say anything?"

"I don't know. Timing. Timing issues."

Across the lawn, David was walking towards them, carrying a blanket, a small cooler, and a large bag from Kate's favorite sub shop. She gave him an excited wave. "David, good timing. Dylan is just telling us about his girlfriend."

"Wait for me." He all but sprinted, then sat on the ground, first putting his jacket down on the slightly damp grass.

"So, we worked in the same lab for about six months, but I didn't really notice her," Dylan said. "Well, I noticed, but she seemed kind of businesslike, as well as *taken*. I just assumed she was taken. I wasn't getting any signals. Unlike Jack, I like to wait for signals."

"Which is why you've had such a lonely existence," Jack said. "The signal is that they're *talking* to you."

Kate tapped Jack's knee.

"So one day, the two of us were doing some data collection and we were in silly moods because it was a beautiful Friday afternoon. Everyone else had taken off and we were stuck in this gloomy room smelling like rats. I mean *we* smelled like rats, not just the lab. Anyway, we stripped off our masks and goggles and our paper hairnet things, and I said, 'Why, Miss Lily, you look so lovely." And she said, 'You too, Dylan. Goggle-free, you have eyes.'"

"Lily," Kate said. "I love her name."

"It's short for Liliana, which she doesn't like."

"So when did you and your Italian girlfriend get together? When did the goggles finally come off?" Jack asked the question for all of them.

"It's been five months, four days," Dylan said.

God, David thought, running the chronology through his head as he realized all the occasions Dylan could have told him and didn't. *Did I take up all the air in the room?*

It was borderline chilly, so he put his jacket around Kate's shoulders. While they ate, they tried to remember the last time she might have had her favorite Italian sub, and pinned it down to Dylan's senior year of high school. Kate could only eat half, and she divided the rest between Dylan and Jack, as she had done countless times before .

"You're chewing with your mouths closed," she said. "I am truly honored."

"It's our welcome back gift to you," Dylan said.

Jack chewed carefully and pointed to his throat as he swallowed. "Kind of an unusual choice, but we thought it would go over better than jewelry."

"Did you now?" she said.

———————⟫●⟪———————

Dylan and Jack walked single-file down the hallway, sent by their mother to "see a good movie or walk around downtown" for a few hours. They navigated the route to the exit, never glancing in the rooms. Long ago, they had confessed that they tried not to look at anybody when they were at the L. "None of us is supposed to be here," Jack announced quite sometime earlier. "So I just pretend I'm not."

They stood by Dylan's car while they figured out who had the keys.

"Why do I feel like having a cigarette?" Jack said.

"Guilt," Dylan answered as he unlocked the car. "Guilt and cigarettes go together." He inched out of the lot, avoiding an elderly driver barely visible over the steering wheel of a large car. "What do you want to do now?"

"I don't know. I kind of think we should buy her some jewelry."

———⟫●⟪———

David and Kate stopped in the kitchen for tea and brought their cups and extra water to a small parlor, where they sat petting two of the cats. After her last sip of tea, Kate said, "I want to be outside, but I need to sleep for a while first. What do you want to do?"

"Follow you."

He did, to her room, where she lay down on her narrow bed. David said he had to answer a few emails and then he'd read. He checked his mail and started a reply, using one finger.

"What is that?"

"A phone."

"Doesn't look like a phone."

"Well, it's more like a computer."

"I want one."

He smiled. "Tomorrow."

After responding to a few emails, he realized he should have brought a laptop. Being away from the department so much had caused a logjam. He gave up and watched her sleep, and then put his phone away, tilted the reclining chair, and soon dozed, dreaming vaguely about both Kate and Jane, with him apologizing over and over, unconvincingly. He forced himself awake and pulled out the *Times*, determined not to close his eyes again.

Kate was awake and in front of the only mirror in the room. He watched her studying herself until she noticed him.

"My neck took the worst of it."

"You have a fine neck," he said. "We're both...I mean neither of us is—" He stopped, but it was too late. She looked away from him, holding herself rigid. "Kate! You can't be angry with me for noticing we're not young anymore."

She relented and turned fully towards him with something close to a smile. "Does this scarf look good or does it just make it look like I need a scarf?" She finished arranging the fabric.

"It's a very pretty scarf. Have I seen it?"

The smile was gone. "My body has changed—no exercise, except pacing, for years."

"You're slim. You're beautiful."

"I'm all covered up. Do you remember how much I used to walk? And the gym. How often do you go to the gym?"

"Two times a week, three if I can. What are you saying, Kate? What are we talking about here?"

She turned her back to him and spoke into the mirror. "I'm saying I'm humiliated. I lost my brain. I was like a child—less than a child—a pet. I was a god-damned turtle. And now I'm dumpy. Maybe that's petty and ungrateful, but I'm going to get Martha to buy me one of those things—*shapers* they call them—until I get into shape."

"You realize that just relocates things?"

Her reflection glared at him. "Yes, David, I realize that."

"Are we arguing?"

"We seem to be, but I have no idea about what."

"That's not true. You're mad that this happened."

"That makes me a horrible person—that I feel more angry than grateful."

"You got screwed. Besides, we're all horrible in one way or another. Only the degree varies."

"We both got screwed."

"Yes we did." He got up and walked to her. He put his arms around her from behind, turned her to face him, and kissed her on the lips for the first time. She kissed him back and then broke away to lean her head on his shoulder.

There was a knock on the door and Jack entered with Dylan behind him, carrying a large bouquet. David and Kate moved apart, as if they were doing something illicit.

"These are beautiful!" Kate said, taking the bouquet Jack held out. "I can't believe you could find such nice flowers on short notice, and you brought a vase for them."

"We each remembered different things about what you like," Dylan explained. "We don't actually know the names of any flowers, it turns out."

"Still, there was no physical violence involved in selecting these blooms," Jack said.

They studied Kate as she rubbed a lily petal between her fingers. She looked up and said, "Thank you."

Later, when the boys said their goodbyes until the following weekend, Dylan said, "I'll call you every day."

"I'll call you at *least* every day," Jack said and then kissed his mother one last time.

"Almost worth it all," Kate said.

———————

David grabbed Jack by his backpack straps as the boys headed for the door. "Remember: not a word to anybody. About Mom being better, I mean. Because it could affect her eligibility to stay in the study. We don't have any idea how long the medication will work, but we *want her on it.*"

"Well, I'll have to say something to Lily." Dylan thought he should be honest.

"As little as possible." David glared at Dylan, then Jack too, and then he hugged each of them, holding on tight.

———————

Lucy's voice was being broadcast through Jane's landline— she must have called on her cell while knocking on the front door. Finally, she heard Lucy use her key and enter through the front and follow the sound of running water. Jane was standing at the kitchen sink washing the few dishes she had used over the last week. Even then, most of the food went down the disposal.

"Jane, why are you hiding out here? You've barely been at work, you cancelled everything this weekend, and you won't take my calls. Tom is ready to shoot David. Or shoot you. He seems to think killing someone is the answer."

Against her will, Jane felt herself almost smile.

"Shall we cry together?" Lucy asked. "Or are you sick of crying? Shall we be mad or cry? I will do anything to help you."

Jane sat silent. Then very quietly, she said, "I feel like an idiot.

I've not heard one syllable from him."

"You weren't an idiot and neither was he. You will hear from him. I know that much."

The silence grew. "I told Tom I might spend the night."

No response.

"He agreed that it might not be safe for you to be alone."

"I'm *not* thinking of hurting myself," Jane said. "I don't want to live without him. There's nothing suicidal about it."

"That's good to know. I'm spending the night though."

"Of course you are." Jane nodded, resigned. "I hope you brought some good drugs because I have to go into work tomorrow and I haven't slept in days."

"Got your back, kid." Lucy started pawing through her purse and pulled out three pill bottles, their labels dingy, and set them on the table.

"Jesus," Jane said, with a small smile. "What vacation was *that* from?"

"I don't know. Mexico?"

The two old friends sat together, mostly quiet, occasionally talking about their work or one of Lucy's kids. Jane cut up an apple for Lucy, and it looked for a moment as if she might eat some herself, but she didn't. Neither of them drank anything but water, and at eleven, Lucy dispensed one sleeping pill. "Grief is so hard to subdue," she said as she gave Jane an extra half-pill.

"Oh, I remember that," Jane said, with a small, bitter smile.

CHAPTER ELEVEN

David drew up a schedule that allowed him to teach his classes, a light load thankfully, and to deal with the most mandatory of his other responsibilities while also taking time off to be with Kate. He left his proposed schedule for Greta to look over before he took it to the Provost. He thought that was the right person. Or maybe there was an assistant dean somewhere who cared about his work hours. Greta would tell him.

When he arrived at the L after work, Kate was in her room sitting at a small desk the staff had set up for her. She had two notepads and Post-its but wasn't writing. He leaned over to kiss her and she jumped a little.

"Sorry. Didn't mean to sneak up on you. What's going on?"

She took two long breaths and then said, "I need you to describe for me everything that happened—everything that changed about me."

David's spirits sank. Would his punishment never end? "I don't want to do that. Do you really need to know?"

"I'm embarrassed."

"You're embarrassed to tell me something?"

"Well, that too. I'm embarrassed by what I said and did. I need to know." She didn't meet his eyes and appeared to hate the topic as much as he did. "I can get caught up on the other things. I'll read all the back issues of the local paper online, and then I'll read one old Sunday *Times* each week."

"I've begun to wonder if that's a good idea. A lot of bad things have happened."

"Well, I'm assuming that mostly bad things have occurred. It will be just like taking a history class, Professor. Except with the amusing parts left in."

He smiled at her teasing and didn't say out loud that she seemed fragile to him.

"I want you to construct a timeline from when I first got sick—what it was like, everything about the boys and you and our families and our house—the neighborhood. Everything you can remember—the parts not covered by newspapers and magazines. But also me, what happened to me." She was standing now and spoke with confidence. "As much as you can. I know it's asking a lot, but I need to know." She looked away from him. "Did people have to help me in the bathroom? Was I still getting my period? I can't remember. I don't want to know. I don't even know what I want to know."

He suspected that if the situation were reversed, he might feel just as determined to know exactly how humiliated he should feel.

"It always seemed to me that you retained your dignity admirably. You paced and you would refuse to go to meals sometimes or to leave one activity for another, but you were mostly quiet. Some of the others talked non-stop and were hard to be around. Do you have any idea why you were so...mild?"

Her face softened a little.

"I have some memory," she said, "of the beginning, I mean. I know I didn't confide in you. I thought I could will myself to stay...present. I thought if I really tried, I could just maintain some plateau of vague and ditzy."

"That sounds like torture."

"Yes, it was. Then, when I knew I was losing ground, I made a vow to not talk. I thought my only hope was to make less of a fool of myself. Maybe I retained some slight shred of control that let me be silent. I don't know." A tear slid down her cheek. "It was probably random."

He needed to change the subject. Maybe it was selfish, but he couldn't do any more of this right now. "Can we talk about home? About you coming home." An expression of fear crossed her face, and then she erased it with something neutral. He counted a full seven seconds before she spoke.

"Soon it will be four weeks since we're pretty sure things started changing, and then we'll make a plan," she said. "Dr. Tsang, you know how he is—so not arrogant. He admits they have nothing to go on as far as guidelines. It's a little like amnesia but not very much, and they don't know much about amnesia either. He just tells me we'll know what to do when the time comes. Does he remind you of Dylan a little bit?"

David was surprised to realize she was right. The differences in accent and appearance had kept him from seeing that his son and the doctor shared some qualities—humility and humor included.

"I feel like I've known him forever. He might be part of this huge breakthrough in medicine, but he'll sit and talk with me about what kind of cats I want to get. Or ask for my advice on prenatal care."

"I didn't know he was married."

"Newly married. But he's very painstaking. As you can imagine, he wants to know everything about the prenatal environment.

Pre-conception."

They both smiled. After he and Kate decided it was time to have a baby, she got pregnant the following week and they spent the next nine months in a frenetic scramble to be ready and equipped. They didn't know anything. They sneered at the expensive equipment. Their first stroller cost seventeen dollars. It turned out it was really only for babies who could sit up, so they carried Dylan everywhere for five months. "I almost forgot!" He stood and headed for the door. "I left something in the car. I'll go grab it." He ran to the car and returned, breathless, with a small black and white box.

"A former student at the store spent some time making the phone company cough up a good number." He turned the phone on and showed her. "What do you think?"

"It's a good number. Easy. And the phone is so…lovable. Even the box is beautiful. Don't throw it out." He shut the phone down and then turned it on, showing her the almost hidden controls. He touched the photo icon.

"Look," she said. "You took a bunch of photos of computers for me. And here you are, showing off an incredibly thin laptop."

"Some guy that writes for the *Times* accidentally recycled it with his newspapers right after he bought the first model." David explained that instead of a manual for the phone, there was a built-in guide. "And you can always go online, where you'll find your question has been asked and answered, though sometimes rudely."

He helped her pick a ring tone and they called each other. She left texts for Dylan and Jack after he explained the current status of voicemail.

"When we were young, we would have killed for voice mail, even answering machines," Kate said. "Anything but the mysterious, unblinking black phone. Or green. Maybe it was green."

⟶⟫●⟪⟵

Jane came to the door, clearly expecting someone else or at least not him. She eyed him with a tight, formal expression. "Hello, David." She looked quickly up and down the street and moved aside to let him into the entryway. Her arms were folded and he didn't even try to edge further into the house.

He stood there. He had no idea how to begin.

She took the lead. "I hear that Kate is much better. I'm very happy for you. One of the researchers even used the word *miracle*."

She waited, perfectly rigid and polite.

"Please don't treat me like one of your clients," he said. They were still standing in the hall.

"Do you think I feel this way around a client?" Her voice was flat now.

"Oh my God. I am so sorry. I don't know why I said that." Of course she was angry. How could she not be? And sad. He had broken her. He placed his hands gently on her shoulders and pulled her against him. "Jane, I'm sorry."

She lowered her arms to let her body relax against his, but only for a few seconds before she pulled away.

"Give me some time," he said again. "We'll figure this out."

She brightened a bit when he said "we" but sank again as if she realized that neither of them knew what he meant by *we*. She took two small steps back.

"I'll leave right now if you want, but I'd really like to stay for a while and talk. I know you're hurt that I didn't call you, and I understand why. I don't know how to convey what the last ten days have been like." She didn't object. "It's felt more like three days."

He headed inside the house, and she followed him to the living room, where they sat facing each other, her expression impartial.

"You're on my mind a lot, but always with the horrifying footnote that I've hurt you. I would have bet everything that I would never willingly hurt you."

"How does Kate seem?"

He didn't see any way not to answer. "Amazingly like herself. Though I think she's pretty traumatized."

"Of course." She straightened out a corner of the area rug. "And it went well with the boys?"

He couldn't stop himself from smiling. "Yes, that was some reunion. That was good." He didn't know what she was waiting for.

Finally she said, "Do you know if you're going to tell her about us?"

Why did he make her ask? He was not good at this. "Of course I will. For many reasons. Not the least of which is that about a hundred people already know. I'm just not sure when or how."

"How do you think she'll react?"

"When we were married—I mean, before she got sick—I felt certain that if I ever cheated, she would leave. But obviously, this situation is different."

"Different. Yes, it is," she said, and she almost smiled at the understatement.

⟶⤛●⤜⟵

Three staff members walked by David's car—it was shift change—and looked at him curiously, but he needed to sit for a while longer. He couldn't execute a quick transition from one woman to another, and he wondered how adulterers managed it. Maybe that was the part they liked: the proximity, the near slapstick timing of the scheduling. He sat until some necessary interval had passed and then went inside, where he found Kate in her room, lying on the twin bed reading a Jane Austen novel he hadn't heard of.

"It's comforting sometimes to read something old. My remedial reading is as grim as you promised." She smiled and motioned for him to lie down beside her, then lay on her side facing him while she read on.

Abruptly, she lowered the book. "What did you do without me?"

"You mean…"

"You know what I mean."

"Mostly I neutered myself."

"You didn't even masturbate?"

He smiled at the naïve question. "Well, that, yes."

"Did you think of me?"

"Not usually. It was too painful."

"Who then?"

"Drew Barrymore once. Kate Winslett more than once."

She laughed. "I don't believe you."

"The Swedish one a few times." Of course she didn't believe him. Did she really think he would answer these questions?

"Ingrid?" she asked doubtfully.

"No, the daughter, Isabella, but her younger self."

"She's not that old."

"Sorry, didn't work. I had to go with her *Blue Velvet* self."

131

"I can't picture what you're talking about."

"You didn't see it. You had to go deliver a baby. I saw it with Don and Martha. They hated it." He was babbling, unnerved. He was in some theatre of the absurd where he didn't want to be unfaithful to Jane. This was nuts. He was lying here with someone who was still his wife, and who he would probably learn to desire again. Yet, in his mind, she was forbidden.

She studied him seriously for a while and then closed her eyes. She rolled over, too close to the edge of the bed, and he pulled her back to him before he dozed off too.

Later at home, David began writing a retroactive diary. He put it all in: bills she didn't pay, losing her car, the diagnosis, the terror, the end of sex, her escapes from the house, the caretaker twins. People who were sick. People who had died. Unexpected divorces. Happy occasions like weddings, graduations, and new babies. He hoped it was okay to tell her so much. After all, she wasn't a starving plane crash survivor who needed to be carefully and gradually fed.

CHAPTER TWELVE

"Did you tell Mom about Jane?" Dylan asked out of nowhere. They were having a beer on the back patio before leaving to see Kate.

"Good question," Jack said, in a pleasant tone. "And does Jane know about Mom?"

"Jane knows about Mom being better," David answered. "I haven't told Mom anything yet."

Jack looked him squarely in the eye and said, "Why the fuck not?"

"She has a lot to take in right now. And things are complicated." David had expected to say something reassuring and completely loyal. Not this.

"What are you talking about?" Dylan sounded more puzzled than angry.

"Yes, what *are* you talking about? This isn't multiple choice—pick all of the above." Jack set his beer bottle down hard on the glass tabletop. "You realize you're not in *Utah*, don't you?"

They looked at their beers. They looked at the shambles of a garden. Dylan said, "I don't think Jack has ever been in love."

"True," Jack said. "But I've been obsessed. I think he's obsessed with Jane. Call it whatever." He made it sound like a crime. "It will pass. It has passed. Mom's here now."

Dylan watched the two of them. In love for the first time, he didn't see the point of arguing, even though staying quiet made him feel like an accessory. He saw Jack looking at him for backup.

"Why are you just sitting there?"

"I'm not just sitting here, but I don't know how to *make* him do anything."

"Christ, Dylan. We're a family. Or at least we were. And you may have noticed—Mom's sort of at a disadvantage here."

"I know this affects you both," David said. "But you can't be part of it. You have to trust me to figure it out." He started cleaning up. "And I'll trust you not to tell your mother. Let's go over there for dinner and you have to act normal. As far as I can see, she's just as smart as she ever was."

"Yeah, she probably already knows about Jane," Jack said cheerfully.

"She's tracked her down and they're good friends by now." Dylan could almost picture this. They all gave something close to a laugh.

"She's probably got Jane fixed up with somebody already." Jack, who hadn't needed his last beer, added, "Just because we're laughing doesn't mean this is over."

David, who hadn't needed his last two beers, said, "Jesus, Jack, are you threatening me? Of course it's not over. I'll tell Mom, and you worry about your own—" He sounded childish even to himself. "Dylan, you're driving."

"You got that right."

⟶∙◆∙⟵

"Here's what I think," Kate said. "It's getting late and you boys had a long day, so we'll say goodnight. You sleep in tomorrow and have breakfast and play basketball or something. Dad will come over early and we'll talk. Decide things. Then we'll all have a late lunch together. Maybe you could bring lunch. Dad will give you money."

Dylan touched her hand. "I grew up, Mom. I have a job. I even buy my own drugs now, instead of stealing money from your purse. I'll treat."

"Okay. Thank you. And I want all that money back, by the way." Kate made herself tall and kissed his forehead. "Good night, rich guy. See you around one."

Jack stepped up to be kissed too. "I don't have any confessions to make."

"I know. Your crimes are too recent."

She stood on tiptoe but could only reach his cheek. Then she took David's hand and walked with them to the exit, waiting while he stopped at the guest book to sign them out. He kissed her and they repeated their goodbyes all around. As he and the boys reached the exit, he looked back to see her still standing by the book and scattered pens. She was watching the boys elbow each other through the door, her smile still perceptible despite the distance.

CHAPTER THIRTEEN

"I brought the thing you wanted me to write," David said. "Do you want to read it now? Should I leave or stay here?"

"Stay here. I'll probably have questions."

She curled up in the recliner, now set upright, and began to read without hesitation. He made himself look away so he wouldn't try to match her expression with any particular point in the timeline. She was a quick reader and before long turned over the last page and shuffled them all into an orderly pile.

"I've been wondering. Do you think we should renew our vows? I mean considering what's happened? It's like we lost and then found each other."

He was mute. Renewing vows was something she had always ridiculed. He looked at her, hoping for some idea of what to say.

"Oh, for Christ's sake. I know you're in no position to renew any vows. Would you just tell me about her already? Or them? I know you must have somebody. How could you not?"

They were both standing now, and he put a hand on each of her shoulders, then drew her close to him. "I've never purposefully done anything to hurt you and I never will."

"Actually you're kind of hurting my left shoulder right now."

He loosened his grip.

"What's her name?"

"Jane."

She leaned away from him, still and quiet, as if taking inventory after a fall.

"Okay," she said. "I'm glad to hear it from you. That part is good, even though I had to drag it out of you. " She shuddered slightly. "Are we a spectacle?"

"We're not young enough to be a spectacle. To my face at least, people have been kind. A couple of people said she reminded them of you."

"What does she think of that?"

"She's flattered, Kate. She couldn't be anything but."

"Well, then, you'd better tell me about her." She had collected herself to the point of sounding interested in a neutral sort of way. "We've always figured things out. We'll figure this out too," she said.

"Let's sit down," he said. She went back to her chair and he pulled up another next to her.

"About a year ago, one insurance company decided they had paid a medical bill in error and wanted their money back. Big money. Let's be honest: Under other circumstances, you would have been the one handling this kind of thing for us, and it was making me a little crazy and I was scared. Jane was the social worker here at the time and she offered to help."

"Here? You met her *here*?"

"I wasn't looking. It just happened."

"Did you fall in love with her?"

He hadn't expected the question so soon. "Do I have to say it? Do I have to say these things out loud?"

"How else can I understand? How else can we make decisions?"

"Okay," he said. "Yes, I do love Jane. I'm sorry, but I do."

He couldn't read her at all.

Finally, she said, "All right. Now we both know what the situation is. That's a start."

She had done nothing to make him feel cruel, so of course that's how he felt.

———⟫●⟪———

They walked outside and the sun, unfiltered by trees, shocked her. David gave her his sunglasses and squinted as he clicked the remote to unlock his sedan. They were going to meet the boys for lunch at a place far enough away that they wouldn't know anyone. It was her first outing beyond the confines of the L.

She stopped walking. "Do I have a car?" she asked.

"I sold it to help the boys with cars."

"That's good. That was smart." She clapped her hands once. "So I get to buy a car. If we're not too broke, I might even buy a new one. I know it's stupid, but I might do it anyway. Or maybe I'll lease one, since who knows how long …. Wait, do I have a driver's license?"

"You do. I renewed it. I have no idea why and it's probably a felony. I just checked no to the medical questions. I knew you weren't driving anywhere. And I just couldn't stand to tell them."

She squeezed his hand and they both stood quietly until she said, "I'll have to practice driving, though. I remember how disorienting driving felt after being inside with a new baby for just a few weeks."

"I've been thinking about what to say to the boys about Jane. I want to let them know that you and I talked about her."

"Maybe that's all there is to say right now. You can't really say more than you're sure about."

David knew this was his cue to say he *was* sure. That he was married again, completely, and that Jane had been a brief and awkward detour. He didn't say any of this, even though he felt surprisingly relieved that Kate knew, and that this mess was no longer his to bear alone. For the first time, he thought he understood why a spouse would confess adultery.

⟶•⟵

Kate pulled into the parking lot, shut the car off, and turned towards him in her seat.

"You had a good idea—for me to try driving back to the L," she said. "Maybe I'm not as far behind as I thought I'd be."

"And lunch went well," he said. "You being out. The boys."

"We still have great kids." She took his sunglasses off, blinked, then put them back on.

"I've read the guest log," she said, "and I saw how rarely my parents and Claire came to see me. Actually for Claire, it wasn't that much different than when I was well, and I understand why. For all of them, I understand. But it makes me think that we can wait a while before we tell them. I'm not ready to see them, and they'll try to come immediately once they know."

He didn't argue.

"Tell me something—why do you think my mother has been so mean to you? She used to be crazy about you. I never would have predicted she'd turn on you."

He shrugged. "I think this thing just floored her and it never stopped. Maybe it helped a little to have someone to be mad at— to get a little break from her grief."

"I'm sorry."

"No! Please don't apologize. Not for any of this. Please."

Neither said anything for a while.

Then she cleared her throat. "I want you to take a few days off from seeing me. Don't come back until Thursday. That will still give us time to talk before the meeting on Friday."

"I can do that. But why?"

"Do I really have to say it out loud?"

"Maybe we just shouldn't say anything out loud." David knew he sounded like a child.

Kate smiled.

———⟫●⟪———

Jane answered on the fourth ring. As always, he appreciated the clarity of one landline calling another. Her voice was sleepy and when he apologized, she didn't deny that he woke her.

"But I'm happy that you did," she added. She waited for him to speak next and, while he wanted to pretend that he had told Kate about her, he admitted, "She made it easy by asking. She was shocked, even though she had guessed, but still shocked. I mean to hear how serious it was."

He guessed Jane was holding her breath.

"But she was kind, very kind. There was no outrage or even what I could call self-pity. You'd really like her."

"I'm sure that's true. Actually, it's already true."

"I have no idea what's going on," he said. "It's only been a few hours since she's known for sure, and now we're not going to see each other until Thursday."

"Why is that?"

"It's what she wanted."

"She certainly understands men."

He wanted to ask about that but knew better. "Then on

Friday, we meet with the team and she thinks the topic will be going home."

"Oh."

"I want you to know that these last two weeks, we haven't had sex. She doesn't seem to be interested. And me, well, I'm a mess. It hasn't really come up. I don't know if that helps with anything."

She didn't speak. What could she possibly say? "Let me know when you do?"

"Look, do you want to get together today or this week? For coffee or dinner?" Then he added, with more honesty, "Or for anything you want."

The pause was long enough that he felt hopeful.

"I don't think I could do that,' she said, "but it's always nice to be asked."

<hr />

David waited at Martha's side door. Don's car was gone. He remembered that Don played cards most Sunday evenings, and it always went later than planned. He could have talked to both of them, but seeing her alone felt more correct.

Martha came to the door with a somewhat fearful smile and brought him in.

"I have some news that's good," David said. "Mostly good. Well, it's all good right now." He didn't sound entirely coherent. The medical team had prepared them with a story, a lie, and now he had to use it for the first time. "A few months ago, the doctors began to question their diagnosis of Kate. There are some better drugs out now for treating the damage from certain kinds of strokes. They decided that her dementia was more from bleeding and related stroke damage. Since then, she's been responding really well to an experimental medication. Three meds combined, actually."

Martha opened her mouth twice but made no sound. Finally, on her third try, she was able to form words. "Did you say *better?* What do you mean?" They were both sitting at the kitchen table now, and she leaned forward and took one of his hands. She dug her nails in. He flinched, but she didn't notice.

"She's alert and she communicates well. She remembers things up until the memory loss got more severe. We're going to talk with the doctors this week about her coming home for a visit."

Comprehension filled Martha's face. She let go of his hand. "I couldn't see her the last time I tried. They said she was being verbal that day and she didn't want to see anyone. I meant to ask you if that had happened to you, but you were away… and then I forgot. It was a few weeks ago and I haven't tried again." Her voice trailed off. "I'm down to only once a month now."

"Stop it. You are a completely loyal friend." Martha burst into tears. She cried loudly, not even trying to speak. Several long minutes went by, and then she went to the sink, where she cried even harder before quieting and splashing water on her face. When she turned back, her face was swollen and pale. She sat across from David and remained there, smiling.

"You're the only person we've told outside of the boys," he said. "You can understand our fears of…fears that the good results might not last."

"Oh no," she said emphatically. "God wouldn't do that to her twice. She'll be fine. We'll just insist on it."

"Kate wanted me to tell you before anyone else. You can tell Don, but only if he promises not to gossip. She really wants a quiet re-introduction to the world." They smiled at this. Don's idea of gossip was to inform a friend of another friend's death. He wouldn't tell a soul.

"She might not want to see you until she's home, but I don't really know. She's really embarrassed about having been ill. I'll ask her about it, and I'll also ask her if she wants to talk on the phone. I got her an iPhone, and it's already like her third child."

"Oh!" Her expression collapsed. She looked at her lap a moment, as if deciding whether to speak her mind, then said, "I forgot about Jane. What are you going to do about Jane?"

David had rehearsed his answer. "Jane is very happy for Kate and the boys."

"Well, that's good then," Martha said, not acknowledging his careful wording. "Of course Jane would understand. She's a good person."

They stood and hugged and she cried again, though when he drew back, he saw that a dazed and happy expression had settled across her face.

<hr />

"I've never heard you express any interest in running!"

Jane had allowed David quick phone calls spaced several days apart, and this time she told him she had begun to train for a half-marathon.

"I wanted something very different," she said. "And the pain helps, in an odd way."

It was her only reference to what he had done to her. It was good to see how strong she was, even though it meant she was pulling further and further away. Soon, someone else would discover her. He would need to learn to tolerate that idea, because he knew he could never learn to not think of her at all.

During this week of his quasi-banishment, he connected with

Kate only once, and she wanted to talk only of her survey of recent history.

"We have an openly gay senator!" she said. "It seems so wonderful and so fast. And no one even cares anymore. It was mentioned, like, once in the paper and then dropped. I can't believe you didn't tell me that, first thing."

"It didn't occur to me to say, 'Welcome back. One of our two senators is gay.'"

She asked him to come to the L Friday morning.

"Friday? What happened to Thursday? You told me to come Thursday."

"Friday's better," she said.

After they said goodbye, he walked through the house collecting Jane's belongings—hairdryer, makeup, and two sweaters. They all fit easily in his dresser drawer.

———>❦<———

David slept fitfully and lay awake at four in the morning. For Kate, was Friday's meeting like the equivalent of an oral exam for a dissertation? Or worse? Did the team want her to stay? Leave? He knew that embarrassment plagued her, though she didn't talk about it much. How did she feel about meeting with Dr. Ratha, who had catalogued her descent? Could anyone be clearheaded in such a setting?

He looked at the empty expanse of bed and tried to picture her next to him. The more recent memories of sharing this room with Kate eluded him, but now the image of a New Year's Eve ten, maybe fifteen years ago played vividly in his mind. She had been dressing for a party and came to show him the outfit: a glittery skirt with a high slit and a low-cut blouse over a pushup bra.

It was an outfit a sales clerk had talked her into, including the bra, which seemingly returned her breasts to their pregnancy size and prompted a moment of nostalgia in him. She looked sexy and self-conscious, but before he could say anything, she left and came back in her robe. "You don't need me to dress like that, do you?"

"I definitely do not need that," he answered, as he untied her robe and reached inside. He began to touch her. "Sweetie, let's wait until after the party. I hate being wet from you and then going out. It takes hours." He backed off, but she said "oh, what the hell," and they had the kind of quick sex people have with two kids roaming the house.

He got up afterwards to investigate the sounds of the boys fighting but, by the time he arrived in the basement, the dispute seemed settled. When he went back upstairs to finish dressing, he found her in a black dress, familiar and comfortable, not cut low or high. By the time the party was over, he had observed every man there studying her.

He had made sure to ration his beers, and when the hosts circulated with champagne, he only pretended to drink, so that in the early morning of the new year, when they came into their dark living room, he was ready for her as she shrugged off her coat and pulled him to the couch. "Listen to our quiet house. Notice the sound of two kids away at sleepovers. I might make noise for the first time in fifteen years." She lifted her hips so he could pull up the black dress, under which she wore only sheer black stockings that reached mid-thigh. He came quickly. "You are just too much for me," he apologized. "Don't worry. I'm almost there." He began to slide down her belly and between his fluids and hers, he couldn't detect any friction, but almost immediately she arched her back to meet him and cry out. She tugged on him and he inched his way up until they lay curved on their sides.

"God, I love New Year's," he'd said and he could feel her smile. And then her voice turned abruptly solemn: "Do you think we'll always be this lucky?" David, for whom the quiet fear of losing what he loved was never far, like gum on his shoe, had lied. "I'm sure of it," he said, his breath on the back of her neck. Then, worried he hadn't been convincing, he said it again.

A shrill noise startled him and he realized that, paradoxically, he must have relaxed enough to doze until the screeching alarm woke him. Relieved that the long night was over, he took a shower and chose his clothes with care, as if he too had some kind of audition today.

<hr>

They ate breakfast in the dining room, or rather, he ate two breakfasts because Kate couldn't eat hers. He ate out of nerves more than hunger and consumed more bacon than he'd ever had in one meal. The meeting wasn't until noon and it was barely nine when back in Kate's room, David came out with it and said, "Do you want to come home?" He didn't tell her about the insurance company cutting off payments soon. He had to know what she wanted. He waited for her to answer, failing to read the expression on her face.

"Of course I want my life back and it must seem bizarre that I'm not eager to leave. But to go back to the scene of the crime, so to speak, is daunting. I want to—of course I do. But I feel safe here. Why, I'm the cream of the crop."

She didn't smile. She was biting her lip and looked uncomfortable. He waited. He believed everything she said, but it felt too slender. He moved to sit in the recliner and said, "I know there's more. There's something you don't want to explain."

"It has nothing to do with Jane."

"Let me guess." He thought he had the essence of it, though the words were sliding around in his mind, just out of grasp. "I think that you're worried that this *miracle* is somehow connected to you being here and staying here. You don't trust the meds will keep working, but you trust them a little more because you're living here."

She nodded.

"You think that if you leave here, you'll jinx it and we'll be home, going through the same horrible thing again. And you think it's irrational to feel that way."

She nodded again. "What do you think?"

"I think these are the times when we veer towards superstition. I'll bet even the docs feel that way. But home is only where you got sick, not what made you sick."

She fit herself onto his lap. "What do we do?"

He stroked her hair as he tried to conjure something helpful to say. "How did you deal with women in labor? When they wanted to leave the room and call the whole thing off? Or they'd ask for medication when it was too late? Or they thought they were going to die?"

"I just helped them wait."

"Okay, I'll wait with you," he said. "We'll help each other wait."

Somehow they were comfortable in the small space, their breathing slow and synchronized, until someone knocked at the door. They both jumped. "I don't need to come in," Mrs. Nowicki's muffled voice said. "I'm sorry that the meeting had to be scheduled for noon. Just wanted to see if you'd like an early lunch or a snack."

David gestured, putting his finger down his throat. "Thank

you," Kate called back. "We're fine, though we might go for a drive to pass the time."

"How much more bacon can they feed us?" David whispered and she laughed.

They did get up then and make their way out to the car. David followed the winding roads away from the L and stopped at the first station for gas. Kate stared at the price but didn't comment. They continued deeper into the suburb to look for a reasonable imitation of one of the downtown coffee houses.

"I wonder if it will be like a parole hearing and I'll be like those old-timers who aren't sure if they want to leave prison. And the doctors won't be sure either because they want me in a controlled environment where nothing will destabilize me. We need each other—the doctors and I. I'm surprised they haven't suggested you move in."

"Actually, Megan did," he said. "Though as a joke, of course."

"Megan? Oh, the child social worker. I love her. Is that her first name? To me, she calls herself Mrs. Something, trying to seem over twenty-one, I think. She's very smart. Is she from the same place as Jane?"

"Yes," he said and nothing else.

She turned and looked out the window for the next half-mile but then turned back and looked at him straight on. "Have you had contact with Jane since I...reappeared?"

"I went to see her Tuesday. To apologize."

"Apologize?"

"I can apologize for hurting her even if I didn't exactly do anything wrong."

"What happened?"

"She listened. She asked after you and the boys."

She was looking out the window again.

"She's prepared to see the end of me. She's very dignified. There won't be any scenes. She would never fight for me."

"She won't fight for you."

"No," he said. "There's no chance of that."

"That *is* dignified," she said, now facing him.

———◦———

Kate decided she didn't feel ready to be in a public place, so they went through a drive-through and headed back, sipping carefully while they listened to a public radio show on animal intelligence. When their dogs and cats were alive, they both believed their animals were craftier than current science would admit. If Kate told him one of the dogs had humiliated himself with abysmal fetching skills at the park, he believed her account of the poor guy's embarrassment, and when he described the herding behavior the older cat had developed to bring him to the treat drawer, he knew she would believe him. She liked his explanation that the cat didn't try it with her because he knew she kept track of his treat schedule, but he could usually con David. "Does that make him smarter than you?" Kate had asked innocently.

"Well, it certainly makes him more organized," he admitted.

———◦———

Dr. Tsang, or "John" as he reminded them, closed the door, and David realized no one else was joining them. "I'll try to call you John," Kate said, "but you are always Doctor, spelled out in fact, and Tsang in my mind."

Tsang sat where he could look at them both. "We thought it was better if you only had to talk with one of us first and then we can meet with the others to see if there are questions or planning items to complete. I think that you're comfortable with me, Mrs. Sanders—more comfortable perhaps than with the others. I mean to say that you've had more contact with me. Anyway, I want to ask you how you feel about the idea of returning home."

"Well, let's see," Kate said. "I have no career and no nursing license, and will probably never be able to get my license back. There's not even a sliver of a guarantee that the meds will keep working, yet oddly enough, even with all the world news I'm catching up on, I feel smashing."

Dr. Tsang smiled. "I'm glad to hear this." He inhaled audibly and said, "Can you talk a little about leaving here?"

"I'm afraid the medications will stop working as soon as I'm home. I'm embarrassed to see everyone who knew me when I was well, and then not well. I'm afraid we'll all be put through this again. But also I think this is like taking off a Band-Aid and I have to do it now and fast." She sat back and exhaled deeply. "I can breathe again. That's a good sign."

David took advantage of the pause to say, "We wonder about the reason Kate's better. I mean, what's the mechanism of action?" He remembered the term from listening to Dylan, or perhaps Kate.

"I'm sorry to tell you that we don't really know for sure. I know that's not the answer you're hoping for, but sometimes the best drugs are the ones we understand the least." He spoke for a while about the mechanics and David caught the phrase *plaques and tangles*, which seemed like part of a poem, and *tau*, which sounded like a religion. "We were expecting some mild improvements based on the animal results but, for a few people, there's been a much stronger effect, as if something has actually been... repaired. We'd like to do an MRI in a few weeks, but the best testing would require..." He offered something between a smile and a wince.

"That you kill me first?" Kate said.

Now it was a smile. "We *would* hate to sacrifice our human subjects. We get so attached to them."

"When will you break the code on the drugs so we'll know for sure?" Kate asked.

"You think this is a placebo?"

"David or somebody said there was a third group that's on another combination."

"We have a number of people who are improved, and I'll be surprised if they're not in the same group as you. If you're doing well when the study concludes, then you'll stay on whatever drug combination is working. I'll make it in my lab if I have to. If we find you're on the placebo, we'll definitely continue *that* too." To address her question, he added, "That's a long ways down the road—nine months at least."

David hadn't even thought about indefinite access to the drugs.

"Tell me your plans, Mrs. Sanders—Kate."

"Well, I'm going to get two cats and name one Anova."

He put his head back and laughed with delight. David looked from one to the other until Kate explained that the word stood for "analysis of variance." "It's how science decides if something really works or not. It's sort of the backbone of comparing things."

"And the second cat? Statistics again?" The doctor seemed genuinely curious.

"If it's a male, maybe Nietzsche."

This one David understood.

"Mr. Sanders—David—I'm not going to ask your wife if she feels ready to go home because I think it's too frightening a thing to be ready for." He looked only at Kate now. "I'd like you to go home today and spend the weekend at home. And," he said, "maybe you'll never come back."

Kate said "okay" so quietly that David saw only her lips move.

Dr. Tsang left and soon came back with Dr. Ratha and a younger man with a long forgettable Russian name, who was usually in other cities at other sites. This must be quite an occasion, David realized. Mrs. Nowicki entered last and, when they finished with introductions and pleasantries, she said, "The room will be yours for the rest of the month so you don't have to move your belongings at once." David thought she looked a little dazed.

Dr. Tsang said, "Either I or someone else on the team will meet with you every week at first. We'd like to see you at Dr. Ratha's office—we don't want you anywhere near the university lab. We'll continue to videotape the exams, but we can also talk off-the-record about anything that concerns you." Everyone took out a phone, tablet, or appointment book and made entries as Dr. Tsang scheduled himself to be at the first three appointments that Dr. Ratha offered. David noticed that Kate finished entering the dates in her phone before he did. The Russian finished last and then asked how the cover story was working. It had been the best scenario the team could come up with, he explained with a note of apology.

"We realize you'll need to tell more and more people once Kate is home. Obviously, people will learn that she's better. We just don't want them to know *why* she's better. It's not comfortable to be less than honest, but it preserves the integrity of the research. With lab animals, we control almost everything. With people..." He smiled. "And yet people are our favorite subjects."

David said, "I've been vague with my co-workers as far as why I need so much time off. I said Kate was having some unrelated health problems, but then I explained it to Kate's close friend the way you said I should. She was too stunned to really dissect what I was saying. But we'll need to tell a lot more people."

Kate said, "I think the story will hold for now. The boys know the truth—and eventually my parents and sister, but that's it. Was it you, David, or one of the doctors—" she looked from one to the other, "who reassured me that people are mostly busy thinking about themselves?"

"That sounds more like me," David said.

"I think that's an observation we can all agree on," the Russian said.

"But eventually you'll have your results, and if the results stay this good, it will be cataclysmic," Kate said, worried.

"We will never release your name. All you have to do is deny you're patient..." Dr. Tsang looked at his tablet. " XT620."

"That's our wedding date!"

"A good omen then," said the Russian, while the others looked carefully blank.

CHAPTER FOURTEEN

"I don't think I see any changes in here," Kate said.

"Is that good or bad?" David asked.

"Neither, I guess. I love this kitchen." She walked the few steps to where he stood and took his hand, then let it go. "Let's see everything."

They walked through the short hallway to the dining room. "Not used much lately," David said. "Like maybe never." She left the dining room, walking ahead of him, studying every photograph and every piece of art along the way until she reached the middle of the living room.

"It looks beautiful. My memory of the house was sort of dim, but just like this. Oh, look at the flowers." She took in all three vases, bouquets that could be straight from a garden. "You had Wilma do the flowers! I'd know her work anywhere." She turned to him. "Who did she think they were for?"

"I told her they were for you. I just didn't tell her I was bringing them home."

"What if I hadn't come home today?"

"I would have brought them to you."

David walked over to his complicated music setup. He had his iPod ready to play the music he wanted, but he didn't trust himself at the controls. He went for the CD player instead and started the machine on track four. Kate walked over just as the first notes began, sweet and poignant.

It seems we've stood and talked this way before…

"Oh! This song," Kate said. "I still love it. It was the second dance at our wedding. Remember how my mother thought it was too sad?"

"I was proud you stood up to her."

We've looked at each other in the same way then…

But I can't remember where or when…

He hadn't been so sure of his idea, but she looked happy, and he lifted his arms so she could slip in close to him. "Isn't it strange we've always liked this one?" she said.

He pulled her closer.

The clothes you're wearing are the clothes you wore…

It felt right to hold Kate again. It was the most they'd touched since she woke. Where was good and faithful David?

They danced more gracefully than he remembered, then broke apart and smiled.

"I felt we needed something ceremonial," he said. "I tried to think of what you might do."

"Well, I probably wouldn't have made you dance."

Kate was home. And she was teasing him.

"But that was a good choice for me. Show me the upstairs."

She admired the guest room—what a feat it had been to afford a house with a guest room—and then the boys' rooms, tearing up at Jack's teen decor. She declared the whole thing far less shabby than he had claimed. "It doesn't look freshly done, but it's not falling down by any means."

"Like those houses we looked at that old people were selling."

"Not even close."

"Good. Tomorrow we'll see the former garden," he said as they headed to their bedroom. He sensed her stiffen as she entered, but then she said, "It's just the same."

She reached for the phone. "I should have called the boys hours ago. I memorized their cell numbers, David. I can call them right now from memory. Can you do that?"

"Were you always this competitive?"

She sat on the bed, propped against the pillows, and called Dylan. David knew this would be one time Dylan would pick up.

"I'm sorry," she said in her soothing voice. "I know. It's been an intense day. We didn't mean to worry you. The meeting went fine and I'm home. No, no, don't come tomorrow. It's too much driving for one day. Let me get situated and you and Jack can come next Friday or Saturday. Will you do that? I love you, too. And Dylan, I'm sorry you worried all day. Yes, I'll call Jack right now."

Her half of the call to Jack was almost identical. "They're a little irritated with me."

"What? They didn't blame _me_ for not calling sooner?" He _was_ guilty, having scarcely given the boys a thought all day.

She brightened. "Actually, they didn't. They didn't mention you. They were annoyed with me. Isn't that great? Isn't that _normal?_" She stretched out the syllables of "normal," making it sound like the most exotic and desirable of states. They were both sitting on the bed now. There was an awkward pause before she said, "We should go back downstairs."

They sat across from each other at the kitchen table—a table they had refinished on winter afternoons almost thirty years before. It had been their first project together. Kate toasted her return with one short glass of wine, and David with a Scotch, the first of three, but he drank slowly, snacking as they cooked together, so he never left his target of being neither sober nor drunk. He cleaned up while she looked through the ambitious recipes, now yellowed clippings, held by strong magnets on the fridge.

He joined her at the table and paged through the paper while she read back issues on her laptop. She periodically read snippets out loud and he was surprised by all that he had forgotten from the last few years of mostly bad news.

She shut down her laptop. "I need to go to sleep," she said. "Where do you want me to sleep?"

He must have looked mystified because she continued, "I mean, would you rather we didn't share a bed? I'm going right to sleep, but still..."

This is so fucked up—she's in her own house. "I don't want to sleep without you. Unless it's not what you want, I mean." He tried to add, "I'm so sorry—" but she cut him off.

"Apologies make me feel worse." She stood. "Just be quiet when you come up, and don't thrash around in anguish. We can talk tomorrow."

She moved to kiss him, aiming for his cheek. He assumed they would kiss on the lips and turned towards her in time to receive a gentle kiss on his nose. Without trying again, Kate went upstairs to sleep in her own home at last.

———⟫•⟪———

When he saw the call was from his mother, Dylan walked from the kitchen into the far end of the next room. Even though his mother's voice was heavy with contrition, he didn't try to hide his irritation that she'd waited so long to call him back. While he didn't say it, it reminded him of his years of anxiety as she became undependable and childlike.

When they finished, he took a moment, as he always did in recent weeks, to absorb the fact that he had just had a conversation with his mother. He had *criticized* his mother. Who thought that would ever happen again?

He joined Lily in the kitchen, where she was still chopping vegetables noisily, as if to show that she hadn't made any attempt to listen. Lily had tried to bring up the topic of Jane, but he couldn't talk about it, and he knew she wouldn't ask again. The subject made him feel like a double agent, rooting for his mother while sympathizing with his father. There was only one road for his dad to choose. Still, he couldn't help interrogating himself about what conditions would compel him to give Lily up. He tried to believe the situations were too different—that his dad should have used up his quota of passion long before he met Jane.

"She's home." The words sounded strange to him. "They're both home. They're going to cook dinner." A tone of amazement crept into the last sentence.

She gave him a happy smile and, looking down at her now laughably oversized pile of tiny slices, said sheepishly, "I think we have enough."

<hr />

On the morning of Kate's first full day at home, David stood just inside Jack's room. Kate had been upstairs for so long that he'd gone to look for her, but she left as soon as she heard him approach. He saw where she had shuffled through the school souvenirs, old term papers, awards, prom pictures, dried boutonnieres, and on and on. Jack's life without his mother was there for her to find. David saw the imprint on the twin bed where she had lain, a yearbook lying open next to the last team photo.

He found her in the living room. She'd stopped crying, but her eyes and nose were raw and she didn't greet him. He waited.

"It's not that I'm ungrateful," Kate said. "I am grateful, but years are gone."

He knew he should acknowledge what she had lost. He should give her permission to feel grief. He should promise to accept her every feeling for however long she felt it. The inadequate words he heard himself say were, "I think this will take a lot of time. And I think time will fix it."

"Time?" She pulled back her shoulders. "Do I *have* enough time left to accept all the time I lost?"

"Maybe it's okay to be grateful about one thing while being sad about another. Or mad at the world."

"I know. I know that. I just don't know how to do it."

"Maybe it's not something you do. Maybe it's just something that happens."

"Can you let me be sad?"

Could he? He didn't know. What he wanted was to somehow travel seven years back and Kate would stay well and Jane would stay a stranger.

"You need to let me know if it's better or worse when I tell you about the kids and our lives when you were gone," he said. "I mean, when I fill you in on things you missed."

"I *want* you to tell me about it. And I want to see the photos and videos. Not yet. Not today, but I will want to. And…"

"And?" he asked. "Jane. Yes. I will talk about Jane."

The phrase he hated, *man-up*, came to mind as he took the stool across from her. "I should have been the one to bring it up today. I'm sorry."

She didn't speak.

"I was finally beginning to think about the rest of my life—that possibly I didn't deserve to be alone, like punishment for something I didn't do," he said. "Maybe that thought allowed me to notice her because I certainly didn't notice anyone before that or when we were married."

He corrected himself, "I mean when you were well. I didn't notice except in the most detached, appreciative way that any man would observe women. Noticing without action. I'm good at that."

He had never been called on to testify to his fidelity until, first Jane, and then Martha had questioned him. Now Kate, only months later, was indirectly asking for that same information.

To say that he appreciated without wanting wasn't a complete answer. It's what you tell your wife, but it's not the whole story. He had always been interested in the lifespan of crushes. His own, of course, were the only ones that he could follow confidently. There had been three since he and Kate got married: an interest in a colleague, then a neighbor, and the last, a friend's wife, all punctuating the first twenty or so years of their marriage. The first time, he was a novice and, as the attraction grew, he thought he'd have to do something about the desire. He thought the feelings had some authority and that eventually he'd be under their command.

But he didn't do anything, even though he was almost certain his interest was reciprocated. And he didn't do anything about the next two either. Sometimes he thought of each woman, in turn, when he was having sex with Kate, but he never felt guilty about it. That was what wives were for, he knew, to be the person you were with, thinking whatever thoughts you wanted, while you weren't out wrecking lives.

He learned that he didn't have to obey these odd, obsessive attachments. He just needed to be careful not to betray anything, not to pay too little or too much attention, not to make anyone else feel excluded from the light of the attraction, and eventually it dimmed or she moved away. The dimming was a better solution because you saw how unnecessary it proved to be to *act*. The heat died down, and your wife was your life again, and you hadn't ruined anything.

She reached across the counter to hold his hands. "I know you had many temptations. I admired your skill. And your loyalty." She broke away and sat back. "Jane," she said. "Jane…When you confirmed you had a lover, I was reading about the tsunami, and that's what kept racing toward me. I mean, a tsunami of possessiveness and jealousy, and I could drown in it.

"You haven't shown any of that."

"It's a good policy not to show everything."

"Did you keep feeling that way? And you're somehow able to hide it?"

"It was odd, but after you let me know a little bit about her, I just couldn't sustain that kind of jealousy. Maybe I don't have enough prima donna in me. You know, look what happened to me, me, me." She started to move her stool back as if to stand, then stopped and said, "I am afraid, though."

He waited until he could talk in a controlled voice. "It's you and me. You know that I love her, but I won't ever talk about it again. It's always been you and me. I've never stopped loving you and missing you and admiring you. I cannot not have you in my life."

He meant it completely. The moment after saying it, though, he wasn't so sure. But it wasn't the kind of statement you could qualify.

She smiled, a sadder smile than he would have expected, and said, "I love you too."

He wondered later if he should have asked her what she was afraid of. He'd been so sure he knew that he didn't think to ask.

———————

Martha came through the side door with a box of tissues in one hand, and when Kate noticed this, she laughed, and then Martha laughed, and they hugged, then broke apart to look at each other, then hugged again.

David left the kitchen, certain neither had noticed him, and decided to go for a walk, then headed back to the kitchen to tell them. When he was a few steps away, he heard Kate say, "Thank you for not sleeping with David. Not that I think you would have, of course." He moved in close enough to hear Martha say, "Maybe it would have been better if I had." He backed away quietly and left.

Halfway down the first block, he thought he saw Jane's Audi. He remembered being surprised at her choice. "Expecting a Prius?"

"Yes," he had answered truthfully.

"It's a fussy nuisance," she admitted. "But very fun to drive." Of course, this wasn't Jane's car. What's the opposite of a stalker? He couldn't think of a word. Except Jane—Jane was the opposite of a stalker.

David would have said he had no plans to call her, that he brought his phone only in case Kate needed him. Without making a decision to call her, he did, expecting to show up as the lonely message of a missed call, but Jane answered on the second tone, and he stuttered twice before saying, "I don't know why I called."

"You miss me," she said. "And you need to talk about Kate. I'm one of the few people you can trust."

"I do need to talk. I feel like I'm useless to her. She's happy sometimes, but she's so sad too. I can't stand to see her grieving over the years she missed with the boys ... or any of it. I keep acting as if she's been away on a long trip." His words came out in a rush. "I know I'm useless trying to cajole her out of her loss."

"Which is almost as big as a death," she said.

"I know that, but then another soothing platitude comes out of my mouth." He stumbled on a curb. "Why are you talking to me about this? How can you be willing to do that?"

"I love you."

David refrained from saying something self-effacing.

"And I feel sorry for you," she added quietly.

"For me?"

"Let's just say I don't envy you." David waited for the walk sign, and Jane asked hesitantly, "Do you have any sense of how much of her pain is due to me?"

"I can't tell. Look, Jane, I'm no less in love with you than the day Kate—"

"Hence my compassion, Dr. Sanders," she said with a mock British accent, and he knew better than to continue.

———◦◦◦———

Jane resumed the loop of reviewing their love affair from start to finish, beginning with her surprise at finding herself in a relationship with him at all. He was so unhappy and mournful that she had guessed, wrongly it turned out, that he would remain loyally bound to the ambiguous state of his marriage. Instead, his pursuit of her had been an unshakable straight line, as if he knew that he needed to be certain enough for both of them. The combination of his loyalty to Kate, muddled by his determination to have her, Jane, wooed her as nothing else could have. She had even felt something close to pride that she could set propriety aside.

She had gambled—not a stupid gamble, but a gamble nonetheless. She would be happy for him. She would not hope for the drugs to fail. She would certainly not hope for David to choose her. And, on some unidentifiable day, she would be happy for him.

———⟶❧⟵———

When he got back to the house, Kate and Martha were lounging on the couch, with two piles of Kate's old clothes between them. They looked happy, but he could tell there had been more crying.

"I know Kate used to like to keep everything," Martha said. "But she's merciless now." She stood and faced David. "I've tried to get her to explain more about the new treatment. She seems short on details. Usually, Kate likes to talk about medicine and science. What's going on?"

David forced himself not to look at Kate. He'd always had the impression that Martha saw through him almost as easily as Kate did. "Science Girl understands more than she's letting on," he said. "But we both feel superstitious about discussing it."

"Yes," Kate agreed. "Superstition is our philosophy of life right now. Anyway, David, Martha offered to bring over dinner tonight. And Don. I said yes. I tried to call you but it went to voicemail."

———⟶❧⟵———

Kate was in the kitchen, showered and dressed, before David

made it downstairs the next morning. He stood in the doorway watching as she paged through the *Times*.

"Is it worth the ink on hands?" she said to herself, not him.

"Don't you miss your parents?" he said. "Don't you want to see them, and Claire?"

"Of course I do." She closed her eyes for a full second. "But I feel kind of like a runaway teenager who's afraid to come home because of all the pain she's caused."

He almost argued. *Don't be silly.* Instead, he said, "I'm going to call them and tell them what the doctor told me the first time— that you're responding to a new drug, you're more alert, and they should come visit." If it were his parents, they'd arrive and then need to be consoled for suffering such upset, but her parents would behave.

"You have to tell them a little more than that, or *they'll* stroke out when I start talking."

"All right, I'll try to prepare them. But we need to decide which story to tell—the real one or the fake one?"

"The real one," she said. "Though not on the phone. They'll understand the need for secrecy. The investigators are hoping to do a larger clinical trial before they make any announcements. Did I tell you that? I can't remember if I told you that." She sounded fretful at the possibility she'd forgotten something. "They would never do anything to hurt me or compromise this," she added. "Anyway, I do really need to see them. And Claire—ask Claire to plan a trip. North Africa will have to get along without her."

"Should I start mentioning to more people that you're doing better and at home?"

"Yes," she said, though she said it slowly. "It scares me to make it official, but I don't want to be trapped at home."

"And you shouldn't have to keep announcing yourself." David

tried to sound genuinely cheerful even though he knew he would hate every encounter. Worse, he realized, some of these people would know about Jane. "I'm going to tell Greta and Tucker personally, and then I'll tell the others at staff meeting."

"Do they know about Jane?"

"Who?"

"Tucker and Greta."

"Yes. They know."

"Oh. I didn't realize. The department—"

The phone rang just then, and she checked caller ID, took the call, and chatted for a minute. He could tell it was Martha. When she got off, he motioned for her to come to him. He leaned close enough to kiss her, but she put her fingers lightly on his chest and moved to the farthest end of the counter.

"I can't do that right now." She began to slice oranges with precision.

"I'm sorry," he said.

"I don't *want* you to be sorry. I don't want to be well again and causing *sorrow*."

"You haven't caused anything!"

She scooped the orange slices into a bowl, glanced at him standing by the sink, then wiped her hands on her jeans rather than move towards him to reach the water.

"I can't think about you yet. And I can't think about Jane. Have you told Ian yet? About me? I imagine he knows about Jane. You need to talk to Ian. That would be constructive."

David took his cell with him to the front porch. When Kate first moved to the L, David assumed it would be Ian's wife who might visit, and she did, once, but it was Ian's name he had seen in the log every three or four weeks, later stretching to six, but still month after month. David started to mention it once and Ian stopped him.

"Too much emotion. You Yanks, always emoting. Besides, it's literally the least I can do."

He gave Ian the laundered version of the story and finished with, "She's been home for two days." This time it was Ian who cried.

⟫●⟪

Sunday, Kate researched cars online, not bothering to ask his opinion. She knew cars bored him. A car needed to start every morning and not embarrass him by being too old or too new. Twice her cell chimed, first Dylan and then Jack. He tried to eavesdrop on her end but only heard murmurs, as if, unlikely though it was, the boys were doing all the talking.

This new intense closeness between Kate and their sons was proving to be a challenge for him. Once the boys had left babyhood, he thought of them, only by virtue of gender, as slightly more his kids than Kate's. When she got sick, the three of them became closer, for unlike divorce, there was no one to blame. Now it seemed a new club had formed.

Kate's busyness was a challenge for him. When he was in the same room with her, he was calm and he felt that everything was *sufficient*. He knew the word might sound damning if he used it out loud, but to him it was a good status. When he left her so that she could talk in private to one of the boys, or because he sensed his presence was irritating, he would feel an ache. He couldn't write or read the paper. He ached for Jane. He tried to pretend he was worried about her, but he had the sense Jane knew exactly how to end something.

Clearly, Kate had limited appetite for his presence. He sought her out with one practical detail or another, such as how to share the car until they bought a second. She was always polite, letting him interrupt a radio show or the article she was trying to finish. He watched her cut out the occasional story, date it, and then carefully place it in a folder. He had the sense she would just as soon be alone, and he didn't want to provoke her into saying it. Several times he looked up from the journal he was skimming to find her watching him with an expression that might seem neutral to others, but which he recognized as her *appraisal*—the look he had seen so often when she was deciding if a fever was worrisome or a child was lying.

"I wanted to ask you something." She finally spoke, with a note of encouragement to her voice. "Do you want to go to the animal shelter with me tomorrow? If I promise not to look at any dogs?"

"Definitely," he said, his spirits immediately lifted by the idea.

He knew she wanted to get back to whatever mysterious things she was doing. How could she already be busier and more focused than he was? "I'm going to the gym," he said. "Are you up for it?"

"The gym? I can hardly stand the thought of leaving the house. It's like this is the only place where I exist right now."

"Then I'll stay."

"No! It feels safe here. I don't need you babysitting me to feel safe."

He changed his angle so he could get a good look at her face, but she wasn't giving away anything.

He grabbed his gym bag and left, but he didn't call Jane and he didn't drive by her house. He went to the gym for an intense workout—the kind that courts injury. Twice, acquaintances stopped by to chat and to ask after his family. Each time he said that Kate was a little better and might be ready to try a visit at home. He would have told them she was already home, but then they would wonder how he could have left her alone. Or would they even think about it that much? Regardless, Kate needed a gradual re-entry into the world—one that didn't scream *miracle cure*. He realized he was becoming a much better liar.

He drove home, tired in a virtuous way. It was, he realized, his fifth week without Jane. He didn't apply an adjective to it, just stated it to himself. *Five weeks without Jane.*

CHAPTER FIFTEEN

David corralled Greta and Tucker. They would be the hardest of his colleagues to lie to but, as he explained the details of the fake diagnosis and new drugs, he forgave himself. *Necessary lies*. Greta and Tucker showed the expected mixture of bewilderment and delight, though their delight was muted by David mentioning relapse three times.

"You mean to say they're not certain why she's better or what to expect from here on out?" Tucker sounded ready to make phone calls and demand better information.

"The boys?" Greta said. "How are they handling all this?"

He looked at her, helpless. He couldn't describe that reunion, or anything about the boys, without crying.

"Of course," she said.

After he described Kate's first days at home, Tucker and Greta became quiet, as if in a moment of silence for Jane. That was probably his imagination. He ended the long pause by giving them permission to spread the word.

"In fact, please do. You're the only ones here I'm making a point of telling directly. I was thinking I'd say something at the department meeting, but I don't want to."

"You do have a Facebook page," Tucker said.

David's account, created many years before, languished

unchanged for months at a time unless Greta went in and added something. Once, she found six-month-old private messages and suggested he email the senders to explain he was too old to alter his mailing habits.

"Well, you don't use Facebook either," he said in his retort, which she answered in that generous way people do when they know they're completely right, "Yes, but I don't *pretend* to use it."

"No," Greta said now. "We'll do this the old-fashioned way."

He stood to end the conversation. He usually didn't like promiscuous hugging which made him want to say *I just saw you a few days ago*, but when Tucker and Greta hugged him in turn, it seemed fine.

⟞⟩●⟨⟝

Kate circled the cat room slowly, not speaking, even to the cats. She circled a second time and stopped in front of seven-month old gray tabbies, one male, one female, and both sterilized young, according to the index card on their cage. The card listed today's date as their release day. The larger of the two noticed Kate and stopped pummeling its sibling. Both cats sprang to attention at the front of the cage and, though he knew it was impossible, David would have sworn they had recognized her.

She talked steadily to them as they presented their heads to be scratched. First, she petted one while the other squirmed, then she used one hand on each until David slipped in next to her and took charge of one cat. He whistled the notes *do you believe in a love at first sight* and Kate leaned against him, then sang, *it happens all the time*, though she didn't take her eyes off the animals.

The cats switched positions and continued to offer their ears and cheeks and chins.

"Do you want to take them out? She said we could."

"No, I can't bear to have the others see that."

That's why she hadn't spoken to any of the other cats. It might indicate to the others that now was their chance, and that would be cruel. Even after all she'd been through, Kate was still faster than he was at figuring this kind of thing out.

"All right," he said. "I'll go do the paperwork, and we'll pack them up. And then the pet store."

After getting fully supplied, they pulled into their garage and he said to Kate, "What are we doing right now?"

Without a pause, she answered, "We're bringing home our first baby. Except it's twins."

"You'll be a great mother."

"And no college to worry about."

After she said this, she winced. Jack's years of high school were almost entirely blank to her and, though she had accompanied him when they went shopping with the list he and David had constructed of what a boy takes to college, she couldn't remember, and she hadn't really helped, but just watched, smiling pleasantly.

He put his right hand over her left one and said, "We can talk about it. The cats are fine right here."

"I don't need to talk about it." She swallowed hard. "It just is."

"Still."

"Still what? Those years are *still* gone. Is that what you meant? They're gone and it's nobody's fault. I know these things."

He caught the menace of the word *still*. It had been his close companion during her descent. Kate is *still* at home. *Still* manageable. *Still* able to communicate.

She leaned across the gearshift and he put his arms around her. They sat together as she cried, wetting his shirt and undershirt both.

———⟫●⟪———

David went into work for the whole day. Kate insisted she was content at home, even though she was stranded without a car. "Go," she had told him. "Work a full day. My days are plenty busy, especially since I need to take at least two naps a day, like the newborn baby that I am."

He and Ian, out of touch for too long, had planned a quick lunch, but David had to call before noon to say he couldn't get away. Instead, they spoke for a few minutes and then Ian, his voice turning serious, said, "Do you see Jane at all?"

He seemed careful not to imply a right or wrong answer, so David answered truthfully. "We've talked a minute here and there. That's it. She's stepped back. She said she's the understudy and her star-turn is over."

"Jane would, wouldn't she? She's a bit of all right," Ian said. In a softer voice, he asked, "Is it okay?"

"Usually." David knew he should stop, but there wasn't another human being to whom he could tell these things. "And then I think of her when I'm not prepared for the idea, and it lays me flat, as you would say. You know, 'the last time we did this—the last time we did that'—and then I'm done for, as you would also say. I think I see her car. I think I hear her voice behind me in the grocery store."

"You and she…the real thing."

"I thought I was so lucky. I thought I was lucky again." Christ, had he said that? He *was* lucky. Kate was back.

"I don't envy you. I do not." Ian sighed. "Well, there's time and all that."

"Yes," David agreed politely, not bothering to mention that

absence seemed to be a terrible cure.

———⟫◦⟪———

Kate sat on the floor, leaning back against the couch David was stretched out on and, with no preamble said, "Was it great with her? Like it was with us?"

"I hadn't touched a woman in years. It was going to be good no matter what."

"So it was great?"

He didn't answer. He sat up, dumping the kittens off his lap. They gave small cries of protest, then went to the other end of the couch. "Come here, Katie. Tell me what you want."

She thought a moment and said, "I want to be remembered."

"What does that mean?"

"I don't know, exactly."

"I need some help here."

"I mean, are you thinking of her? Am I mixed in with her right now?"

"Oh, Kate, does it really matter?"

"It *does* matter."

"Why?"

"Why does *anything* matter? Because otherwise what the hell are we doing here? We don't have to *resume*. We're free agents. You understand that, don't you?"

"Free? Free to do what? I love you, Kate." He heard himself almost yelling and started again, softly. "I love you and I want you. I think you sort of want me, which is good enough right now."

She turned to face him straight on for the first time. "I want a cigarette. If I could, I would smoke a cigarette right now."

"Well, you're free, right? You can smoke."

"I might." She got up from the floor and he made room for her on the couch. Her face softened. "You waited so long for me."

"I don't think I was waiting. I just didn't know what to do."

"Those beautiful grad students."

"Do I ever remember to tell you that you're beautiful? You're as pretty as you were at sixteen."

"You didn't know me at sixteen."

"Oh, yes I did. All the guys knew who you were. I watched you. And then I lost you in the metropolis of the university. I went to a lot of bad parties until I found you."

She scrunched her forehead as if she was counting something. "My high school sweetheart?"

"In a stalker kind of way," he said, and he put one hand on her cheek. She held it there.

Then she got up, walked towards the stairs, and began to climb them slowly. David jumped up and followed her so closely that when she paused to straighten a photo of the boys on Halloween, he stopped short and bumped against her. She leaned into him from the next higher step and started a little when she felt his erection. "We'd better get you upstairs," she said.

In their bedroom, she stood facing him, her expression uncertain, and he began to unbutton her shirt, his hands shaking slightly. Freed from the last button, she shrugged the shirt off and led him to the bed. He lay on top of her and they kissed, eyes open. He pulled away from her to unsnap her jeans and work the zipper. It had been decades since they began to make love while still dressed. In movie after movie, the man, even with a struggling victim, easily pulls the woman's pants off, but he didn't see any way to do it without her help, and just as he had that thought, she lifted her hips and tugged on one side while he did the other.

He tossed her clothes aside and then scrambled out of his

own. She waited for him to unclasp her bra, remembering he liked the job—it was a high school thing, he had told her. It made him feel like he was getting away with something. Naked now, he lay down again, his weight half on her, and she said, "Welcome back."

It wasn't the sex of their previous life, but it was sex—until David thought she winced. He withdrew, prepared to use saliva or perhaps just stop, but she produced an unopened tube of lubricant from the bedside table. The foresight reassured him. She wanted him, or at least wanted to want him. He let himself relax and finish, then used his hand. She did come once—so briefly and quietly that she seemed like another woman—and then she moved his hand away and held it with both of hers.

"Well, at least that broke the ice," she said.

"God, yes," David said, and then they both started laughing, having noticed for the first time that both kittens were staring at them from the doorway. "Do not climb on this bed," he said authoritatively, but Kate was already up and the cats sprinted toward her. Kate grabbed them, set them outside the door and closed it, then got back in bed and lay close to him, her head against his chest. It was a few moments before she spoke.

"When did you miss it most?"

"All the time," he said. "It was god-awful lonely here. Everywhere, really."

"I mean before you met Jane. When did you miss it most?"

"Oh," he said. "The gym." It wasn't exactly true, but he didn't think full disclosure was required.

"Is the one with the breasts still there?"

"I'd forgotten about her. No, she's gone. Possibly why I don't get there as often."

"So you're saying you want me to wear cute workout clothes next time."

"Would you do that? How about right now?"

"Oh, I think I'm done for today." Her tone was apologetic.

"That's okay. I don't have many second acts either anymore."

"Even with Jane?"

"Even with Jane."

"I guess time didn't stand still for any of us."

CHAPTER SIXTEEN

"Can we just get together to talk? I need to know you're okay." David realized too late he had forgotten any small talk or even a greeting.

"I can't be the person you cheat on Kate with," Jane said. "And I can't be your friend."

"No, I know that." David knew he sounded despondent, the most unappealing of emotional states.

"Jack called me."

"No! I'm sorry. Was he rude?"

"He was lovely. He wanted to know how I was. He wanted to tell me that he thought you and Kate were going to be good together again."

"He shouldn't have called you."

"Of course he should have."

"You take his side as if he has an actual position here."

"I know what it's like to be cheated on."

"I am not cheating on Jack," he said, with his jaw clenched, knowing he sounded petulant.

"I'm not sure that's exactly an accurate thing to say. Are you sure you know where you stop and the boys begin?"

He wasn't actually angry with Jack. He had to admire him for going after what he wanted, not playing it safe but taking David on. He used to think Jack had too much confidence, but maybe, what he had seen in him was bravery.

"You'll be okay, David." She made a small sound that could have been a cry, stifled, then she paused. He could picture her collecting herself. In a quiet but sturdy voice, she said, "Absence makes the heart forget."

"I don't think that's true."

"Yes, it is. You'll see." Her voice was even smaller now, but resolute, and they said goodbye.

He loved the goodness in Jane, and now he couldn't have her precisely because she was good. Was *he* still good? He had been good at being untested. He had rigorously avoided temptation—that most slippery of all slopes—and there was goodness in that. Even now, he knew he pushed her to see him because it was safe: He could count on her to turn him down. It wasn't entirely fair to ask her, but he couldn't think of any other way to talk about how much he loved her. He had reverted to a primitive gender role in which he pursued—and she maintained—virtue. She was almost entirely gone from his life except for brief phone conversations that would end soon. He knew she was being kind, letting him have a small fix here and there before her final absence.

He was almost home before he remembered the groceries. He turned around in someone's driveway while the owner looked out curiously. He went back to the store, where as usual, he could only remember two of the three items. It didn't matter what the trio was—*60 Minute* segments, movies, a gift list—you only remember two.

At home, he pulled into the garage and sat, his phone in his palm as a prop so he could say he had just taken a call or gotten an important email, but Kate didn't come to check on him. How surprising to learn that loving her again did nothing to stop him from loving Jane. In fact, he didn't even really forget her except for brief moments when Kate was right in front of him. He supposed that eventually the fire, unfed, would cool. Regardless, he couldn't have Jane believing she was interchangeable, or that what happened hadn't happened. Because it had.

He sat, his eyes closed, for what seemed like a long time, and though it wasn't, it was long enough that he was ready to go inside and hold his wife, and laugh together about something, and make dinner together and get back to the business of starting their lives again.

———>●<———

The Ambien hadn't worked, and now it was too late to take anything more. He'd been drinking multiple glasses of orange juice and water, which meant he had to keep using the bathroom just outside the kitchen, flushing only every second time, in the hope that their old house plumbing wouldn't wake Kate. He didn't pretend to be doing anything; there was no newspaper spread out or essays to grade, just him sitting. He thought he should go to bed soon, even though, like anyone with insomnia, he hated lying awake next to someone sleeping. Before he had a chance to move, he heard Kate say softly from the doorway, "What can I do?"

Happy to provide an answer that was completely true, he turned and said, "Nothing. There's nothing you need to do." And then, with the manly conviction he had learned to use during terrible thunderstorms or while driving on snowy roads, he said, as he had many times to his wife and young children, "We're going to be fine." And maybe it was true.

———>●<———

In the middle of their mother's first week home, Dylan called Jack, and when he didn't reach him, tried again a few hours later and then an hour after that. He knew Jack barely looked at his phone, so he didn't actually expect a return call.

"What's up, Dylan. Did somebody die?" Jack sounded worried more than sarcastic.

"Not that I know of. I just wanted to see how you're doing."

"Okay. Kind of weird, though, for you to ask."

Jack was right. They weren't quite at the point of having a close friendship now that their time together had to be arranged with effort. Growing up, it was easy when all one had to do was throw a ball at the other. Or one would come home to find the other parked on the couch and soon they'd be talking—maybe only during the commercials—but talking nonetheless.

"Yeah, you're right. I don't really care about you. I actually want to see what you think about *them*." Dylan also wanted to know what Jack thought about Lily coming home with him to meet their mom—perhaps not this weekend but sometime soon. He didn't know if he'd bring it up because then he'd have to admit he was afraid she would relapse before Lily had a chance to get to know her. Jack wasn't big on that kind of negative thinking. Or to be more accurate, Jack knew how to worry too, but he was a worrier who believed those kinds of statements should be left unsaid.

"Mom seems good. I call her cell. She won't talk about Jane." Jack sounded indignant.

"Imagine that. Your mother doesn't want to talk to you about her husband's lover."

"She shouldn't *have* to talk about it. I realize he had to come clean, but it should be an asterisk by now and I don't think it is, or he wouldn't be hiding from us. Have you heard from him?"

"I called once about the car insurance," Dylan said, recalling the quick and awkward conversation. "But other than that, no."

He decided not to say anything about Lily.

⟫●⟪

"Kate, where are you?" he called loudly.

"I'm in the living room," she called back. "Come in here. I guarantee the cats will follow you. I think they've been waiting. You should have seen them when they heard the car pull in."

He went to find her, the cats one moment in front of him, then circling behind. She was sitting in an armchair, and he sat on the corner of the couch nearest her. She gave him an anxious smile.

"I need to say something and you just need to let me say it." Her voice was tight and low. "You and I, we've had a lot of happiness together. I mean, maybe more than the normal share. Not that we didn't deserve it, but we've been very lucky too. I admit I occasionally noticed men that I thought would be fun to have sex with, but I never imagined loving anyone but you. I mean, after I finally met you."

He had no idea where this was going.

Kate took a deep breath. "I won't be the one to make you give up Jane, like she was... " She didn't finish her sentence and added less forcefully, "And you know I'm sort of lost sexually."

"But that could change." *He should have said something different,* he thought. He should have said it didn't matter.

"I'm not going to mess with the medications."

He'd never asked her to. Where was she going with this?

"I don't want dutiful David, honorable David, David the martyr. Maybe it's arrogant of me, but I want to feel loved by

183

choice, not obligation." She took in a gulp of air. "I don't think you're going to stop loving Jane."

"You know I'm not leaving you. You can insult me for it if you want, but—"

"I think you know that's not what I'm talking about."

Know what? And then he knew.

"No way!" That was all he could manage. Surprise was muffling his vocabulary. She waited for him, and he continued, calmly this time. "People end up hating each other. I don't want that for you. For any of us. And I won't live like some reality show—"

"I don't *give* a fuck if you're embarrassed," Kate said. "I lost my mind for what—five years? I don't even know exactly how long I was gone. I can spend my remaining time replaying it—suffering over it, or I can work really hard at not caring. Not caring what people thought, or what I said or how I looked. I was always smart. Whatever my flaws, I was always smart. And then I wasn't. I was empty and stupid."

David stood, pulled her from her chair, then held her in a tight hug as he whispered, "You were always beautiful. And dignified." Maybe it wasn't always true, but he could make her believe him, and he said the words again, changing the order, but the same words, like a prayer. He held her and she cried, but finally she leaned into him.

Then she drew back, fished for a tissue, and blew her nose quickly before saying, "I don't plan to have sex with her or with the two of you."

He stared at her. Had he always been this bad at predicting what she would say?

"No, maybe I will. Maybe I'll wake up lesbian tomorrow. Look, I know you're trying. Trying not to think of her, trying not to call her, trying to feel nothing but lucky."

There had to be many questions he should ask her, but he could only think of one: "Why are you offering this?"

She looked him squarely in the eye. "Because you are trying so hard. And because you are so damned sad."

———⟫•⟪———

David drove home late the next evening and, at a four-way stop, found himself in a trance, perhaps waiting for a non-existent red light to change. When he came to, it seemed that the other drivers were also lost in reverie, and even the drivers second in line in each direction hadn't honked. Finally, one took his turn and the rest sorted out the order, slowly it seemed to David, like a well-ordered folk dance. Was it providential—watching people negotiate and share?

He found Kate in the kitchen reading a recipe, a presence that felt equal parts familiar and impossible, and set down his laptop and briefcase, propping them against the wall. The laptop slid quietly to the floor but he left it.

"I can learn to forget her," he said firmly.

She shook her head. "You're not really very good at that."

"Are we talking about this because you love me? Or because you don't? I know you don't want me. I understand that."

"I want to want you," she said, using the same words he had imagined. "I want things like they were. Do you doubt that I love you?"

"Well, there's habit and then there's love."

"Sometimes habit *is* love."

"Perhaps you mean love is a habit?" They seemed to be talking nonsense. "Then explain jealousy. The thought of you with anyone else has always made me crazy. *I* would *not* be making this offer."

"No one ever really knows what they would do," Kate said.

He walked across the kitchen and sat across from her at the counter.

"Are you resisting because you only want one woman—and it's Jane?" Before he could answer, she said, with some panic in her voice, "Are we still married? Did you start a divorce?"

"Jesus. No, I did not start a divorce. You think I would have hidden something like that?"

She looked down at the table, embarrassed. "That was horrible of me to say. I don't know where it came from."

He stood and walked the few steps towards her. She stood too and he put his arms around her. After a while, she tilted her head back to look at him. Then she said, "Haven't you suffered enough? Wouldn't you like a long stretch without suffering?"

He didn't like to hear that his pain was visible when he'd spent so much effort hiding it. "You have to think for both of us."

"*Casablanca*," Kate said, and then added, "I wish I didn't love you so much."

"Also *Casablanca*, but why?"

"Your grief wouldn't hurt me like it does." She gave him a sad smile.

"That's not *Casablanca*, is it?"

"No, just me."

"And *your* grief?"

"I don't have any grief that can be fixed."

They were quiet, and then she stood up very straight, the way she did when she wanted to seem taller. "You know, the problems of three little people don't amount to a hill of beans in this world."

He didn't speak.

"Just because it's a movie line doesn't mean it's not true," she said.

"It's *not* true. Your illness killed me. It killed everyone who loved you. Or even liked you. Maybe the world didn't care. But *your* world cared. And now you think that with your optimistic ways and this idea that everyone can get along—you think that your *generosity* can fix this?"

She took a few steps backwards. "If you don't like my *generosity*, then you have a problem. I am *not* going to be your cross to bear. I am *not* your ticket to the Good Husband Club. And this may seem weird to you, but you do *not* get to decide this by yourself. This is my problem too, and I have a say in it. And Jane has a say. And we are *not* going to pretend she doesn't exist. Or that she isn't the person you would have spent the rest of your life with."

She walked quickly to the kitchen door, but turned back before she crossed the threshold. "Fractured," she said. "Whether you admit it or not, you are torn in half."

⫸●⫷

David stayed in the kitchen. She hated being followed. They hadn't had many fights, but when they did have one, he would want to fix it right away, to say anything to stop the kindling, the slow burn of disagreement that was sure to combust. Her way worked, he had learned. If he didn't pursue her, she wouldn't leave the house and he could find her later, and instead of him placating her, they would talk and something would be worked out. "I need to live in real life," she would say. "It's okay if we're mad at each other. I'm not going anywhere."

He loved Kate. He loved Jane. He wanted Jane so much it almost seemed he could make her materialize, like how in a dream when you feel pain or sex that's as real as anything awake. And even when he tried to picture a different turn of events in which Kate got well and he hadn't met Jane, he found that he couldn't imagine not knowing her. He could imagine giving her up, but despite their short time together, he couldn't imagine her out of existence.

He went upstairs to Kate. That she was in their bed registered again, as it did every night. There were only brief moments when he forgot the surprise of it. She was already asleep, and he lay close, but not touching, as he spun the possibilities around in his mind and watched her sleep until morning.

———◦———

"Cherstyennikov," the researcher said. "Vlad Cherstyennikov. But Vlad is fine. Or Chad. Or Brad. It's a hard language." They began the checklist of symptoms a spouse might observe.

"Has she taken wrong turns while driving?"

"I don't know. I guess I should let her drive more."

"Has she asked questions that were just answered?"

"No, it's me that does that."

"Has she been able to follow instructions or a recipe?"

"Yes," David said. "She's bored, so she's been trying new things."

"Good. That takes a lot of concentration. Is she making excessively long lists of to-do items or reminders?"

This one scared David. "Well, she's a list person. I don't know what's excessive. It just seems like her, though. Like regular her."

He read *People* in the waiting room until Kate finished with Dr. Ratha and Dr. Tsang. He didn't know who any of these people in the magazine were, even the writers and musicians. He must be older than he felt. Kate found him staring at the crossword puzzle, which could have been in another language.

She waited to speak until they were alone in the stairwell. "Based on their body language and cheerfulness, I'd guess the others are still doing fine too." She shook her head once. "It's more than cheerful. Those guys are excited. Excited and scared, I'd say."

He gave a whoop and hugged her. "A future," he murmured in her ear.

"Possibly," she said. "But at the least, a present. Just having some *now* counts too."

He tugged her hand and they sat down on a step. He wasn't about to make her bring up the topic. "You don't know that Jane would say yes," he said.

"It's maybe not even likely," she agreed. They heard the landing door open and moved over to let two people in scrubs trot past them. "And I'd need to start kind of slow. I need to fill my time with something other than researching the lost years."

"To use our word from the other day—why are you being so *generous?*"

"I don't mean this to hurt you, but I can't embrace everything the way I did. It's not personal and don't analyze it too much—just accept it. And then there's what if I get sick again? You realize I could still get breast cancer or something else. I'm not immune just because I have this. You may think we can reconstruct our previous life, but I think it's impossible, or wrong, and possibly bad luck."

"Had," he muttered.

"What?"

"*Had* the illness. Not have." She dismissed his distinction with a shake of her head. "I'm sure I'm going to like her. I expect her to be a nicer version of me."

"I don't know," he said. He stood and offered his hand to help her up, though she didn't need it. "It's early days. She's probably been on good behavior."

———⟫●⟪———

They drove towards Jane's house. "Should you have called first?" Kate asked.

"She would have told me not to come."

"She is definitely nicer than me."

They stood together on the porch until David inhaled deeply and rang the bell. He knew that the Jane who had been married to Charlie would never open that door, but apparently the Jane who loved David decided everything is possible. She let them in and guided them to the kitchen so she could turn off a burner. They all tried but failed to smile.

"At the risk of making this even more surreal," Jane said, "I want to say that I have definitely heard a lot about you—and I'm very, very happy for you and your family."

"Thank you," Kate said.

Everyone looked at their feet. Jane's were bare. "Kate refuses to let you go," David said, "to let me..." He tried again. "She doesn't think you and I have to be over."

"What did you say?"

He repeated it.

"I don't understand. I thought you came here to meet me—that you were curious."

"I wouldn't indulge myself like that," Kate said, in a kind voice.

"But what are we talking about here? I know this isn't a prank, but why do I feel like it is?"

"We want to find a way to make this work," David said. "A way where no one is hurt. Jane, I understand completely if you're insulted or you think it's crazy. Say the word and I'll leave. But if you love me as much as I think you do, maybe we could consider it. Consider the three of us, I mean. No, the two of us. And the two of us. I mean dividing time. Dividing whatever needs to be divided. Still being us, as much as possible." He looked at Jane, who still seemed stunned but less confused. "Should I explain it more?"

Jane gave an almost imperceptible shake of her head and turned to Kate. "What is he talking about?"

"I don't seem to be able to pretend that I wasn't gone—or that everything's fine now and you don't exist. It doesn't feel honest. It doesn't feel safe. It may not be rational, but it feels unsafe to try to go back to what David and I had. And David," she went on quietly, "now he's hurting again. He's lost someone again. And I just don't see any reason for it."

Jane seemed to be trying to catch her breath.

"Now, we don't have any details worked out. I realize you have every right to be with someone who's only with you, and that's not what's being offered. And maybe you don't want to negotiate holidays or weekends. I don't know. Maybe David and I will end up getting divorced."

David felt a sudden pain in his chest.

"But I don't think we will," Kate added.

"I can't decide if this offer is flattering or crazy, or both," Jane said. "And I can't picture very clearly what either of you envisions. I do think it may be the kindest thing anyone has ever offered me—well, it's certainly the oddest. I have no idea what to say."

Kate suddenly looked exhausted. "You know, I think I need to go home." She swallowed once, hard. "David, maybe you should stay here. If Jane wants you to. If you want to. Obviously, you both need to talk, and you can't do that with me here."

Kate left the kitchen, and David mouthed *wait* to Jane, before following Kate through the front door to the car. She leaned against it, then pulled him close and kissed him.

"You don't have to do this," he said.

"I know that," she said. "And I know the idea came from me and no one else. All I'm saying is that it's possible. But you don't have to go back inside. And this is Jane's choice, too. She may have already locked every door. But no matter what you and Jane decide, my life isn't going back to the way it was." She kissed him again.

He heard himself say, "If I'm not home in an hour, pick me up at work tomorrow and we'll have lunch."

"I will," she said.

He watched her drive off. If the door was locked, he'd walk home. He went inside without knocking and found Jane still in the kitchen, leaning against the sink, a glass of whiskey in her hand. He sat on one of the tall stools by a counter half-covered with her neat piles of mail, newspapers, invitations, and receipts. For the first time that evening—the first time in weeks—he took her in: the glossy dark hair looking almost black, compared to Kate's blondness, Jane's unlined skin with a hint of olive, and the dark, dark eyes. Still barefoot, she wore a denim skirt, almost to her knees, and a fitted V-neck tee shirt with, unusually for her, a half-inch of cleavage. Of course, he realized, she probably thought she was going to have an ordinary evening at home.

"Somehow," she said, "I needed a drink." She gestured at the bottle but he shook his head.

"Did I dream that?" she asked.

"I don't think so."

"She's very lovely. And funny. And unusual."

"She is."

192

"I'm thinking of running away with her," Jane said.

"I've never doubted that I'll end up alone and miserable."

"Maybe," Jane said. "But not tonight." She walked to where he was sitting and stood between his thighs. One tear made its way down her cheek.

"Why are you crying?"

"Because I can only agree to right now. Tonight. And that's probably a mistake too."

He inched forward on the stool and they began to kiss, slowly at first, then ferociously.

She broke away to say, "Just this once." Then she said it again.

He pulled on three tiny snaps that started at the v of her shirt, exposing an almost transparent lace bra. He had a quick fear that she was dressed for someone else but lost the thought as she undid his belt. He imagined they would make their way to the bedroom, but she turned off the kitchen light and pulled him towards the floor.

Later, they moved to the bed and talked in whispers through-out the night. The next day, he'd be unable to reconstruct the conversation. They each slept a little, but not at the same time, so one of them was always awake, as if on watch.

Kate stuck her head in his office door just after noon. He motioned her in and she shut the door and leaned against it.

"So, how are you?" she said.

"Then, it's okay to talk about this?" He quickly added, "Of course, it is. It has to be." He moved from his desk to the couch and motioned her over. How to begin.

"It was good to see Jane. Usually people know when something is ending, but she and I didn't know. It was more like a car accident or something." It had been. Fast and terrible. "You made a big impression."

"I imagine."

"She thinks you're sincere, but she doesn't think you know what you're offering or how it would feel. For you. You understand—she's not in the business of hurting people." They both turned sideways so they could look at each other straight on. "She hasn't said yes." He was sure Jane wouldn't say yes. Last night had just been a long-delayed goodbye. A *formal* goodbye. Or official. There must be a vulgarity to describe what happened. He couldn't think about losing her again right now. He needed to think about what he had—the woman who was here.

"You need to tell me what last night was like for you."

She closed her eyes briefly. "I won't pretend it was anything but strange. I wondered, have we fixed things or ruined things? I started in on writing descriptions for our photos. For the first time, I looked at the pictures you took of me when I was gone. Before you stopped. I still can't believe I'm back. But I think I'm starting to believe it a little bit."

"And me being with Jane?"

"I made myself think of you and her making love. The picture was kind of fuzzy. I don't think I'm much of a voyeur. I ended up picturing *us*. I wonder if we'll ever be like we were." She looked away. "I was kind of something, wasn't I?"

He wanted to touch her, but it didn't seem as if that was what she wanted. "You were, Katie. You were something."

Now she moved towards him and lifted his arm around her. "Thank you for not saying something consoling."

She drummed her fingers on his thigh and said, "Your turn."

"It was good," he said. "I know you can understand that well enough. I tried to just let myself be there, but of course, the question was hanging: Am I cheating? I'm breaking rules but not your rules. Am I sleazy? Is the whole idea lurid? I didn't answer any of these questions. But maybe they're not for just one of us to answer."

They were quiet. His office phone, and then cell, rang several times, alternating.

"You probably need to get ready for class, and you didn't get any lunch."

"I don't mind."

"What I would want," Kate said, as if she had just come to a decision, "is for you to only be gone two or three nights a week at first, maybe just two in the beginning. Until I make something of my time—make some new friends maybe. Later on, we could add more days and divide the weekends. Holidays will take some work. Jane can have Valentine's Day, though." She smiled.

That didn't surprise him. She didn't like either sentiment or spending on demand. "I don't think this is going to happen."

"Then I've made things worse."

"No! You let us say goodbye. Things will be easier now." He wanted to say *I promise*, but he didn't.

———⟫●⟪———

Errand by errand, Kate began to tolerate being out of the house, though she avoided places and times when she thought she'd see people she used to know. "You're not on parole," David teased her, but not very forcefully. He understood self-consciousness. It was more or less a new state for Kate—she'd always had an ease he lacked—and he wasn't the one to talk her out of it. He was happy when she said she was ready for the freedom of a second car. The boys came home for the event.

"Man, I hope I never have to sell cars," Jack said. "The stakes are too high on every sale. I couldn't master the art of not scaring people off."

"Well, you could sell to young women, at least," Kate said.

"Actually, I think I would sell to their boyfriends and ignore them, and of course they would hate being ignored and would try hard to please me."

"That's a good strategy, but finish college anyway," David said.

They drove in silence for a few minutes until Kate said, softly, "How did I come to stop driving? Was it a big fight like you hear about?"

David gulped audibly. "It was one of my first lies. Every time I tried to discuss your driving, you argued with me even though you had gotten seriously lost a few times. So finally, I told you that a few neighbors had mentioned they saw you driving and you seemed confused. I didn't like lying. No one had actually said anything, but I knew they would. I also told you that I saw you almost hit a dog."

He looked over at her but she didn't react.

"I moved the car over to Martha's, and you didn't ask any more. Later, when I said you didn't drive, the doctors didn't think to do anything about your license. I realized they might have misunderstood and thought that you had never driven, but I didn't clarify things. I didn't see any reason for the state to be involved."

Kate nodded twice. "None of us has anything to feel bad about," she said. "Only that it happened."

At the third dealership, they checked out a four-year-old BMW.

Dylan said, "I don't know why, Mom, but I see you in this one. And *Consumer Reports* doesn't hate this year. She should drive it, don't you think? And if it turns out to be needy, you can drive Dad's boring car while he gets this one fixed."

"That seems fair," David said. "Somebody in this family should have a sexy car. And just think, I'll get to drive it when it's broken." Both Kate and Jack voted for paying the asking price— *out of simple human compassion,* as Jack put it.

Five days later, after the car was paid for and prepped, David tried to feel celebratory about the milestone. If he had ever hoped that seeing Jane one more time would make it easier to lose her, he would have felt let down. Instead, he wasn't at all surprised when the weight of her absence settled in on him again. He *was* surprised that he and Kate were able to talk about it. "How are you doing?" she asked one evening. "With not seeing Jane. It's almost three weeks. I can't speak for you, but I feel kind of rejected."

"I actually get that." They were both able to give a small laugh.

"I mean, I'm not romantically rejected like you are, but still, it's almost a little embarrassing. The unwanted grand gesture. Or offer—whatever it was."

"I know. Maybe it's kind of funny. Or will be."

"Yes," she agreed. "Someday it will make a great story to tell nobody."

Now he felt even more determined to hide his sadness from Kate. It would be the worst of outcomes for her to both offer her husband and then witness the refusal. Hiding was difficult. There seemed to be new layers of loss this time. His cell phone was now an object of misery. He had promised Jane he wouldn't contact her, and she never showed up on the small screen, though without his reading glasses, he sometimes hallucinated her name or number. No friendly texts. No interesting articles forwarded. No animals adopting other species. No news at all about or from Jane. He understood cyber-stalking for the first time—if it were an option, no doubt he'd be doing it, but her online presence was almost nothing. It took everything he had not to drive by her house.

There was one thing now that was different, and in a good way—he could write. He was tackling a weightier topic with this book: a history of anti-war movements in the U.S. He might call it *The Wars Against War*, and he found himself able to write with a concentration from earlier years, before Kate got sick, when he could lose himself in the effort and four hours would pass like two. He had made good progress today until he came back to consciousness with a start and called Kate to say he'd be twenty minutes late. He was never late, but she didn't ask, and they made good time down to the dealership, where they tried to follow a tutorial of the car's highly engineered tricks. Neither of them could have even started the vehicle without instructions.

David suddenly felt panicked as Kate prepared to drive away on her own. He wanted to follow her to see how well she drove. He wanted her to go straight home so he could call her in a few minutes to check. Why did she even need to go out? Couldn't they make a life with her confined to their house or block or neighborhood? Why risk the world again?

When he did call her just before his afternoon class, she was safe, of course. He wished he believed the *of course*. When she asked why he called, he hadn't prepared an excuse and could only say he didn't know. She wouldn't enjoy that kind of solicitousness.

He worried enough that he came home a little early, thinking he would surprise her, but she wasn't there. It wasn't long before he heard her pull into the garage and then join him in the kitchen, still flushed from the gym.

"I didn't see a single person I knew, or who knew me. This town is bigger than I remember." She began to look through the cupboards. She reached and stretched, looking for something to make with only three ingredients and one pot, she explained. She pulled out two cake mixes and a can of icing, all five years past their expiration. He could have gone to help her but watched her instead, her body contained in form-fitting black pants and a tapered knit top in a beautiful color he couldn't have named. "You used to wear baggy clothes for yoga."

"They don't do that anymore."

"Oh," he said. "Are there men in the class?"

"Today there were four." She had stopped looking for food. It seemed unlikely either of them was going to cook. She drank a glass of water quickly.

"I miss you, Kate."

"It means a lot to me that you do."

"You know that I'm available just about always, right?" Did she blush or was it residual exertion? "And I'm fine with just using your body without regard for your needs."

"That's a good joke. You have never ever done that. Even if I said it was okay."

"You'd be surprised." She had yet to ask for details about the downward arc of their sex life, and he hoped she wouldn't choose now.

"Well, we could try that, " she said in a neutral voice.

He couldn't read her expression. "Now?" he asked encouragingly.

"I should take a shower first."

"Not for me," he said

"It'll take two minutes. Really."

⥼●⥽

She couldn't come. "That's okay. It doesn't matter to me. Remember, I'm just using you."

And paradoxically, as sometimes happens, she relaxed enough to not try, and her body figured things out, quietly and with little fanfare. He finished quickly and they broke apart to lie facing each other.

"That was a nice surprise," she said, "but I won't be able to come again."

"You're about 10,000 ahead of me."

"You did the math?"

"Men are very competitive about sex."

They lay quietly. She had the sheet up under her armpits, something he didn't remember her doing.

"This is nice," she said. "But I'm getting up."

He joined her at the bathroom sink and they brushed their teeth, eying each other before spitting.

"Why are we brushing our teeth?" he asked. "I'm very hungry."

To his mirror image, Kate said, "I called for dinner before I showered, and the food will be here soon, and I don't know why I'm brushing my teeth. What a waste." She rinsed. "Did you know some couples won't buy a house unless the master bath has two sinks? And to think, we don't even have a master bath."

"You must have seen that on HGTV."

"You've heard of HGTV?"

"Treadmill at the gym."

"I've watched it at home a couple of times. I wouldn't tell just anybody that." She put her finger to her lips to hold him to secrecy.

"You need a job," David said, and then realized it was true, or would be soon.

We're all doing fine, David told himself. He was working and writing, and Kate seemed less shell-shocked each day. They heard from the boys much more often than when he was on his own or when he was with Jane and, as Kate joked, that made it all almost worth it. When he wanted to cause himself pain, he would imagine Jane going out with younger and richer men. Or any man. He would imagine someone touching her. He drank more on those evenings. Sometimes he thought he saw her or her car, but it was always one of those lovelorn tricks of the brain, so it took a long second to trust his senses when she turned out to be two people ahead of him in line at the coffee place. He never went there at night, but they were out of coffee for the morning. Kate hadn't wanted to come with him.

He stepped out of line so that Jane would see him as she moved away from the counter. He watched her finally realize it was him. She must have been so sure this hour of night was a safe way to avoid this possibility.

They stood facing each other. "I'm going to leave," she said. Her voice trembled. "It's not that it isn't good to see you." She said this nicely. "But I'm going to leave."

"Yes," he said. "I understand. Nothing's changed, but I understand." He held the door for her.

He forced himself to get back in line, though his mind was on such high alert that morning coffee now seemed superfluous. He wondered where she was going at this hour carrying two coffees. When he was two-thirds of the way home, his cell lit up. He saw her name, or at least thought he did, and pulled into a Walgreen's and parked.

"It's you," David said. "How are you?"

"How's Kate is more to the point." Jane couldn't quite believe she had called him. She'd helped enough therapy clients with strategies for *not* making these kinds of calls.

"Well, there are a lot of valid questions here," he said.

"I thought..." He could hardly hear her and turned up the volume. "I thought I was good until I saw you."

He took in an audible breath but didn't speak. He hoped she'd say something more. When the silence went past what he could tolerate, he said, "I know you'll have a good life without me. A better life. There's no way I can pretend to make a case for you and me."

"Look, are you sure you want all these complications? Kate is great. I mean, I believed you before, but still, meeting her, it seems like a pretty full life." She had called him in some kind of trance state and with no agenda. Or maybe she wanted him to retract the offer. Maybe she hoped he would say or do something that would free her.

"How are you?" he asked again.

"Oh," she said. "I'm in trouble. I'm afraid I'm in real trouble."

"Are you sorry you met me?"

It was a question she had considered many times and she told him the truth: She tried to imagine they had never met, but it turned out she couldn't allow any scenario in which she didn't meet him and love him. "It would be so easy if I were sorry."

Silence. He was afraid to say anything in case he stepped on her next words. He was afraid anything he could say would sound like begging.

"One month," she said. "We'll try one month. I have no idea if this will work. Will it be enough? Will it be a continual frustration? I will not live in Jealousy Land again. That much I know." Need seems to follow love, she thought. Women start out so independent, but soon they're waiting for the phone call.

'One month," he repeated.

"If it hurts Kate, it stops," she said. "And no one else knows except people we can't stand to lie to."

"I can lie for you," he said. "If I have to."

———⟶⦾⟵———

"I ran into Jane," he told Kate. He had thought of only saying that Jane had called, because to call after the accidental meeting would seem too spontaneous, too unplanned—not to be trusted. But instead he told her exactly as it had happened. "One month," he quoted. "And not if it hurts you."

"I thought you looked different when you came in the door," Kate said.

He hated to think he was so transparent, though he didn't think he was, except to her.

"She must have tried so hard not to contact you," Kate went on. "There's not even the small comfort of calling and hanging up like in the old days. You can't hide anything now."

He hadn't tried to picture that. He had imagined Jane moving on to a new life with someone who wasn't him. He also couldn't imagine what to say next, so he said, "Okay, Katie, here we go," and she seemed to think that was fine.

———⟶⦾⟵———

A few days later, David left work and drove the other direction from home. He knocked and waited and then used his key to let himself in the side door. When he called out, Jane came to meet him, carrying the mail and newspaper. "I used my key," he told her. "I hope that was okay."

"You're right. I need rules. You're not a husband. You're not a friend exactly. Lucy would knock and wait before she used her key. What are you?"

He was glad to see her take his question seriously.

"I think that if I know that you're coming," she said, "then you can use your key, but if you're not expected, then you should knock."

"And wait? And leave if you're not home?"

She nodded, pleased to have a policy. "I'm glad you're here, though—for many reasons—but first, could you look at the tub drain? How could it work one day but not the next?"

They went to a big box store to buy a replacement, along with a new splashguard for the garbage disposal. Lucy's oldest child had somehow sent the current rubber circle into the works of the thing, and then turned it on. While Jane was off looking for something, a neighbor came up to David to say he'd heard the good news about Kate. Just then, Jane joined them, tile cleaner in hand, and the neighbor, looking studiously polite, backed away quickly, calling out *nice to meet you* as he left. "I don't think he thinks I'm the housekeeper," Jane said.

She didn't seem to care who the neighbor thought she was. *He* was embarrassed, but that seemed a small price to pay.

Installing the splashguard went quickly, but then David spent enough time with the tub stopper to know she needed a plumber. "Really, I'm mostly good at remembering historical events," he told her. They made dinner and ate in the kitchen, ignoring the landline that rang several times. "I'm sure it's just Rachel from Cardholder Services," Jane said. "She's stalking me."

"I know her well," David laughed. "She's such a bitch. That touch of menace in her voice—the veiled threats. *This is your last chance.*"

"She can't help it. She's programmed that way."

After dinner, they moved to the living room, and Jane turned to the presentation she was giving the next day on the placebo effect. "I need to go through everything twice more. I just need forty minutes and then I'm all yours."

"I'll bet you're letter-perfect already."

"Yes, but I never stop there."

A few feet away from her, David pretended to read but, after fifteen minutes, she put her files down and said, "This is ridiculous. I can hear your thoughts. Let's go to bed. I'll just get up a little early tomorrow."

"Bed?" he said. "When we've got a perfectly good floor right here?"

"Do not push your luck," she said, and she began to turn out lights.

Later, after she cried out and then caught her breath, she pushed him a few inches away from her so she could see his face.

"What?"

"I still can't believe you're here," she said.

She wasn't the only one.

———⟩●⟨———

At home, the family scattered, Kate to take a nap, David to work in the study that they once again shared, and Dylan and Jack to the driveway to play basketball, the net gray and tattered but still usable. David listened to the sound of the ball and hoped their elderly neighbor to the west wasn't home. She had let them know years before that the marathon games annoyed her; now, however, she was kind of deaf. For him, the sound was welcome; it carried the message *home safe, home safe.* Once, he had surprised Kate by asking if she heard the same reassurance, but she had never thought of it, and like their neighbor, had to work at not being irritated by the sound. "Though I do like it when they're home," she said, looking at him oddly. She and David had been pleased to the point of silliness when Jack called the day before to announce he and Dylan were on their way.

"It's a surprise, but we wanted to warn you so you could go buy better food or whatever you do before we come home."

David finished his goal of grading ten essays, most of them good, and found the boys in the living room, sitting near a properly made fire and stripped to their tee shirts because it wasn't very cold out. While he and Kate had been unavailable, the cats had bravely come out of hiding and were sniffing the boys' feet, then hiding again before pouncing. Anova climbed Dylan's chest and positioned herself precariously on his shoulder. Fred tried to bat her off. "I had no idea cats were so..." Jack searched for the right word and ended with, "cute."

"Then you are not spending enough time on the internet," Dylan told him. "And you're not following those links Mom sent you—the cat break-dancing in the mirror, the mother cat hugging her baby."

Jack looked guilty. "It doesn't take long to take someone for granted, does it?"

Dylan frowned. "It doesn't. But maybe that's not a bad thing. Maybe it means we're optimistic."

"Either that or naive," Jack countered.

Kate came in the room carrying the three most recent photo albums and a glass of water.

"I couldn't nap, but I had a lovely time looking at these. Now we have to go through them together."

David could tell she'd been crying, but he didn't know if Dylan and Jack would notice the signs, which she had tried to cover up with eye makeup. She sat in a chair they had saved for her and put the albums on a side table. She changed the order of the pile and then lined the books up carefully before she looked up to speak.

"Boys, we need to talk about some changes." They both sat up straight, Jack rigid, as if ready to fight.

"I think you know that for your dad, meeting Jane wasn't some casual event. He and she love each other, and they had every reason to believe that I wouldn't get better. And if I have a recurrence, the doctors can only guess how to treat it."

She took a sip from her water glass. "I think of myself as having died," she said. "There was this dead person sitting, walking, staring. It wasn't really me."

"You're getting a divorce?" Dylan said, his voice equal parts surprised and baffled.

"No one is getting a divorce," David said. "You don't even need to think about that."

Jack said to Kate, "Are you going somewhere?" sounding like the fifteen-year-old she had left once before.

In first grade, Jack had discovered divorce: "Does everyone have to get divorced? How long does a divorce last? Do you know when you'll get divorced?"

"No. No one's going anywhere. I'm trying to be brave enough to tell you that we think there's a way that Jane and Dad don't have to be so hurt and sad and—"

"You're going all Utah on us," Jack said, getting it before Dylan did. "That is so *bent*." Jack's voice was shaking. "This is so stupid. So unnecessary. So embarrassing."

"Yes, it may be all those things, and I don't expect you to give us your blessings. We just don't want to hide and lie."

"There's just no way?" Dylan said. "No way to go back to how things were? To fix this thing? Dad...?" The last word plaintive and childlike.

"*This* might be a way to fix it, is what we're hoping," David said.

"Fix it for *you!*" Jack shouted. "What about Mom?"

He began to cry silently, and Kate moved to squeeze in next to him. She put her arm around his shoulders, and he made a gesture to shrug her off, but she held him tighter and he let her. He stopped crying and pulled up his tee shirt to wipe his face.

"We think Jane is with the program," Kate said, "though understandably, she might not think this is entirely fair to her."

"Well, Mom, you might not think it's all that fair either," Dylan said.

"It's what I want. I can't be everything to your dad anymore. I cannot live day after day picturing him alone again if I get sick. You need to know that Dad would give Jane up for me—he did give her up. I've met Jane and I plan to like her. I think she might already like me quite a bit." She used her thumb to blot a tear on Jack's cheek. "This will work, honey. We're into the second month. It will work, and there won't be a trail of broken hearts."

David wondered if the more likely outcome was that there would be three or more hearts broken in new and confusing ways. He let Kate's story stand: that he had given up Jane—when really Jane gave him up, and so quickly that he was hardly tested. Would he have been ready to lie and cheat if Jane let him? But she wouldn't, and he had stayed home to love Kate, which was not at all hard, while he waited for the attrition of Jane and for the wanting to become less demanding. Eventually, he knew, it would have become difficult to conjure Jane's face, and he would betray Kate only by occasional dreams that were wanted and unwanted in exactly equal parts. The other possible scenario? If Jane had been willing to cheat? This was not the moment for rigorous truth-telling.

"Okay, so I think we all know that this thing is not going to work," Dylan said, "but in the meantime, *how* is it going to work? Do you draw a number every day? Is there a rotation?" He looked somewhere past Kate's head as he spoke. "And what does Mom do while you're gone? Wait? Think?"

"*Imagine* things?" Jack said.

"So," David began. "Two days a week at first. At the most. When Mom's settled in and busier, then we'll look at weekends, holidays, all that."

"Pilot project," Dylan muttered.

"Yes," Kate said. "Call it that. I like that better than 'going all Utah.'"

She left then for the kitchen. David wanted to follow but didn't. He and the boys sat without speaking. Jack reached for the remote but thought better of it.

"I'm sorry you're dragged into this," David finally said, "but you're too old not to be honest with. I miss the old days too, you know. But maybe your mom is right that we can't make it be like it was."

"Home maintenance!" Dylan said, as if playing a trump card. "Are you going to do the guy stuff for two houses?"

"I don't know. Possibly. By the way, we've agreed not to research this kind of thing online."

"You'd probably just get porn," Jack said.

No one laughed.

After vetoing a few suggestions (too many bikers, too many aging stoners), the brothers ended up in an out-of-the-way bar where they wouldn't see anyone they knew. They settled into a booth and Dylan said, "Did you see this coming?"

"No way. I had the impression Jane had just stepped aside—like, 'Sorry, wrong seat, I'm really in Row G.'" Jack started to say more, then stopped and said, "Weird shit, but who knows?"

"If I had to pick someone who could maybe handle this, it would be someone like Jane," Dylan said. "But Mom? What's in it for her?"

"Maybe it's what she said—less responsibility. And I think people don't get so crazy jealous when it's all above aboard."

"If it was Mom's idea—and I do believe that—then she's pretty much in control of the thing," Dylan said. "I don't mean that in a bad way. And it does make the idea seem a little bit possible."

"Well, if Dad wasn't ever going to get over Jane—"

"I don't know if he would have." Dylan thought he should explain the dopamine hypothesis to his brother—help him understand the activation of their dad's reward circuit. How even his love for their mother and his joy at her return could face strong competition from the new, unanticipated stimuli that was Jane. Dylan wanted to say that if he were told to give up Lily forever or the city of Chicago would be destroyed, he'd have to think about it. And he might just say "screw Chicago." But it wasn't his job to lobby for his dad.

"Then I guess Mom either doesn't love him any more," Jack

said, "or she loves him a whole lot."

"I wonder if it's some mixture of the two."

Jack frowned. "Do you even know what you mean by that?"

"I think I mean that she loves him a lot, but that it's different now, or it feels different to her. That there's some change that lets her see Dad's side and Jane's side without making her nuts. I wonder, too. I mean, he did move on. He did fall in love with someone else. Not until years had gone by, but still, how do you just pretend that didn't happen? Mom's not big on pretending."

Jack was unusually quiet before saying, "The only part I really hate—I mean the part I hate most, so far anyway, is...I really, and I mean really, do not like having to think about our parents' *sex* lives."

Dylan agreed. "It's a terrible thing. And it seems about to get a whole lot worse."

"I want things back..." Jack said, but he didn't finish.

———⇒►●◄⇐———

"I should call Jane later. She'll be wondering." David wanted Kate to know before he called. No matter what his wife said, he planned to be very careful. He knew how it felt to imagine oneself to be left out. It never felt like imagination.

"She's got to be curious about the boys' reaction," Kate said, and then went upstairs to take a bath.

He didn't expect to find Jane at home, but maybe he had a chance calling her cell. He noticed they both left their phones on a lot more and had become adept enough to answer in time. Of course, he was always slightly on edge expecting bad news from Kate or about Kate. Jane answered on the second tone, her voice barely audible over loud music.

"Am I allowed to ask where you are?"

"I'm at an old-fashioned key party. Let me just see who I've agreed to go home with." She waited a beat and said, "Oh, no, I am not leaving with *that* guy. Hold on a second. I'll walk somewhere quieter."

He heard the background sounds muffle.

"I'm in the bathroom now. How are you?"

"Well, I'm pretty sure you're not at some weird swapping party, which is good. I'm not jealous. I just don't want to catch anything."

She laughed. "It's a card party. I came for the pizza and powdered donuts." She waited.

"Kate and I talked to the boys. They are not fans of the idea."

"Do they hate me?"

"No. They hate *me*."

"I suppose they would, but they could also be profoundly annoyed that I'm willing to be part of this."

"They think Kate's crazy and they hate me. They didn't really focus on you."

"Yet."

⸻

Kate spent the next morning looking at photo albums, one son on either side. "It's interesting how often you two don't agree about where a picture was taken or even who's in it," she observed.

"It would help if I had labeled any of them," David said from behind the couch, where he perched periodically to see what they were looking at. "Maybe you could go back and do that now. From wherever you left off."

"I did some the other day," she reminded him.

Dylan and Jack seemed to be frozen, waiting for him to leave the room, so he did. Later, Kate made sandwiches for the boys, and they left five hours before they would have if things were normal.

"I'm sorry," David said, after they drove off.

"I'm glad they don't try to fake it," Kate said. She leaned against him. "Look, you don't have to come home. Like this week, when you go over there. I'll be with Martha all evening. Stay over. That's better, don't you think? As long as I know what your plans are. And I think you know that I don't see your time with her as some once-a-week…"

He knew, thankfully, that she wouldn't be able to say *booty call*, even if she knew the phrase. *Thing* was what she eventually came up with.

They moved to sit on the living room couch, first clearing off the albums and newspapers.

"Has it really been okay for you?" He forced himself to continue. "I know it's just a handful of times. I feel like I'm intruding to ask again, and I don't even know what I want the answer to be."

"It's better than watching you missing her and trying not to show it, and I don't say that to make you feel bad." Quietly, she added, "I've not been in pain." And then, "What about you? Do you feel guilty—in any direction?"

"I've felt guilty about you for so long, maybe I can't even tell if I feel some higher level of guilt now."

"Guilty? You mean when you met Jane?"

"No, longer. Like maybe we had an argument and it triggered a bunch of brain chemicals and that's how it began. Maybe if I'd admitted sooner that you were ill, something would have helped. And then meeting Jane. I didn't so much think that I was doing anything wrong, but I still felt guilty. They're not always the same thing, are they?"

"You don't really feel responsible for what happened to me, do you?"

"Not in any way that makes sense," he said, "but I think maybe guilt can be a way to stay close to a person, a tie to someone who's gone." On the word *gone*, he saw her blink hard.

"And now? With Jane again? More guilt? New guilt?"

"Maybe I should, but I don't seem to. Only because you know, and I'm not sneaking. Does that make me shallow and greedy?"

"I think you're sort of brave."

"What?"

"I mean you risk disappointing both of us, and I don't mean mostly about sex."

"Yes, two people to let down. I just can't make myself worry about that right now."

"I'll tell you this too. It's sort of embarrassing, but it's you, David—I can tell *you*. I think it's been just the smallest bit arousing, as if something broke through this asexual state. Does that sound perverse? Or childish? Like how Fred doesn't want the cloth mouse until Anova touches it."

"Childish? No. But perverse?..." he said, talking into her silky hair. "Yes, perverse, though in a good way. For me, anyway." She laughed and he thought perhaps he should make a move and then smiled to think of planning a strategy to seduce his wife of decades to whom he used to be able to just say *I want*. He felt her relax against him and heard her breath rise, then fall, and he let her sleep for a few minutes until his arm went numb. When he extricated it, she woke and they stood, and he watched her climb the stairs slowly, like a child long past bedtime.

Now that David always had use of his car, their mornings felt deceptively like the routine he and Jane had before Kate came back. He found Jane in her kitchen, holding a sponge but not using it. She didn't eat breakfast, and he was finding he could skip it too.

"You know, we never really got a chance to talk about living together," he said. "I never heard your answer to that idea. Is it even fair to ask now?"

"Everything. I would have said yes to everything."

Her willingness to lay herself bare made his heart race for a beat or two.

"But as for the new question, I can't tell you what the minimum is that will work for me. One day a week? Three and a half days a week? Does it even matter, if I keep expecting a call from you or Kate saying there's been a change of plans?"

"First of all, that is not the new question. No one is asking what your *minimum* is. Second, you say that Kate or I will flake out, but you don't actually sound pessimistic. About us. About you and me."

"I plan to learn to live in the moment." She smiled. "And yes, the contradiction is intentional."

"So we need to live in the moment—and we do that by…careful planning?" he asked rhetorically.

They made a date for three days off—their last chance before Kate's parents' arrival.

When he got to class, the lecture hall was mysteriously locked. He opened it and the students camped out in the hallway climbed to their feet and streamed in to hear his talk on the unknown abolitionists. To most of them, it was as if he were recounting a cable news story. The topic engrossed them, but it was all news to them, the details too full of conflict and ambiguity to survive into popular history. A few asked such smart questions that he thought, as he sometimes did, that he would do this part of the job for free.

After class, he called Kate. She'd spent the previous evening with Martha. He was pretty sure he knew what had taken place.

"We weren't in the mood for shopping. We just talked. It seemed like the right time to tell her. About the plan—we have got to think of a word for it. You know, I think I've shocked her before. I mean, this is a woman who went through the seventies without smoking pot, and she was clearly not prepared for this. She wouldn't comment—she refused to give an opinion. Whatever she thought or felt, all she did was grab my hand and say it was good to have me back. I hope Don doesn't have a heart attack when she tells him."

It seemed to David that he had a choice here: to be flooded with embarrassment and self-consciousness—exposed in a dreaded and dreadful way—or to…just not. To not go that familiar route. To be somebody different, not necessarily an improved version of himself but just different. Someone who planned to make this thing work, and with some confidence and kindness, not just towards others—he was good at that—but also towards himself.

"Thank you, brave one," David said. "It was right to tell her."

"I wouldn't be doing this," she said, "if it was something I couldn't talk about."

"Yes, I understand that. It only works if it feels valuable. And possible." This way of seeing things *was* starting to feel possible. "Jane is good," he offered. "Tentative, as you can imagine. Sort of expecting a change-of-heart phone call from you. Or me."

"Understandable."

He heard their doorbell ring. "I'll see you after work. We'll prepare for your parents' visit."

"And we'll do that how?" But she laughed after she said it.

CHAPTER SEVENTEEN

David and Bill shook hands, but then mutually turned it into a hug. David was struck as usual by how much taller he was than Bill, who, even just a few feet away, seemed by sheer command to add four inches to his height. Bill looked his age again, as if some of the premature withering they'd all experienced had dissipated. Perhaps his grief had eased as he'd had increasingly less contact with his daughter's condition. David watched Eve as she waited her turn—if he squinted, he could see Kate superimposed on the still lovely woman. When Bill released him, Eve took over and wrapped him in a long guilty hug, or so he imagined. "It's been so long," she said. "Too long."

David took a breath and said, "I haven't really prepared you very well for..." and he saw their faces, already tight, collapse. "No!" he added quickly. "I mean I haven't prepared you for the... improvements," he decided to call it. "In fact, we're not going to the L. Kate's actually in the house." Bill set down the larger of the two grocery bags he was carrying, then took Eve's arm and they started up the front steps quickly. Eve tripped and Bill said, "Slow down, Eve. Remember the no-falling plan." They walked carefully into the house, where David caught up with them, banging luggage against the door molding as he led them to the living room.

Kate stood by an armchair. "Hi, Daddy," she said sweetly,

and then, "Hi, Mom," her eyes clear and focused, though with the glisten that precedes tears. Eve dropped her handbag and Bill let the small shopping bag he was carrying fall—something in it resounded, possibly broken, but he didn't glance down. They walked slowly towards Kate as if afraid she'd disappear like a hologram.

"I'm feeling a lot better," she said. "The new medications seem to be working."

Bill knelt down. Whether his legs gave, or he was praying, wasn't clear. Kate knelt beside him and took his hands. Eve melted into the closest chair, placed her hands on Kate's shoulders, and kissed the top of her head, a series of little kisses, as one does with a baby, mouthing "you're back, you're back" into Kate's hair. Bill had yet to utter a sound when David began a quiet retreat.

At first, he only went as far as the kitchen, but the air throughout the first floor seemed thick with the intensity of the reunion, and he soon felt short of breath. He went to the basement, little used now, and watched sports highlights on the last of the old squat TVs.

Much later, he heard footsteps, and Kate found him watching the end of a two-year-old basketball game. He roused himself to a seated position and she sat next to him, looking both exhausted and slightly manic. Putting his arm around her, he could feel her quivering as adrenaline started its delayed reaction. He breathed along with her, trying to slow his breath each time. Soon, her breath matched his and he felt her begin to calm.

"They're unpacking the groceries they brought. We won't have to shop for a while. They also brought a cooler with some things they made. They must not know you cook now." She glanced at the muted game, then back at him. "I didn't tell them about Jane yet. It seemed like my dad was ready to ask, but then he didn't."

"Do we even want to tell them?" he said. "We don't have to—unless they move here—which is entirely possible now." David thought her parents *should* move near Kate, safe and close, for their last years, but he knew Bill and Eve were the type that didn't plan on dying—or even becoming old-old. *Mind over matter*, he could picture Bill saying, as he did when confronted with something unpleasant like stuck lug nuts or a pulled muscle. He had been the last to admit Kate was ill. Even Jack could talk about her illness sensibly before Bill did.

"Of course, we don't want to hide like we're ashamed," he said seemingly contradicting himself. "Look, Kate, I've been worried about something. It's important to me that you know that I do not think I deserve this. It would bother me if it seemed that way."

"Is it possible that if all kinds of bad things happen to us that we don't deserve, then it's okay if something *good* happens that we don't deserve either?"

He pulled her towards him, held her too tightly, and then relaxed his grip.

"I'll tell them tomorrow morning," she whispered.

"I'm in if you want me," he said. "Always good to have something to look forward to." And they both stood to climb the stairs.

After dinner, David and Kate helped Kate's emotionally exhausted parents maneuver their luggage and get settled at the inn where they had stayed during each visit since Kate first moved to the L. David had understood right away that they couldn't stay in the house without Kate, and no one tonight suggested they change their plans. They all needed a break. When he got back, he found Kate in bed, still awake, not quite vibrating like earlier but too wired to sleep.

"What would help you?" he asked, and she said, "Some educational TV. Maybe history—history always puts me to sleep." She wasn't joking. When she was pregnant and plagued by insomnia, she'd say "talk history to me," and it would work, though he realized more from relaxation than actual boredom. It wasn't that Kate was uninterested in history; she just couldn't retain the information. Periodically, she'd say, "I still don't get World War I. And the War of 1812—why don't I even remember the sides?" She hadn't properly understood that the Panama Canal connected two oceans. One time he asked her what she did while history class was going on around her but she didn't know that either.

Now he laughed and turned on the History Channel. "Christ, it's about Caligula. That's not going to work."

"How about *Raymond*? Is *Raymond* on?" As usual it was, and before the end, she was asleep. David waited for the epilogue and then he fell asleep too.

———⟫●⟪———

Eve and Bill sat on the couch and studiously avoided making eye contact. Kate sat in an armchair kitty-corner from them, and David balanced on one arm of Kate's chair. He could see she was beginning to lose patience.

"I don't have a better way to explain this," David said. "I don't really have *any* way to explain it." He found it never helped to repeat things when someone is angry. First, Kate laid it out for them, and then he told them the same few truths: that it was Kate's idea, and that he never would have left her. They could believe him or not. "Look, this might last for one more month. It might be a terrible idea. But we didn't want to hide it from you."

Eve opened her mouth but then pressed her lips together and Kate spoke instead. "If things were reversed, who knows if

I would have gone all these years without someone? You do not have permission to question his loyalty. You could hardly even bear to come see me. David didn't tell me that. I've seen the visitor logs. I understand, and it's *fine*. I'm glad you didn't torture yourselves more than necessary, but..." She was slightly out of breath. "But do not judge him." Her voice softened. "It wasn't my fault that I got sick, but it isn't anybody else's, either. They love each other. He can't just *fire* her. I don't mean that he couldn't, but that isn't—" She stopped and sat back in her chair. "I agree with David that this could turn out to be impossible, or short-lived. I mean, how often does this kind of thing ever, ever happen? Back from the dead?"

Her parents inhaled sharply at those words, and then Bill, looking only at David, said, "This is insane." He looked from David to Kate. "I don't know where to begin."

"I don't want you to begin. We understand that you hate this. We know it might not work. We're not foolish people, no matter what you think." Kate looked her father square in the eyes. "We're going to look at photo albums now. You can help me label some of them, and...there may be a few of Jane in the most recent one."

"Then we are not looking at photographs," Bill said.

———⟫●⟪———

At five o'clock, Kate and her parents emerged from their cloister and joined David in the kitchen, where he had the ingredients for gin and tonics lined up and ready to mix. He studied Bill and Eve, their expressions changing from moment to moment as they alternated between the euphoria of yesterday and the depressingly unwelcome news of today.

"The kitchen held up well," Eve observed. She had helped

with the last remodel many years ago. "I don't think you'll ever need to do much to it again."

Kate laughed. "Are you saying we're getting on in years?" Eve placed her palm on Kate's cheek. "You are still so young. Trust me on that."

David served the cocktails, with a plain tonic for Kate. "Unless you'd like a real drink, Katie."

"I think I would—a half-strength real one."

"Do you think it's all right?" Eve said, but Kate didn't respond.

David moved everyone and their drinks from the counter to the kitchen table, which was set with flowers her parents had brought, along with crackers and nuts he had arranged. Everyone was still standing and David must have had that look that people get before making a toast, because Eve said, "Wait, I want to say something." Without looking at her husband, she took a gulp of air and said, "I don't want to fight about this anymore."

David almost jumped, surprised again at the speed with which Kate's mother changed sides.

"I don't want to be angry anymore. I hate it, but I can pretend she doesn't exist—and maybe after awhile, she won't." Eve finished and waited.

Bill looked only at his daughter. "I think you deserve more." He didn't sound angry. "I think you deserve everything. This is a bad bargain for you."

Now David could see that Bill was angry—furious in fact, despite the lack of drama in his comment. He'd had a boss like that once and had been fooled a few times before he learned every tic and tell. Bill's eyes narrowed and something throbbed in his neck. David sensed he was trying to come up with a threat, but what threat did Bill have except to withhold his love?

"How can you be so sure how long either of you would have

waited?" Kate asked. "And it wasn't even really waiting! It was…
hopeless." She looked in her lap. "And I'm not sure I could dispose of someone I loved. Could you? How can anyone know what
they'll do? More important, I shouldn't be defending him because
you shouldn't be criticizing him. David was—I mean is—a wonderful husband." She looked only at her father and asked, "Why
would you want him to lose somebody again?"

Bill shook his head slightly but didn't speak.

"Daddy, do you remember the first night of our honeymoon,
when David and I missed our flight to Mexico because neither
of us had noticed the gate change?" She went to kneel beside her
father's chair. "Do you remember what I said when I called you?"

"You thought it was an omen, that it meant you'd made a
mistake."

"Do you remember what you said?"

"I hope it was something wise."

"You said, 'Don't be an idiot, Kate.' Then you said, 'I hope
David didn't hear what you just said to me. He's the best human
male you've ever dragged home.'"

One quiet sob, then another, escaped Kate.

"At one point, you did have the most terrible taste in men,"
Eve said.

Bill stood, drew Kate to her feet, and held her. "Please don't
cry, Katie. I can't watch you cry."

David wondered if Bill's anger had been calculated—a nego-
tiating stance—though what they were supposed to be negotiat-
ing he couldn't imagine. No, he realized, the anger was real. Bill
and Eve's submission was only about not making Kate sick again,
about not causing her stress—about never running the risk of
being the one who did or said something that could later be seen
as *pivotal*. It wasn't genuine agreement. It was more like a game

of hot potato—*I won't be the one to trigger a relapse. You* can disagree with her if you want, but I'm just going to say, "Yes, Kate. Whatever you want, Kate."

No one could stomach what he and Kate were doing. Maybe Dylan hated it less than Jack, and somebody would hate it the most, but no one was going to feel even neutral about it. They were tolerating it because they loved Kate. She had never been an easy person to win an argument with, and now she was untouchable.

Bill said, "Katie, this...situation is for—it's not really our business. I don't ever need to meet her." He gave the start of a smile and added, "Unless it's to catalog the many ways she is inferior to my daughter."

Eve was crying now too. Bill let go of Kate, though they stood hip to hip for a long time, and then all four of them began to move about the kitchen.

—————⟫●⟪—————

A few days after her parents left, Kate and David went together to Kate's outpatient appointment. Impossibly, there was already a sense of routine about it. They agreed later that neither of the researchers seemed tense.

"Dr. Tsang said that he couldn't tell me how the others were," Kate reported. "But he had a big smile when he said he couldn't tell me."

"Did he ask you about sex this time?"

"He did. So, I just gave him a smile. And he laughed."

—————⟫●⟪—————

David dreaded Claire's visit less than Bill and Eve's. Still, he was glad when she took an international call that occupied the short trip from the airport. "I can't go." Kate had begged off. "I cannot do this in public." It was only after they pulled up in front of the house that he took Claire's hand and said, "We don't need to go over to the L. Kate's inside. She's been home on a trial basis. There's been some improvement." He saw her begin to take it in. "Actually, Claire, there's been a lot of improvement."

They got out of the car and walked slowly towards the house. She seemed frightened.

"It's okay. It's not a joke. I would never joke about this."

"I know," she said.

Once in the living room, it seemed at first that Claire was at least going to be able to stay standing. Then he saw the telltale signs of someone blacking out and ran to grab her. Seated, her head cleared. "Jet lag,' she said. "Yes," he said. "That must be it."

Kate watched, her tears diverted by Claire's collapse. Claire, though, began to cry and cried for fifteen minutes, only stopping when she got the hiccups. Kate comforted her and helped her hold her breath, but Claire was too wrung out to manage it. Finally, David went to the kitchen and brought back the sugar bowl and a spoon. "It's kind of disgusting, but it works."

It did work and, when the women were settled and ready to be alone, David left for Ian's house, where his friend, lonely while Daphne was in England, was glad to see him.

"If I go out and have any fun, my delinquent kids will have a party," Ian predicted. "And you haven't seen a teenage party until your house is Facebooked."

Ian and Jane had spent one morning and two evenings in each other's company and he approved of her. "If Kate's mother is 'old twin, then Jane is kind of 'dark-haired Kate,' don't you think?" he asked David after the first meeting. "Kate would be flattered,"

Ian had said. "Of course, if she could be flattered, then she'd be well, and the flattery would lose its appeal." He had seemed to be seriously trying to follow this line of reasoning.

All Ian knew now was that Kate had a new diagnosis, was responding to different treatments, however temporarily, and that her time at home was going well. Someday, David would tell him the real version. After their first beer, when David said, "We need to talk," Ian said, "Christ, please don't make this bad news."

"You decide," David said, and then he told him.

Ian stared at him. "You fucker. You crazy, lucky genius. I do not believe it." He squinted at David. "I do not believe it. A mare and a spare."

"Jesus, Ian. It's not like that at all."

"Oh, it is. It is so flippin' like that." Ian studied his beer label. "But not together, right? Strictly couple stuff?"

"Yes, Ian."

"You sure you have time for all this?"

David didn't answer, just looked at his friend until they both grinned. David had no idea if he could manage all this. Would Kate find the *idea* worked for her but not the reality? Would Jane tire of it soon? He wasn't about to say any of this.

"All right then, just don't frighten the horses, mate, and you'll be fine."

David had to laugh. More horse metaphors. Then he remembered.

"There's one more thing."

Ian looked at him dubiously.

"If this thing works out, it will become known, but not by you. If I hear that you've gossiped about this, I will personally beat you up."

"Oh, come on, David. Have you ever even hit anybody?"

David thought for a second. "No."

"You do have those large sons, though."

"Ian, I know you'll tell Daphne, but if she gossips…"

"You going to beat *her* up?" Ian gave a short laugh and then went silent. David wasn't sure how to read his expression. It wasn't critical. And he didn't sense any envy. It was wonderment, he decided. Just neutral wonderment.

———

Claire was gone. "She went out," Kate said. "She's mad. She seems to think we've agreed on this plan in order to mess with everything she believes in. "I waited all this time to have a man of my own—an unencumbered man—and now you say that isn't important? You're more evolved? You're too amazing to be confined by marriage?"

Kate took a breath. "There's more. She's always admired our marriage—though she made it sound more like a punishment—admiring us, I mean. I've had to hear about your marriage for 25 years. I've waited for the right man so I could be you and David. And now you say it was nothing?'"

He took a seat next to her.

"What I'm thinking is that I do not want to be the big sister anymore. And I don't think I should have to be. If I lost…whatever…five years, six, then we're kind of the same age. I do not want to be a role model. I do not need to be admired. I don't even need for *you* to be admired."

"That will come in handy," he said, "because, except for Ian, I am slipping way down the list of admired—"

Claire came through the front door just then, carrying wine-shaped bags, which she put down carefully on the coffee table.

She gave David a stiff smile and pulled an ottoman close to her sister.

"I'm obviously not about to lose you again—even to this. Maybe we don't need to talk about it anymore. Maybe we can pretend just a little bit. I plan to pretend that there's zero chance you'll get sick again. I can pretend about this too. I know that's probably word for word what Mom said, but I don't care."

David stood up and collected the bags. She looked through him, but he said, "Thank you," then left them. For the rest of the afternoon, he heard periodic laughter and excited conversation, just below audible. In the early evening, he went into the living room where Kate and Claire were curled up, each on an end of the couch. When he returned with a water pitcher and three glasses, the sisters were asleep, their feet intertwined, both with a cat insinuated in the small space between their backs and the couch. Neither stirred as he covered them with the oversized cashmere blanket Claire had brought them many years before.

He doubted she would ever come for Thanksgiving.

———◦———

Dylan wished he felt more excited about his parents' visit. He supposed he was happy for whatever peace they had found in their domestic triangle, but today's get-together was poor timing for him. He was in a good relationship, which must in part be influenced by his parents' marriage, but now what he had seemed to have a tameness to it. He felt kind of prematurely old and staid. No, to be accurate, he only felt that way when thinking about his parents—or in their presence. He knew he didn't want anyone else instead of Lily. He was sure he didn't want anyone else *along* with Lily. It must be vanity. He just didn't like feeling more conventional and less adventurous than his mom and dad. It wasn't natural. It made him want to do things he never did, like get seriously drunk. Or high. Or try the four-year old ecstasy that was in the freezer back at his apartment. What he wasn't going to do was talk to Lily about it. At least not today.

He made his way to the living room in time to hear his parents as they reached the last few creaky steps and stood in front of Apartment 4B. He thought he heard his dad panting slightly. "I'm not knocking until I catch my breath." He definitely heard his dad say that. Dylan opened the door and said, "We heard you staggering up the stairs," as he gave his parents quick hugs.

"This is Lily," he announced and she stepped forward to be introduced. "They grandfathered in those stairs," she said as she shook their hands. "They're not the right rise. Sometimes I sit and rest halfway—not if Dylan's watching, of course." Everyone laughed.

"So I hear it's only to be 'Lily' and not the long form," David said.

"I was thinking maybe it could be Lilana on first reference, like they would do in the New York Times," Lily said. "But only Dylan can sing it." She smiled at Dylan.

"Sing it?" David said, looking at his son.

"Later," Dylan said, and Lily led them into the living room, which was decorated nicely in a post-graduate but not fully grown-up style. "I'm good at finding things on Big Trash Day," Lily said in answer to Kate's compliment. "And you wouldn't believe what students throw out at the end of each semester—or maybe you would. I forgot you live in a college town too."

"We made tea and cute sandwiches," Dylan said. "So we can stay in for lunch. It happens to be Parents' Weekend and there's no parking anywhere." They toured the small apartment—a tour empty of embarrassment about the fact that Dylan was more or less living there. No attempts had been made to collect and hide his belongings. Though really, David thought, by the time he and Kate were halfway through college, some of that fuss about living together had died down already, except for a few fundamentalist parents, and the only thing their disapproval seemed to gain for them was a gap of years when they didn't see their kids.

During lunch, Kate and Lily talked intently, somehow drifting into a private conversation despite the small party of four. Dylan and David suspended their own desultory discussion a few times and just watched, trying to overhear enough to identify the topic—it seemed to be Lily's doctoral program. Dylan helped with the dishes, gathered two textbooks and his laptop, and the three of them said goodbye to Lily. He rode with his parents to the small apartment that he had cleaned for their visit. He still felt the need to flee back to his place sometimes, though he was learning that if he just waited out the feeling, the anxiety that he sometimes felt by being close to Lily began to seem like a normal thing—a price everyone pays for letting their life depend on someone else.

"The sheets are clean. Well, I haven't slept on them since they were washed. Is that the same thing?"

"It's good enough," Kate said.

Dylan got them settled in and left for the library. "Lily is too distracting—she hardly has to study and keeps *talking* to me. I tell her I don't get this stuff by osmosis the way she does, and she pretends to understand, but it's just better if I go to the library." They made plans to meet downstairs to walk to the restaurant Dylan had called two weeks before, worried about all the other parents in town. He showed them how to make coffee and then left them to themselves. David and Kate settled in at the kitchen table with mugs and the newspaper.

"So?" David said.

"She's lovely…and easy to talk to. She treated me like a person instead of a mother—*and* like a person in full possession of her faculties."

"Our daughter…do you think we've met our daughter?" David's tone was light and they both smiled, but he saw the tell-tale glint in her eyes and knew he looked the same. Embarrassed, each reached for a section of newspaper and they read quietly until Kate put her cup in the sink and moved to the living room, where she curled up on the futon, which was neatly folded, couch-style.

"Did you buy this for him?" she asked as David moved to sit next to her. The futon creaked dangerously.

"Yes, when he got his first apartment," David said. "Man, this place is so nostalgic. Am I the only one who feels twenty-two again?" She smiled but didn't answer. His hand began to roam and she whispered, "This just seems wrong. Wrong," but she didn't stop him.

"Nice of you to wear a skirt," he said, as he moved his hand higher until he reached the v of the small band of silky fabric. He took his time. They weren't going anywhere, and he didn't need anything—just to remember being young and alone with a girl he liked. He had forgotten the pleasure of this near-voyeurism. Kate's breathing quickened without him even disturbing the elastic, and then she let him continue, but just for a moment before she took his hand away. She opened her eyes and looked at him quizzically, but he said, "No, I'm good—that was a freebie."

She smiled. "You are so not twenty-two."

PART III
ORDINARY TIME

Kate and Jane sat on Jane's couch, a barely touched bottle of wine in front of them. The trial month Jane had signed on for had elapsed and then a second and a third, with the weeks now split into four days Kate and three days Jane. "That's all I want right now," Jane insisted, surprised that she meant it, but she was falling behind in everything. Time with David often still felt like a very long date. He displaced her regular life, like a teenaged love affair.

Waiting for a *30 Rock* rerun, they had the volume turned low on the unwanted show that came before. Kate counted out cashews four at a time and ate them, each time claiming they were her last. Something on the screen caught her attention, and she mimicked the just audible, disembodied male voice talking over the mute thirty-year-old L'Oreal model: "See up to ten years disappear in a stroke!" Kate repeated. "They think we're that stupid."

"Do you buy that stuff? Do you do all that?"

"I barely wash my face. Though if I'm around and aware these next ten years, I could see myself getting more interested."

The two women looked at their shoes, scattered on the floor.

"What's the highest heel you ever wear?" Kate asked.

"Probably two inches. I tried spikes a few times, but I always felt like a prostitute. Plus, I fell off them once. A clumsy prostitute." Jane stood and balanced on her toes. "I don't get it. Wanting to be looked at that much. In college, once, I was waiting at a bus stop near school." She had never told anyone this story.

"You remember those days—most of us didn't have cars. The bus stop was next to a long light and I saw the driver of the first car staring at me. I mean he *stripped* me. I'd been looked at before, of course, but never anything like this. The light went on and on, and he started making these movements with his mouth. I turned away but that almost seemed worse. After this interminable time with him all over me, the light changed and he pulled away, really, really slowly, and someone from school who'd been just a few feet away, not a guy I knew, came over and said, very sympathetically, that he couldn't believe how the guy had looked at me. He was being sweet, and he was extremely shocked, but it embarrassed me even more that there had been a witness. As if it had been my fault. I know you know what I mean. Later, though, I was kind of glad he saw it, and I wondered a few times what he did with what he learned."

"Did you ever wish he'd said something to the driver?"

The question surprised Jane, and then she felt surprise at her surprise. "No, I never thought about anyone helping. For that matter, why didn't *I* say something?

"Yes, why don't nineteen-year-olds know exactly what to do?" Kate glanced at the TV and back at Jane. "David says you don't confide much."

Jane watched the start of the next ad while she considered this. "I think I got out of the habit because Charlie didn't. He was probably afraid he'd divulge something incriminating, so we kept it pretty superficial. And Lucy tells Tom too much, so I have to be careful there."

"How come you can talk to me then?"

"How can I not trust you? You don't seem to want anything from me, except that I not cause your husband pain. Where else would I find such a friend?"

"I know that joke! It's a lovely therapist joke."

Jane's voice turned solemn. "I was very good at being single and at having casual relationships, and occasionally even casual sex, and at being alone in between the...casualties, because it seems to me that a woman has to be skilled at being on her own. The quality of available men—well, the good ones are always married—" She stopped, stricken, to wait for Kate's reaction.

Kate waved her hand. "Don't give it a thought. The whole time I've been with David, I have never—underline never—met an unattached man I thought I could be interested in. Every crush or fantasy I ever had was about someone who was married, or the equivalent."

They both let these words sink in.

"I don't want to be alone again," Jane said.

"I don't think that will happen," Kate said.

"I know we have no idea how long this will last," Jane said quickly. "I'm not a rose-colored-glasses kind of person. Any one of us could find things to object to. Even David."

Kate raised her eyebrows.

"I know that's a little hard to picture," Jane continued, "but still. And then there's me. Every time I'm in a relationship, men start coming around. Plus, maybe it sounds predatory, but it's just a fact that before too long, men our age will start being widowed."

"Breast cancer," Kate said solemnly.

Jane nodded. They each knew several women in the midst of,

or just past, their treatment. "Well, here's to the impermanence of the unknown," she said as she raised her glass, but Kate didn't raise her glass. She was looking at Jane with a question.

Jane replayed her words and realized how she had sounded. "I don't mean that I'm using David as a stopgap until I meet someone else. I know it must have sounded that way, but he's not just *anyone* to me."

Kate still didn't speak.

She would have been a good therapist, Jane decided. "But it's true that if I meet someone else, I'd be out of your hair, right? I mean, I am the third party here."

Kate sat up straighter and leaned forward. "I'm the third party too. And I could get sick again and be out of *your* hair. But I don't think this will work if we each think that way. I want you to tell me: Have I made you feel like you're not as…weighty as either of us?"

"Christ, no. You've been totally generous."

"He's not mine to give," Kate said.

That was a new thought for Jane, and one she would need to think more about later. "I know three things," Jane said firmly. "I am not hoping to meet someone else. I am not waiting for you to get sick. And we don't know what the fuck we're doing."

Kate laughed and they took a ceremonial sip. She pushed the cashews out of reach and Jane turned up the volume for the start of their show. She held onto the remote and hit "rewind" a few times after their laughter made them miss the next quick line. "How can you pause a show that's being broadcast—one that's not a recording? Dylan said you could do that, but I didn't believe it." Kate looked from the remote to the screen, puzzled.

"I don't know. You just can."

"But how do you catch up with yourself—with the start of the next show?"

"I don't know. I never seem to care about the next show. Ask Dylan maybe."

"It's like time travel," Kate concluded.

"It is, but you can only go backwards and not forwards, sort of like life. You can remember things, but you can't predict much."

After watching the episode's epilogue, Jane turned the TV off. Kate started to gather her things but stopped and, then with a half-smile, said, "What was David like?"

"You're fishing for compliments." Earlier, Jane had almost asked if David knew Kate was here, as if one or both of them was somehow cheating on him. She had stopped herself at the first syllable. It wasn't her job to manage this thing, or rather she would manage her part of it, and the other two would manage theirs. David must know that Kate being here was a possibility.

"Maybe it's not fair to ask, but tell me anyway," Kate said.

"Overwhelmed. Miserable. Funny. Handsome in an exhausted, sad way. I thought he was great from the start. But it wasn't clear he was at all available."

"But he was, wasn't he?"

"I don't know. I mean it's hard to be miserable and available simultaneously. I think meeting me took him by surprise. And maybe even if he didn't think he was ready, he could at least welcome the possibility, when it happened without a round of grim *dating*." With a light still glowing on the TV, Jane flicked the remote again. "Okay, a question for you, Kate: If David had—and I mean *if*—I know it's not likely, but if he had been unfaithful... *before*, what do you think you would have done?"

"I would have left him," Kate said. "He had absolutely no reason to cheat back then, and I would have left." Then she smiled and said, "Or not. I don't know. He would have paid—I can say that much."

Jane found Kate's certainty, and then her ambivalence, consoling. "Let me ask you something else. What's in this for you? I don't mean the three of us—I mean you and me. We seem to have drifted into a friendship."

One day their carts collided at the grocery store. Then, peering at each other's food choices as people do if they don't stop themselves in time, they saw each had the coffee David liked, along with grapefruit juice and green bananas. They smirked and then let themselves laugh, their carts blocking the aisle. They agreed to meet at the cafe just past the checkout and talked for an hour—"I didn't buy anything frozen, did you?"—and then continued to meet every few weeks to talk, and once for a concert David couldn't attend, and another time when Jane tried Kate's yoga class. Kate told David about it from the start, and he said, with a touch of resignation in his voice, "I'm surprised it took you this long."

Now, in Jane's living room, Kate answered her question. "I'm lonely, but it has nothing to do with David. I used to have a lot of friends, and now the only one I'm comfortable with is Martha, and sometimes that's hard too because she knew me when I was well. The friends who stayed away feel guilty, and they don't believe me when I say I don't blame them. It's tiresome. It's not their staying away that bothers me. It's what they saw before they stayed away. So we're embarrassed and awkward for different reasons, and it doesn't work anymore."

"Do you feel any of that around the kids?"

"If I thought they were dwelling on how I was then, I'd be horrified. But I think they've pushed it out of their minds. They worry about me, but I think the current me is who they see."

Jane took a gamble. "And David?"

"David, well, that's harder. I say to myself, 'He watched you deliver two babies.' Of course, that inelegance isn't the same, but still, there's less room for vanity after pushing out a baby. If I let myself think about being sick, I'm very embarrassed, but I never feel like he remembers me that way or is haunted by that version of me. He's more worried about reliving it. Me here, but gone again." She shrugged. "We each need to coexist with our particular demons. But I've read my chart. You and I didn't interact at all. I'm a new person to you. Almost, anyway." She paused to give Jane a chance to say something, and when she didn't, Kate finished with, "And we have so much in common, after all."

"I set you up nicely for that one, didn't I?" Jane said and picked up her wine glass. "To friendship," she toasted. "Odd or not."

⟞⟝●⟞⟝

Jane came over the next evening—their first time together in the family home—and the three of them sat at the kitchen counter. "No alcohol," David insisted. "We'd be sure to mess up the scheduling." Kate had a wall calendar in front of her with invitations and notices paper-clipped neatly to the current month as well as the next few. David was still at Jane's three days a week. The plan was to eventually go to three days one week and four the next, but all of them thought Kate still didn't have had enough going on in her life for that.

David and Jane thought consecutive days would be better for them, but when they tried to plan around Jane's schedule, they realized that on too many occasions he'd be waiting at her house until she came home shortly before bedtime. He didn't mind doing that once in a while, he had told her the third time it happened. "But it can't be often. I'd probably feel like you were just using me for sex," he said, and not entirely to make her laugh. So for now, his one evening class and Kate's still uncomplicated life meant Jane's schedule dominated the division of time.

"Are we going to get away with this?" David asked. He hadn't planned to say it. "I mean, am I really going to get away with this? Without hurting you both? Without punishment?"

"What's behind all these questions?" Kate said. "Is this guilt talking? I think you know I can't help you with that any more than I have. Is this just you, David? Waiting for bad things to happen. Or self-consciousness?"

"It's not guilt. And it's almost never self-consciousness, though there's some of that. And why wouldn't there be?" David had never touched her in front of Jane, but he reached for her hand now and held it between his. "I just worry that it will wear on both of you. That it will feel like rejection instead of choice."

"You could feel a little rejected too, David," Jane said. "I mean, here are two people you love who are telling you they can get by with less of you. Maybe that's what you're after here. Maybe neither of us fought hard enough to be the *one and only*."

David didn't think he had ever been interested in the kind of fight she described, but it sort of felt like she had him here. "Okay. I couldn't have attached words to it, but yes, there is, within this amazing state of being wanted, also some not-being-wanted. Some familiar feeling of not being completely necessary. The old parent-thing, I realize. You know how parent-things are. As soon as you think they're gone, they're back." He looked at the ceiling.

Kate touched him once on the shoulder. "You need to trust me," she said. "I love you with all my heart. It's true that my heart isn't exactly like it used to be, but whatever is there is yours."

Jane leaned forward and waited until he looked at her. "It would be so easy for me to find a man I didn't want. I've found so many of them already. It's you, David. Yes, it's complicated, but it's you, and I don't think I can do anything about that."

He was embarrassed. He had thought he was speaking about his fear of hurting them, but instead they had uncovered something in him. It wasn't significant—more of an artifact, an old feeling attached to something new—but he was reminded that nothing about this venture was predictable. It made him wonder what else lay ahead.

———>>●<<———

David came home from work and walked through the house, hunting for his reading glasses and, if he were honest about it, looking for and worrying about signs of a possible relapse. Jane or no Jane, losing Kate again was not a tolerable thought. He tried to be strict with himself about not dwelling on it. Self-flagellation didn't have the appeal it once did. There were, of course, the occasional nightmares, but he didn't hold himself accountable for those. Some days, the anxiety was so strong he wanted to follow her to see if she was driving in circles or talking oddly to strangers. He knew that even if he had left her for Jane, she'd still be in his life, and everyone he loved would be ruined by the loss of her again. And now, even Jane's life, he knew, would not go unscathed. It was too late for that.

On his second pass through their office and the kitchen, he had the frightening thought that he was seeing Post-it's in greater numbers, but when he looked at them closely, he saw that they weren't references to *forks* or *stove* but instead, *Xerox last year's tax return/find flash-drive* or *check flexible spending account* and he smiled, spared. This was just Kate taking care of the numbing details of modern life. From a small pile of bills, he pulled the solicitations from the local and national Alzheimer's groups. He'd write those checks. She shouldn't have to do that.

His gratitude didn't stop him from saying later that evening, "I continue to really dislike how you load the dishwasher." He made sure to keep his voice pleasant.

"I can't believe you care about something that small. You have dish-loading OCD."

"If you don't care, then why don't you do it the way I like?" He had never made this point before. He had always backed down, always let it stand that he was the petty one.

"Because I'd have to think about—" She stopped for a second and started again. "Because the issue betrays the fact that you don't think I'm perfect, and we were always based on the idea that you thought I was perfect." Her smile was sheepish.

"Perfect for me, Katie. I only meant perfect for me. Not incapable of annoying."

He watched her move the dirty bowls to where they ought to be.

———⟫●⟪———

Dr. Tsang explained the newest phase of the study. "Sadly, this is my last time to be at your appointment. You'll be followed by Dr. Ratha now that this phase has ended, and there will be only one visit a month. I can tell you that everyone who responded well is still doing well. We were sad to learn that one person had a serious heart incident, but we knew he had pre-existing heart disease. That he survived this time is probably due to the fact that he could communicate his symptoms. At any rate, we'll break the code in about six months and end this next phase of the study. Of course, you'll remain on the regimen you're on now."

"What about publicity? We're still living in fear of a national news blitz." David asked this but he knew he spoke for Kate too.

"We did issue a very guarded press release when we filed the last interim report, but it hasn't attracted much attention. Perhaps there have been so many 'breakthroughs' that proved to be false hopes that the media isn't as interested in us now. It will still happen, but maybe we have more time than we'd thought. Still," he said, "don't let down your guard."

"I'm glad that crying wolf has worked to our benefit so far," Kate observed. "And on the subject of the meds, I should tell you that lowering the tricyclic has been useful. I forgot to say that last time."

David sat straighter. She hadn't mentioned a change in medication to him. He knew they weren't talking about the experimental drugs, but still, he hadn't expected to be cut out of a treatment decision. Now he did a double-take on her choice of *useful* and realized she meant sexually. He had noticed that the last few times, sex seemed less effort for her. Apparently, her chemistry was being restored to something closer to its original state. Did their "arrangement," he wondered, hinge on Kate's reduced interest in sex? He didn't think that a woman's desire for sex—at least with her husband—ever increased past middle age, but what was predictable about any of this?

"Well, that's good news," the doctor said, and then a small chirp came from his pocket. "My phone is telling me to leave for the airport," he said reluctantly. "You will call me anytime if you need to?" He offered his card to each of them. "I think you know that I mean this." He and David shook hands, and he hugged Kate one last time. "It's been a pleasure, Mrs. Sanders—Kate. It's been a pleasure working with you. I will hear of your progress through the team, and I will always be thinking of your health."

To David, he said, "You are a very lucky man."

If there was a way to decipher an additional meaning to the statement, David didn't know what it was.

CHAPTER EIGHTEEN

Sometimes, David worried that Kate felt guilty for having gotten sick, almost as if she had cheated on him and, as if by returning, *she* was the interloper, not Jane, and that it was Jane who had some degree of prior claim.

"You aren't the only winner here," Kate said to him one day, apropos of nothing they were chatting about. "I needed a new friend—a post-illness friend—and you sort of handed me Jane. I like her. I like who I am around her. She has this sort of completing, non-needy presence. And smart. I've added her to my short list of people—my parents, you, Ian and Martha, the kids—I always want to hear their opinion on something before I make up my mind."

"For you to say that out loud, is so…not just kind, it's generous. And it makes me think that maybe I'm not a burden—that our messy life isn't a burden."

"You have to understand," Kate said, "I'm not afraid of this. I'm afraid of getting old—and of not getting old. I'm afraid of Jane leaving. I'm afraid you'll die too young. But the three of us, I can handle. Someone has always loved me, and it's almost always been you. What we're doing doesn't burden me or scare me. Everything else does, but not this."

Still, not long after, when he didn't offer to cancel an overnight trip to Chicago with Jane for a big-deal fundraiser Kate had told him about too late, they argued.

"You said you'd make sure this didn't cause trouble for me,' Kate said, misquoting him, perhaps innocently, perhaps not.

"I said I'd leave her if you were in pain, but you're just *inconvenienced*. Do you want this to be a union shop? And you have seniority? That's not how we set things up, but is that something we need to talk about?" They were standing at opposite ends of the kitchen, and he could see the tension in her hands. She had never thrown anything at him, but he took a step back reflexively.

'No, I don't see it that way," Kate said, "though I wonder what Jane would think."

He gave her a look, harder than he meant to, and she added quickly, "I would never say anything."

"She's not a prop or a character in some script you wrote. You must have known these kinds of conflicts would come up. But I meant my promise: If this ever becomes something that makes you sad, I won't let it go on."

"No, I don't think that's what I mean. I have to pull my thoughts together." She poured herself some water, but then held the glass without drinking. "I think you may be right about annoyance. And some boredom. I feel terrible admitting to boredom. Am I used to life already? Jaded? Why can't I treasure every moment, like a dying person?"

"Because you're *not* a dying person. No more than the rest of us. You're one of us now, more or less. You can't survive on gratitude and amazement alone."

Seeming to replay his last sentence, she now nodded. "I need to fill my life more. I need to *use* it. Yours is already full. But if I do the same, are we going to have room for each other?"

"You need a full life anyway, with or without Jane," David

said. "We used to scramble to see each other. Remember when you were working one of those stretches of days, and I left work to bring you lunch?" They'd had quick and furtive sex in her windowless consultation room, surprising both of them.

"I thought about that a lot later on," Kate said. "It was nice to have a true fantasy."

"So, Kate, do you want to stop this?" He tried to convey that there was no right answer.

"I didn't want to wake up and find you in love with someone else."

Was their grand experiment over?

"I don't wish her gone. It could happen, but I don't wish for it now. There's something to be said for doing something wild— something you never imagined. I don't have to like every minute of it." He crossed the kitchen to join her, and they both leaned against the sink, facing each other.

"This can go either way. I'm stronger than you think."

"I know that. That's not something I ever doubted." She gestured with her hands, and he reached to steady the glass she was holding just before it overflowed. "Sometimes I worry that we've ruined Jane's life in some yet-to-be-determined way. But then I decide we've just changed it. Or rather Jane chose to change it. Then I worry: Did she really have a choice, given the force of love…and your irresistibility? And tell me this: Has anyone ever successfully defined free will?"

———>•<———

David came in through the garage to the kitchen, where he found a pot of water boiled down to an inch and the radio playing to no one. He turned off the stove and went looking. There wasn't another sound to guide him, but he found Kate in the upstairs bathroom, still kneeling near the toilet.

"You threw up?"

She nodded.

"Are you sick?"

"It's a panic attack. The worst should be over."

"You've had these before?" Her skin was a terrible shade, and when he touched her arm, he felt the clamminess left by a cold sweat.

"This is the third. They're a new thing." She raised her head. "I thought it was a heart attack the first time, just like you hear. But then I did the nurse thing and realized what it was."

"I'm really sorry. I haven't had one in decades, but I know they're horrible."

"Yes."

"Do you think it's from the medicine? Or is it about something?"

"Dr. Ratha is pretty sure it's not the medication."

"Good. I'm glad you talked to him. I feel bad you didn't want to tell me."

"I never think there's going to be another one. I thought I could will them away." They sat for a moment, and he stopped himself from offering empty reassurance. He offered silence instead, and it seemed to be what Kate needed.

"Maybe they *are* about something." She wiped her face with a dry washcloth. "I had just begun to let go of the certainty of relapse. Or at least I thought I had. I was feeling so…myself. Not unworried but less worried. I guess I don't know if that's why it started, but that's when. I didn't want to tell you. I cannot bear to be the sick one again."

"Did it ever happen when I was with Jane, and would you tell me if it did?"

"I was at home all three times, but you weren't with her. And the only thing that happens away from home is that it's become hard to drive. I have the sensation that I'll be hit at any time. I almost hallucinate about cars coming at me."

"Okay, that's good to know." He recalled something. "You know, I read somewhere that those sensations can increase with age. Which would account for older drivers crawling along." She smiled. "If this happens again—the panic attacks, I mean—would it help if I were with you?

"Maybe. I don't know."

"Next time, you need to find me. I'll cancel class. Whatever." That definitely got her attention. "I worry a lot about relapse. Maybe we need to be more open about it—worry together."

"You've *never* cancelled a class."

"Exactly. I've earned it. And I'll come home if I'm with Jane. She won't give it a thought."

"She will. What if she thinks I'm being manipulative?"

"Oh, Katie." He brushed her hair away from her face. "She trusts you. She's not like that, and she trusts you."

<hr/>

Kate proposed to David that they take dance lessons. "Social dance, not ballet or anything."

"No, I don't think so," he said warily.

"That's fine. Jane said she would go with me if you didn't want to."

David gave a startled yelp. "Okay, so now I'm competing with Jane for time with you?"

"Yes," she said nicely. "That wasn't my plan, but I guess so."

"What's next? Are you getting a horse?" He made himself

go through the motions of resisting her, when really he was too happy to care about the details as long as he could be with each of them. If Kate wanted a horse, he would get her a horse. *Empress Kate, may your reign be long and powerful.*

As time passed in this new odd normal, Tom and Lucy, quasi-family to Jane, moved through the stages of horrified, then stoic, and now resigned, as they witnessed their friend happy again. Jane invited them to brunch at her house, along with Kate and David, which David thought might be too much, even for his open-minded wife, and she did pause long enough to say, "What's the worst that could happen?"

David, normally so good at imagining just that thing, said only, "nothing." He couldn't see anything bad happening. The morning was awkward for the first hour but sociable and noisy in the second, and he felt that he was forgiven by Tom and Lucy, though he wasn't sure if it was for staying with Jane or for not leaving Kate—he guessed they wouldn't have been able to decide exactly.

He had no clue which of the women first suggested the idea of the five of them meeting for dinner downtown—in public. In the past, he heard one side of the *arranging* phone calls, but now full-blown plans were presented to him for his perfunctory approval. For this milestone, they arrived in five different cars, something they realized as they showed up one by one at the table—David from interviewing a possible new hire, and Tom from a job site where he was placating a demanding couple—the only type, it seemed, who ever want a house built. "They're freakin' perfection-ists," Tom said. "That's why they do it in the first place. They think that perfect exists."

"Well, my interview with the young hotshot went great," David volunteered. "At one point, he said his only concern was that the community might be too conservative for him, at which point everyone looked right at me. Every single person looked like I was supposed to get up and tell my story."

"What did you say?" Kate asked.

"I asked the hotshot, 'What is it that you're planning on doing?'" The other four laughed loudly. "Same thing happened at my meeting, and then we moved on. He can ask some of the others tonight when they take him out for dinner."

They were quiet for a moment and, in the lull, Kate said, "Do you find that you don't remember much about your early experiences with sex? Like who you did what with first? Oral sex especially—it should be a milestone. I don't remember much of the details, and it makes me kind of sad."

Tom said, with phony solicitousness, "You mean you used to remember and now you don't?"

Kate made a face at him. "No. I've never been able to remember."

"Me neither," David said. "I must have had to get her drunk first, whoever she was."

Lucy and Tom looked at each other. "It wasn't him," Lucy said. "But I don't know who it was." Tom shrugged.

The four of them looked at Jane now.

"I do remember," she said. "We were very young, and I thought he had invented it. And, I think you're all tramps."

Amid the laughter, Lucy said, "Why do you ask, Kate?"

"It just makes me a little sorry that something like that is gone."

Tom said, "I should probably tell you, Kate, that we have

sort of an unspoken rule that we—Lucy, Jane, and I—don't talk about sex. It's one way we keep the incest taboo going between me and Jane."

"Though the first firewall is that you're repugnant to me," Jane said sweetly. Tom sputtered into his wine as she batted her eyes at him.

"We've obviously given up on taboos," said David, "We just say whatever we want."

Lucy raised her hand. "Let's list all the things that we know have happened to us that we don't remember."

"No," Tom said decisively. "It's only interesting if it's about sex. Otherwise, forgetting isn't remarkable at our age. Not any more, anyway." He lifted his glass to toast Kate. "Plus, my theory is that we don't remember details about sex because we were the first generation where it wasn't such a huge deal. It was something you did sometime between the first time you hung out with some-one and the third."

"You slut," Lucy said genially.

"I'm not going to take that too seriously, though I am eter-nally grateful," he said, as he leaned over to kiss her. "But what I was leading up to is that for us, technology is our virginity, so to speak. That's what we remember: our first email, first time we heard *www* or Wikipedia or Google—all of it."

David joined in. "I clearly remember the moment I heard two guys from the Geology Department talking with awe about the World Wide Web. I had never heard of it. As you can imagine, the History Department's always the last to hear things."

"I remember my first awareness of email," Kate said. "My famously smart cousin sent an invitation for something, and it said on the reply card that you could also use electronic mail to respond, and I thought: 'Well of course, she's invented a new kind of mail.'"

David was enjoying himself. He scanned the room and didn't see anyone he knew. Nor did he see anyone watching them with interest. When Kate got up to use the bathroom and Jane soon followed, he wondered why, but was distracted by Tom and Lucy describing their oldest child's detention at school. "I would like to hook her up to a lie detector," Lucy said, "because everything she says sounds plausible, but not much of it is actually true."

"Lie detectors aren't accurate," Tom said. "Especially with sociopaths. Did your boys lie?"

"Of course," David answered promptly. "But not nearly as much as I did at their age. My parents were so self-absorbed that I used to lie just to dare them to concentrate on me long enough to catch me. I told them once that I'd been chosen to skip a grade of high school, and they believed it, even though no one had ever skipped a grade in our school system." He drained his wine glass. "Since leaving home, though, I've hardly ever lied."

He remembered then that Lucy knew the real story of Kate's recovery—and presumably Tom did also—so they knew he was currently involved in a large network of lies. David was surprised to be going on about himself, especially on this topic, which was making him a little dizzy. Was he telling the truth about lying? Or lying about being honest?

———◦———

Jane found Kate at the mirror, brushing her hair and mouthing the words to the endlessly repeating Spanish language tape. After checking the stalls to be sure they were alone, she said quietly, "Listen, why don't you and David go home together? I know it's not what we planned, but..."

Kate froze. "No, I'm fine. Why?"

"The way you were reminiscing, I thought maybe you needed him around tonight." It pained Jane to make the offer. She had been waiting almost a week to be alone with him, though she had been the one who'd been unavailable. David finally asked if she kept her life so frenetic to avoid depending on him. He understood why she would think this was the safe way to do things. But he didn't like it. He understood it and he didn't want to argue about it, but he didn't like it. "Do you think I don't miss you? Do you think that because there's Kate, that you, Jane, are just an enhancement?"

Sometimes she wished she were more adventurous or more attracted to Kate. She admired her enormously, but as everyone learned at some point, admiration wasn't enough. She couldn't picture the two of them together, and never had the slightest hint of it from Kate, and certainly not from David.

"Well, that's a kind thing to say," Kate answered. "But I'm fine. And I wouldn't expect you to change your plans. I mean, I don't outrank you."

"I wasn't referring to rank, just to need." Jane smiled. "Yes, I am that magnanimous."

Kate squeezed Jane's hand. "What I was really trying to talk about is that, as I come to grips with losing those years, I also run up against all the other normal forgotten events. Memory is so loosely knit. It helps a little to know that others can't remember things either. Except you, Jane, with your inventive boyfriend."

They made eye contact in the mirror and Jane said, "We should ask David to warn the boys to make note of their first blow-jobs before it's too late." Kate's eyes went wide and she laughed explosively at the usually reserved Jane, who, equally surprised, began to laugh too, their laughter fueling more laughter until Kate, weak and breathless, went to sit on a gaudily painted chair. They calmed themselves and began to leave when Jane remembered the other reason she had come to the restroom. "Who cares about sex? I actually forgot to pee," she said, and their laughter started again as Kate waved goodbye.

Jane arrived back at the table just as Tom said, "What I really get nostalgic about is drugs. I miss drugs. Sort of."

Lucy looked surprised. "Would you really smoke pot again?"

Tom considered Lucy's question seriously. "I mostly miss it when I watch people in movies getting high. But I'm not sure that's the same thing as wanting to do it myself. And then there's our teenager and soon-to-be-teenagers."

"I miss feeling a little out of control." It was Kate who said this, but they all had wistful expressions.

"I'm sure you all did acid," Jane said. "I feel really unhip, but I never did. It wasn't like I was being careful or good. I don't remember ever getting a chance to turn it down." She sat up straighter and said with some pride, "I remember cocaine, though. That was everywhere. Twice was enough for me. Erroneously inflated self-esteem is not my thing."

"God, yes," David said. "I mean, no thanks." It had been everywhere. Every party. Movie plots. It practically came out of the faucet. "I think I still have insomnia from my long weekend."

He and Kate exchanged a quick look. Their cocaine-fueled three-day binge probably hadn't even been a binge by coke standards, but afterwards they agreed they were done. "I don't want to go down this road," Kate had said, and he said he thought that he had been following her, and she said, "I know that's true. Let's make new friends." And from then on, it was alcohol and nothing else.

Lucy turned Tom's wrist over to look at his watch and he said,

"Can you take care of the bill, Lucy, while I go do some business with the busboys?"

"We can't afford drugs," Lucy said. "We have to pay the sitter."

David paid for Jane's meal; he stopped her demurral with one firm gesture and then walked Kate to her car.

"I'd say that the fun part outweighed the weird part by a lot," Kate said. "But what about you?"

"It did," he said, and he could hear the surprise in his voice. "We had too much to talk about. I didn't have time to worry the thing to death."

She gave him a chaste kiss, then he drove to Jane's, stopping for gas first. The door was locked—Jane must have locked it out of habit, so he got out his key, but she reached the door before he needed to use it. She was wearing a black slip or nightgown—it was hard to tell—and her skin looked beautifully pale in the light coming through the windows of the dark kitchen. He set down his briefcase, newspaper, and sports jacket before embracing her. "Hold on a second," he said, breaking away. He pulled out his phone and rifled through a drawer to find a charger. "Why don't you wait for me in bed? I have to brush my teeth. And floss. Did you have something stringy stuck in your teeth too?"

"I can't talk about floss right now."

A few minutes later, he called out from the bathroom, "Do I have time for a quick shower?"

"No," she said, her voice firm across the distance to the bedroom. "You do not."

———⟫●⟪———

One day, David and Kate had a squabble and briefly disliked each other. By bedtime, he couldn't remember what they'd disagreed about, but it felt like a necessary milestone had been crossed. Claire didn't come for Thanksgiving, which was so normal that David had never mentioned the possibility to the others.

When he finally told his parents the good news about Kate, they were effusive with delight, and he held his mother's interest for an entire conversation, and part of a second one. There was no reason to tell them about Jane—he didn't crave their attention that much.

After their first visit, Bill and Eve called several times a day. David answered the first few times and they interrogated him until Kate reached the phone. She waited as he answered their questions in monosyllables before saying, "You know, she's standing right here." Then he started making up Kate's memory feats. "She just recited an entire old 'Mad Men' script verbatim. She can multiply four digits by three digits in her head." Finally, they laughed, and he put Kate on. "You have to talk to me like I'm normal or I'm hanging up," she said.

Kate still researched any event someone mentioned from her lost years, but on one Sunday, David watched her pay six dollars for the Sunday Times and read nothing but the *Style* section. Kate and Jane came up with a low-maintenance plan for the backyard, and the boys came home for Mother's Day and dug. Sporadically, one of the insurance companies spat out a check to the L and Kate would spend three hours undoing the mistake. "Do you not understand this is me talking to you?" he heard her say once in disbelief.

David took Kate to a dance club he had learned about by asking around, embarrassed but determined. She taught him some moves before they left the house, and they learned a few more during the quick lessons the host taught every half-hour. He was glad to be told exactly what to do. Driving home happily exhausted, they decided to go once a month.

"Would you mind if this is something just you and I do?" Kate asked tentatively. "Not all dancing but dancing like this?"

"God, I love you," he said, without any explanation, and when she added, "though we should tell her, of course," he said it again.

Jane ran a 10K but then stopped training and went back to the treadmill. Running was too public. Good, David thought, glad as always to be a man, and guiltily aware of how thoroughly he studied women runners. He didn't want her unsafe, and he didn't want men looking at her.

Jane's friend Winston (he had changed his name from Bob) joined the three of them occasionally for movies or dinner when his big pharma boyfriend was traveling. Winston had a crush on David, which David didn't seem to notice, and Jane never mentioned, knowing that Winston's crushes were like a virus that would run its fevered, harmless course. One afternoon, David arrived at Jane's and they cooked dinner together, went for a walk, and didn't make love that night. One of them was too tired or had a cold. They talked into the night about his research or her new contract or something in the news too vexing to go unexamined. The next morning, she said, "I didn't think that would ever happen," and he said, "It always happens."

<hr />

David came into the kitchen one evening, laden with the usual devices and bags, plus a bouquet of flowers. Kate was wiping fingerprints from cupboard doors, and it took her a moment to hear him over the earnest tones of public radio. She turned the volume down and started when she saw the flowers.

"Is there an occasion?" She went to take them. "They're

gorgeous. These must be from Phoebe's stall."

"Yes," he said. "And no occasion." Kate seemed more excited than flowers could account for.

"I thought maybe you could read my mind," she said.

"I know we've established how bad I am at that."

Without telling anyone, Kate had interviewed for a half-time position at the university, and the offer had come through that morning. "It's in the Biology Department, the collaboration with the linguistics program that we read about."

"Animal communication."

"Yes, Randall Trevino. He'll have to call me support staff of some kind to free up a little of the grant money. I offered to work for free. Do you know what he said?"

"No," David said, feeling some small alarm.

"He said I'm too young for that. He said maybe he'll cut my pay later, but for now I need to be paid." Kate was idly swiping at smudges. "It was kind of a strange interview. I don't think he's even hired anyone before. He actually asked me to name my biggest weakness."

He laughed. "What did you choose?"

"I said that I talk too much and I interrupt people but that I'm always working on that. And I'm too honest at times so I hurt people's feelings. Also, I can be impatient—like most of the time."

"What did he say?"

"He started laughing halfway through. Then he asked for my biggest strength and I said I can usually make people laugh."

He congratulated her and then added, "If you have any thoughts of reapplying for your license, I'll do anything I can to help you." He wished he hadn't said that.

Sounding both sad and resigned, she said, "I don't think so. If I don't trust myself, then I wouldn't be very persuasive. At least

I can't kill anyone in the new job. I'm not even working with animals—just coding the video. The animals are in a sanctuary in Georgia."

"I'm sorry," he said and he was. She sounded determinedly cheerful, but he could guess how it felt to go from helping women with something as powerful as birth to observing other people's work. His thoughts were also on Trevino. David was vaguely aware of the man, having seen him interviewed on "Nova" shows and local TV. He couldn't remember how old he was or anything about his reputation with women. Without meaning to, he laughed out loud. "Are you making fun of me?" Kate asked.

"Absolutely not. I'm ridiculing myself for thinking I can control or predict anything. Or anyone. And for never knowing what you'll do next." Maybe Kate's boss, or an older student, would fall for her and complicate David's happy life. In her previous life, she had worked almost entirely with women, and that had been more of a luxury for him than he realized. Did he even know if he remained his familiar jealous self? Maybe he was changed too.

<hr>

"Mine is more haphazard," Kate said, speaking of their house—hers and David's—though she used the pronoun *mine* to be polite. It was a Sunday afternoon and Jane had stopped by to go through the calendar.

"But it has life to it, even with the kids gone. Mine may be more *perfectly decorated*"—Jane drew the words out as if it was a criticism—"but it sometimes feels like a stage set—waiting."

"Well, you haven't had young people putting your silverware down the garbage disposal and shooting baskets in the house."

Jane smiled. Apparently, David had never mentioned repairing her garbage disposal. She knew Kate didn't mean there was damage or scars, but that houses have an essence. Her house used to feel fully occupied even if she was the only person there. That had changed, and sometimes it was only after David arrived, looking a little guilty and then pleased, that the house truly came alive. Need follows love. It always does.

She had thought that just not losing him would be enough. And it usually was enough. Well, it was enough to prevent terrible pain. Was it enough for a full life? She didn't know yet. Are busy and full the same? Sometimes she couldn't be with David when she wanted to, but that was true for a lot of spouses.

On the other hand, there had been a few times recently when she surprised herself by wondering what Kate was up to—and might David want to wander on home because she, Jane, was all talked out from her week of hearing sad things. The second time she went quiet on him, he noticed and said, "I know that look," and went into work for three hours. When he returned, they made love and then watched a movie. She could be married to a lot of people who wouldn't know her that well. Still, the future lurked, with its less busy years and unromantic needs that would multiply with speed.

David came in through the garage and heavily put down a bag of water softener salt. Both women jumped a little. He poured himself a cup of coffee and refilled theirs.

"We were going through the Symphony schedule," Kate explained. She pushed the brochure towards him. "Do you think someday we'll all want to live together?" she asked no one in particular, her tone idle.

"But whose house? I really like my house. Too, I mean," Jane said.

"I love your house. And I love my house," Kate said.

"Now this is just an observation," David offered, "but it is interesting that you're willing to share me but not a house." It really was just an observation. He didn't necessarily mean to promote the idea of living together.

"Is that what you want?" Kate said.

He wanted to choose his words carefully. He felt, too often, like a guest at Jane's house. He had explained this to her recently and told her he wanted to paint her laundry room. She had never gotten around to covering up a bad shade of mauve. "I need to change something—make it mine too. She said fine and he should surprise her. They laughed at the idea of her not caring what color he chose. Still, he couldn't imagine the three of them living in one house. He supposed the schedule and the decision-making could stay the same, but there was no part of his mind that could picture the three of them roaming the halls like a Peter Sellers movie. Maybe later.

He didn't know much about the sex lives of the elderly, but it was his impression that things wane significantly. Not that he would wish for it, but maybe then they could live in platonic happiness, like siblings—siblings who chose each other.

"I don't think I do, for now," he said. "Except for one thing." They looked at him curiously and he realized his next words would disappoint them. "I hope to get old someday and my appetite for cleaning gutters and maintaining snow blowers and turning over packed soil might diminish." Seeing Kate begin to speak, he added, "I know, Kate, you were going to learn how to do all that stuff in case something happened to me."

"And for the sake of fairness."

"Okay, but it never happened. And I don't want to do half of all the stuff you do anyway."

"Like remembering your parents' birthdays?"

"Exactly. And donating to every food drive. And _gifts_." He shuddered. "And all of the paperwork. Organizing the recycling. I missed you, Kate—every recycling day. Really, I just threw most of it away."

Jane listened to David tease Kate and wondered if she could be alone in one bedroom with the two of them in the next. How could anyone know such a thing in advance? No, she knew. She knew that what they had worked only because of the distance and privacy. This unlikely equilibrium would be easily wrecked.

David and Kate seemed to be waiting for her to say something, so she announced, "I think this went very well for a first discussion, and I believe we can table this topic for now. I'll make a note on the calendar that we can talk about it in a year." She spoke in an exaggeratedly businesslike voice as the others laughed. "Wait. I just thought of something: In my defense, I have a snow plow guy now. We just haven't had any snow."

"I did not know that," David said. "And I realize you don't ask me to do these things. I just can't _not_ help when I'm there. Or maybe I'm not there, but I think you need help. You are good with a shovel, though. But a snowplow guy—thank you from the bottom of my heart. I don't care if it makes me sound old—thank you."

———⟫●⟪———

They were making love—not something that happened more than every two weeks or so. Kate, who like him, rarely spoke, whispered, "It's okay if you have thoughts of Jane…I mean, I don't want you to feel guilty. It's not like we really control our thoughts. So, if you think about her when we're..." Uncharacteristically demure, she finished with "doing this."

"Doing this?" David teased, mostly to buy some time before reacting. After the first time he had questioned her, he had only asked Kate once more if it hurt her to picture him and Jane. She had brushed off the question with *I haven't changed my mind.* She had never asked him to buy a new mattress or even which side of the bed Jane had slept on. Didn't she care? Did she want to needle herself? Perhaps she only cared about *now.* For now, she was healthy. Now her husband was in their bed. Now she was loved, and while their history and children were part of the equation, it was still love and not duty or handcuffs.

He knew Kate would have let him leave and wished him well, but how can you leave a woman who loves you that much, and who you have loved and now love again? He had the thought months earlier, and it occurred to him, again, that she even took some degree of pride in the fact that he had fallen in with Jane, that he had been able to sidestep the highest order of correctness—and then pride again later when he said yes to something outrageous. She *liked* this new version of him—this man who could tolerate making people he cared about angry, who could withstand gossip of an unknown flavor—a man who would accept more than his share.

He never asked Jane about any of this either. He was certain she experienced something ranging from simple awareness to pain at the thought of him and Kate, and he also believed that she felt his absence, though she never let on. He was sure she would say, *It was my choice and it's my responsibility to deal with.* He knew that Jane might find someone else, though he never had the sense that she was looking. If that happened, he planned to behave well, but as Kate liked to remind him, no one ever knows what they'll do.

He thought sometimes that if he had loved Jane more or better, he would have kept Kate's offer to himself. He'd been selfish—or—he had let Jane make her own decision. There were two ways to look at it. But it was done, and he mostly succeeded in not thinking about losing her. He couldn't make himself dwell on menace like he used to—except the fear of Kate relapsing. That was with him and, he knew, with her. She didn't talk about his retirement or grandchildren or old age.

Now, before he had a chance to answer, Kate said, "I think about her sometimes. Not that I'm making love to her, but that I *am* her and you're making love to me—as her. I guess I'm just saying that we don't need to pretend she doesn't exist."

She had explained to him long ago that women are so inundated with the sexualized female image that they can easily picture being someone else. So their fantasy isn't that they're making love to another woman, but that they *are* another woman—being made love to by their husband—or whichever male they've invited into the fantasy.

It confused the researchers at first, and they mislabeled it lesbian attraction. Such a transmutation had never occurred to David, but it made sense when she explained it, and more and more sense as he later studied the volume of stimuli that, while directed at men, couldn't fail to affect women too.

What he said now was, "Good to know. Turn over."

"Okay, but why?"

"How else can I pretend you're her?"

She laughed, as he knew she would, and pulled him towards her. She began to move again and he moved too. He had never confided any fantasies to Kate, though he always had the sense she wouldn't have minded. Now, she had brought Jane into the room, and while he believed her that she didn't suffer over the idea that his thoughts included Jane, he wanted to last a long time so he didn't think about either woman for a while, and then he did, and they came at the same time, which they used to do easily, but hadn't for years.

He waited for his heart to slow and then said, "I think it's just possible that I will never need Viagra."

They turned on their sides and he held her. "Jane and I don't do anything you and I don't do." Had he said that right? "I mean we do the same things."

He couldn't see her face, but she sounded pleased when she pulled his arm tighter around her and said, "Well, you always were more of a frequency guy."

"And never bored."

"I want to ask you something." Kate directed this to David, though Jane was present too. In fact, they were in her living room; David and Kate had walked over one beautiful Saturday afternoon to return a coat she left in David's car.

"You can have anything you want," David said promptly.

"Really? What if I wanted us to become foster parents?"

"Then I guess then that's what we would do."

"Well, it's a dog that I want. I know we said we'd never have a dog again, but I want one. It might have to be a puppy because of the cats."

"I've never had a dog," Jane said quickly, "I might want one too."

"You want a dog? That's a surprise," Kate said.

"Why! I mean, why?"

"You like things so nice—kind of perfect."

"So do you." Jane said this as David watched, amused, as if he were following a Ping-Pong game. Back to Kate. "But I've lived with young children—I got over it."

"I'm still going to think about it." Jane had already been thinking about it, about what would give her house the feeling of inhabitation it too often lacked. Having a dog meant she would have to stay home more. She would have to decide if being home and having more time for David was a good or bad thing.

"Why a dog, Kate?" he asked. She spoke of the future so rarely, and a dog was definitely a future-oriented concept.

"I want to do *everything*. Learn to sail a small boat alone, be outside in a hailstorm, stay up all night once a year—but not on a plane. Raise a dog again."

She was definitely talking about a future, however odd her list was. David tried to appear to be considering the dog idea in a fair, unbiased way, until he heard Kate say, "I also might want to have sex with a new person before I die. Someone I like." She looked at Jane and smiled. "A man."

David put his water glass down hard. "No. Absolutely not." Both women stared at him in disbelief. He had completely forgotten the possible new him who might not be jealous.

"Look, I met Jane when you weren't...around. And then you came back and gave permission. I didn't ask. You insisted. There was no contract or quid pro quo." He spat out the last three words. "I've always hated the thought of you with anyone else. Why would that have changed?"

The women seemed to know that Kate's longing meant nothing negative about him. And he knew it too. But he didn't want anyone else to touch Kate. Or Jane. It wasn't fair or rational and he had no veto power. If it happened, it would make him crazy, but wasn't all happiness just a moment, a slight turn into some crazy-making loss?

Without giving any sign she heard him, Kate said sadly, "I probably wouldn't meet anyone."

"There's the internet." Jane offered. "Do you really have to like him?" David glared at her. If this conversation had taken place in the first weeks of their experiment, he might have guessed that Jane wouldn't mind if Kate paired off with someone else, making him and Jane a couple by default. Now he only saw a helpful friend; her expression was guileless, her amusement and fondness open and transparent. Good for her and Kate. But she was annoying the hell out of him.

"When I was young, it just had to be someone really good-looking and hard to get," Kate said.

"So you were easy to get?" David asked. He and Kate had never wanted or needed to discuss this topic, but here it was.

"I was easy to get for someone who was hard to get," Kate said, her voice matter-of-fact. "Besides, promiscuity is just a way to travel for people who don't like to leave home."

"Ani Di Franco," Jane said. "Good one."

"David was the first really attractive man I met who didn't seem to know it, or use it. He was kind and sweet."

"Is that really a good thing?" David asked, worrying, not for the first time, that it wasn't.

"Oh, yes. That first night after you rescued me at the party, I decided that I would marry you. That's why I didn't have sex with you then. I was afraid it'd be too *fast*—remember that word? I didn't want to be too fast to be considered someone to marry."

"And I thought you did it to torment me."

"Wait," said Jane. "Rescued? What's that about?" So, taking turns interrupting each other and, despite having never told the whole story to anyone else, they remembered the facts identically.

Later, David wondered if Kate had introduced this topic—he didn't know what words to use—*taking a lover*—to deflect him from his opposition to a dog. He didn't think she was that strategic. She probably wanted both a dog and a novel sexual experience. Regardless, it had worked, and the dog now seemed like an entirely harmless idea.

CHAPTER NINETEEN

David was in a bar in Phoenix with a group from a historians' conference, his first since Kate's return. Every surface seemed to be laminated, and the air-conditioning was set on destroy-the-planet cold. A chair from another university, Floyd Franklin, must have started drinking in his room after the last meeting.

"I thought you'd bring one of your sister-wives along with you," Floyd said, though in a pleasant tone. "Or both. Too exhausted? Looking for a third?"

Kate wouldn't come with him. "I can't shop that much," she said, and Jane, apologetic, explained, "Maybe San Francisco, but not Phoenix. Tell me if you have any meetings in Sedona, though." So here he was, alone and apparently fair game.

Franklin's line seemed rehearsed. No one laughed. David skipped the part of trying to figure out who gossiped and thought only of punching him. His right hand began to quiver. He could so clearly imagine the satisfaction of hitting the guy's fleshy jaw. He wanted to defend himself. He wanted to tell Floyd to tend to his one wife, whom David had met at previous meetings, and who struck him as lonely and ignored.

"Yeah, they're both really, really busy," he said finally, and everyone started breathing again. Tucker raised his glass. "To love and history. To history and love." A few minutes later, Franklin, sitting on a chair added at the end of the booth, left to use the bathroom. Three of the remaining four threw down a pile of bills, hoping to exit the bar and have dinner somewhere without him. "We'll tell him we thought he had left," Tucker said. "He's on that early panel."

"No, I'll stay," said the fourth, a quiet man whose name David hadn't quite gotten. "I have to work with him. He's not a terrible guy—terrible social skills, though. You go. It's fine."

When the remaining three settled in at a new place and had drinks in front of them, the youngest, Aaron, whom David had met just that day, raised his glass. "To David, who almost hit Floyd Franklin but decided words are better. If only history were more like that."

"Hear! Hear!" Tucker said. "But it would have been great. Really great."

"Sorry, man," David said. "Maybe next time."

Later, watching the weather on the oversized screen that nevertheless produced the usual bad picture, he was glad, of course, that he hadn't been an asshole. And he was happy to be without a roommate. He always paid whatever premium the cost-cutting university required for a single room, knowing his chances of decent sleep disappeared with even a non-snoring, congenial roommate. He saw that it was, as promised, snowing at home, and he thought about Jane and Kate, sleeping or perhaps lying awake, listening for the comforting back-and-forth of the snow plows, as lovely a sound as a late-night train whistle.

Hearing the plows, he always felt taken care of—not by God but by the idea that people had civilized themselves to the point of pooling their beads and selecting some strong men to clear the roads so the business of living could continue. He hoped the men would finish their routes in time to radio each other so they would know whether to meet for breakfast at Big Boy or Steak and Shake or Jessie's Chuck Wagon, in business for ninety years, which was too small to hold them all comfortably, but where the waitresses would fuss over the exhausted men, and one would give her nephew, the newest member of the crew, a proud kiss.

He was glad to know that if there were more than a few inches, Jane's snow guy would come, and the neighbors would take care of Kate if the snow was too deep for a shovel.

He watched the screen for a few more minutes. The weather in Florida wasn't good either—citrus—and then fell asleep. His last thought was to wonder if there were other men in the hotel not watching porn. Do men buy porn and watch with their col- league-roommates? Were there others who didn't want to peruse the selection? "No titles will appear on your bill," the enticement read. *Good one-line poem,* Jane would say.

Then he slept.

—➤●◄—

Kate and David and Jane had been out in public with Tom and Lucy a few times and with Dylan and Jack twice, but they had never gone anywhere just the three of them. David couldn't remember whose idea it was, but there was a band that rarely played that they all wanted to see. "We've probably been in the same crowd listening to them or dancing near each other," Kate said, sounding pleased at the idea. David wanted to not care what people thought, and he believed he was doing better at this since his moment with the history conference *arsehole.* Ian had liked the story, outraged on David's behalf, and surprisingly not disap- pointed that David hadn't hit Franklin. "You were angry enough to, mate. That's enough for me."

And now, faced with the big night out being planned around him, what was his choice? To stay home? Neither Kate nor Jane had volunteered to drop out or scare up other friends, and why should they? Why should they be the ones to give, and give things up, to always *alternate*?

Still, sitting at a small table they'd been lucky to grab, David felt self-conscious. The large bar managed to be a place where the college crowd, post-college cohort, and baby boomers coexisted peaceably, and he would know a good twenty percent of each category. The lead singer was a former student, charismatic and smart. Kate would have delivered some of the young ones. Jane probably knew their grandparents. He tried to savor the micro-brew he was sipping and feel the music, which was as good as he remembered. Apparently, it was irresistible. Kate wanted to dance.

"I don't want to be a spectacle," he said pleadingly.

"We're a spectacle already."

"There are degrees," he said. He saw that Jane was watching them with interest but didn't speak. "Besides, what would Jane do?"

"She'll dance with us—or with that professorial guy who can't stop staring at her." Kate raised her eyebrows and nodded slightly to the right. He made himself not look and saw that Jane didn't change her gaze either. He doubted there was such a man waiting to pounce on her.

"That's fine. I'll dance with Jane then." Kate nodded towards the moving bodies—all ages represented. "If she'll have me." Jane stood up promptly and the two women moved through the crowd to carve out a space.

Left alone, he saw a group across the room—a hiring

committee from another department, showing a candidate the town nightlife. Several of them were watching Jane and Kate and then turned to study him before glancing back at the women. He looked away and saw that Don and Martha had arrived and were approaching him on their way to the dance floor. Martha reached the table first and leaned down to say in his ear, her voice low and intense, "For God's sake, David."

He had never heard her use the word in an unofficial way. "I'm not a fan of what you're doing, but either do this or don't. Don't you *dare* waste a moment on embarrassment." Kate had been close-mouthed about what Martha thought of them. "Less outraged than Claire, less sad than my parents—more mystified than anything" was all she would tell him. Martha took his hand and he resisted at first, but it would have been more obvious to fight her, so he stood and followed her and Don onto the dance floor, where he surprised the women.

Kate gave him a happy grin and Jane smiled and backed up a little to make room for him. He danced, unsure as always when not holding a partner, about what to do with his arms. He had studied others for years but never satisfactorily answered the question. He had even Googled the subject, and it helped to know that the topic was under discussion. Hold them up, he'd read, but it was hard advice to follow.

He heard the opening chords and worried that his former student was teasing him—the band didn't do many covers. *I've got seven women on my mind.* The student's mother worked for Jane and Lucy, and he would know the situation. Just then, the singer found David in the crowd and tipped his hat. It didn't feel like ridicule. The middle-aged dancers sang the *ooh ooh ooh* parts, while the young ones bounced and looked amused, though by the fourth repeat, they joined in too. The band knew how to prevent people from leaving the floor, and the three of them danced for a long time until they were sweaty and out of breath. When the pace slowed, the sign that a break was next, they found their table and sat, flushed, exhausted, and oblivious to any observers.

After Kate caught her breath, she said, "Do you remember, David, how the boys said once that they didn't actually hate seeing us dance? They didn't go out of their way to watch us, but if they didn't avert their eyes in time, it was okay. We played it really cool, but we were so flattered. It made me very self-conscious at the next family wedding, but it was worth it."

He remembered how embarrassing it was to learn he was being so openly judged by his kids, though happy to be given what was, for the boys, high praise. "I do remember," he said. "I think they were talking about you."

"Self-deprecation is not your best trait," Jane said, but she was smiling.

When the band resumed, the dance floor became so crowded that they stayed seated and listened. David realized with some shock that he couldn't remember where he would be going after the bar. He knew it had been decided. How could he tune out information that was so completely interesting to him? He had been trying to become a better listener and a more careful speaker so that he didn't repeat himself or say, "I could have sworn I told you that." He was continually working on listening without tuning out midway through. The more immersed he had become in writing his book, the more he had to fight the temptation to compose sentences in his head when he should be listening.

Despite his intentions, had he actually become careless, habituated to this undeserved bounty? He felt Kate press her leg against his and he had his answer. In the next minute, Jane said she'd have to be leaving soon. *Of course.* Lucy and Tom's babysitter with the curfew—Jane was taking over so they could stay out late. He had been told this information and then didn't store it in his memory. David believed, and this was not false humility, that each woman will tire of him if he acts as if he's more important or valuable than either of them. In fact, they will probably band together and leave him. He did not want to be a man who treated a woman as if she were invisible or inaudible. He wanted to be a good listener, and not just good for a _man_. He would take tonight's lapse seriously.

Jane watched David, who seemed to be concentrating on something—he looked like he was doing a math problem in his head. She hoped he was having a good time. He worried too much about others' opinions, and yet he seemed to have let go of that tonight. Jane knew she would have been glad to hear him pull in her driveway later, but she also felt able to leave them here without anguish. Needing less is a form of wealth, she decided, and perhaps just as important as _having_. When she stood to leave, he stood to walk her to her car. She tried to dissuade him—"I'm parked so close"—but Kate insisted and David wouldn't back down. At her car, he leaned into her, and without looking to see who might be around, kissed her and said "I love you," even though it wasn't their custom.

———⟶●⟵———

Later that night, he and Kate sat on their front porch, not talking. He was quiet because he was marveling at the sweet strangeness of the evening, but Kate, it turned out, was quiet because she needed to tell him something.

"While you were gone, at your meetings, I was with someone," she said, and took a deep inhale, as if she'd been holding her breath. " Once. Twice. I mean one evening."

She had spoken so softly, he made her say it again.

"I won't make you ask questions," she said. "I'll tell you and you'll have to stop me if you don't want to know."

"Tell me."

"It was William." He noticed she said *was*.

"I think you know him a little. The relatively new guy from Kansas. You know how quiet he is. And his wife left him last year."

David remembered him. They'd served on a committee together, and William was so shy that it was hard to notice either his absence or his presence. Anything he said was smart and well received, but then he'd lapse into silence again. *Of course* he would confide in Kate. His misery made him talkative and more interesting, she explained.

"It wasn't pity," Kate clarified. "He's smart and attractive and I knew he wouldn't do me any harm."

"Well, he might fall in love with you."

"That isn't harm in itself," she insisted. "But anyway, that isn't what's going to happen."

They sat in silence. David thought he had never heard her make a more naïve statement. She looked miserable. That was something.

"So, I know we aren't even now," he said finally, "but are we even now?"

"This wasn't about payback or scorekeeping."

"What was it about?"

"I did it because it's the kind of thing almost everyone wants to do. And I thought I could do it without losing you." She looked up and met his eyes. "But I couldn't do it without telling you."

"Right. Afterwards." He sounded aggrieved and suddenly didn't like himself very much for it. "So, Kate," he went on, but gentler, "It was…was it what you were looking for?"

"Well, someone new…you and I both know how much fun that was, before we met. I was sort of old Kate. I mean young Kate. I mean Kate before…all this. He was kind of amazed. I guess his wife found sex a lot of work. And the results were unpredictable."

"Amazing Kate," he said, and he knew he sounded a little sad.

She moved a few inches closer. "I think maybe this will benefit you, David. Us. Though maybe not tonight. I get that." They sat quietly for a while longer, and then she went inside.

By the time he got to bed, she was asleep. As he lay close to her and watched the rise of her breath, he took note that his mind hadn't tried to picture Kate and this William. Perhaps he could keep that up. Leave her that much privacy. The thing he thought would kill him, he realized, may not have made him any stronger, but it didn't seem to have killed him. Yet. He gently shook her. "I'm sorry, Kate. Please wake up. Please." He said it again louder, and she roused herself with a soft groan.

"Is this something you want to happen again?"

She turned over to face him. "It would be bad for him," she said. "He needs someone to love him. Maybe someone to help him be more lovable. I can't do that."

It sounded to him like exactly the kind of thing she could do.

"That's not what I want anyway. I don't need *more*."

But wasn't that exactly what she had done? Gone out and gotten more?

———⟫⟪———

Dylan was tired of thinking about his parents. The night before, Lily asked if he thought there was anything between his mother and Jane. He had been trying his best to convey that this question and the entire topic were off limits, but her curiosity had gotten the better of her. When he protested, she looked guilty. "Okay then," he said. "So we're done with this topic?" They were in bed just before falling asleep, and it was their first time together that day.

"I'm sorry. I just want to understand things. I didn't mean to upset you."

He supposed it was natural to be fascinated, and she didn't have his same aversion to the specifics. He turned to look at her. She covered herself with the sheet and then contradictorily said, "I could make it up to you."

"Tomorrow," he said. It would be something to look forward to, and maybe by then his parents would be out of his head. Lily kissed him once before they both rolled apart. As they were drifting off, he said sleepily, "I think she only likes men. My mom, I mean. That's my understanding."

"Not that there's anything wrong with that," she said. She was asleep before he had time to laugh.

Dylan had always considered his parents completely conventional people who married somewhat young and never strayed, either romantically or from responsibilities. He would call them both enthusiasts, but that only came after the last dish was dried and the lawn was short again. His father wanted to be good, and no matter what the everyday rebellions of his youth, Dylan knew him as responsible and considerate—colorless qualities that instead seemed desirable and to be copied. When neither he nor Jack made it past Webelos as Scouts, he knew his dad worried they were missing out on the finishing touches of their moral development. "Look, Dad," he had argued, desperate to be free of the regimentation, chanting, and general dorkiness of scouting, "we're being raised by an Eagle Scout. That has to count for something."

What did it mean that a man who needed to be good, who *was* good, was now so entangled? He and Jack very much wanted their parents to go back to how things were; no one wants unusual parents, especially parents unusual in a new way. He was surprised and baffled to find himself drafted to not only cooperate with, but also explain this plan they'd cooked up.

Perhaps there was a lesson somewhere—something to learn about marriage and love. And friendship, he realized. He had long ago understood his parents as lovers, but perhaps he hadn't begun to understand their friendship. Maybe what seemed like an embarrassing failure of fidelity was, in a different light, not a lapse of anything. Would leaving Jane have been a heroic act or obedience to convention—an obedience that left his mother with a lovesick man who needed to be good at any price?

Dylan didn't think of Lily as a friend yet. To him, she was everything, and someone who was everything couldn't also be a friend. But he knew eventually things would settle down and something else would settle in, taking the place of extreme new love—from rapture to routine. That's what the brain research says.

Lily and he were new enough that he could think they'd be exempt. But probably not. If they were lucky, they would have friendship. He used that word now when he thought about his parents—how they didn't like to beat each other at games, how nice his dad was when she dinged up the car. How his mother wouldn't warm up to his father's parents no matter how hard they tried to charm her, which made them try even harder and ignore his dad even more. She was polite. She remembered their birthdays and engineered regular contact between them and Dylan and Jack, but she did not forgive them for wounding David, and she loyally refused to be charmed.

———————

The next day, Dylan wasn't entirely surprised to be interrupted by a rare call from his brother. Family issues were in the air and, in any event, he would have called Jack soon. Jack had timed his call for Dylan's forty-minute lunch break, and Dylan set his sandwich aside to listen.

"I've been studying with someone, Erica, and she asked why I seem so post-traumatic. Did my parents go through a horrible divorce, or what? Through all the years of Mom being ill, no one has ever asked that. They seemed to accept that I'm this dark—or maybe it's light—cynical person. No-drama Jack."

Dylan was surprised to hear this. He had always felt Jack's grief to be visible, though of course he had his own grief to guide him. He'd heard various adults worry about Jack too, but he supposed young people wouldn't see it or would mistake it for some appealing detachment.

"Well, what are you doing? I mean what do you think she sees?"

"I didn't think I was doing anything, but—and this is going to sound stupid—but at least recently, since Mom came back, I realize I've been keeping everyone safe. Well, Mom mostly. You all seem to be having a lot of fun. Everyone's in love with at least one person. So I'm like Grandma, worrying for all of us, but what good did all her worrying do? I think I'm like the sacrifice—I won't get too happy—so long as you don't punish my mother. So hooking up is okay. It's…" He paused here but finished gamely with, 'It's nothing."

Dylan understood how Jack might feel it wasn't safe to be

happy. He wouldn't ridicule this superstitious bargain. Scientists are as prone to superstition as anyone. They just recognize it for what it is. He knew he could give Jack a pep talk—offer to share the worrying, gently expose the superstition. But what he thought Jack wanted or needed to do was tell him about Erica. So he said, "Who's tutoring who?"

"Who?" Jack said, and Dylan got the joke. In the old days, their mother would have said, "Whom, Dylan. The second one is the object." Now, luckily, she didn't care about that kind of thing. Dylan had the impression that she wanted to spend as little time as possible mothering them, as if friendship—there's that topic again—with her sons was the thing that counted most now.

Jack proceeded to describe to him in great detail, and with reasonably correct grammar, about his new acquaintance, whom he had never touched and who seemed interested in him—not in acquiring him, but in getting to know him, and how he found he could remember their conversations almost verbatim.

Dylan stopped himself from offering platitudes like *just take it slow,* because if he had learned something recently, it was that he didn't know anything predictable about love. He had thought that he didn't want to have a child before thirty, and that he would always be completely strict about birth control, and then a few weeks ago, he and Lily were completely stupid about it, and he felt more curious than worried about the outcome. It didn't seem like a disaster, and if his mother were to be around to meet her grandchild, that would soften the blow of his master schedule being disrupted. But mostly, he just didn't feel very in charge of things.

Of course, he and Jack had wanted his parents to choose *normal* and status quo, to reunite without complication. He had thought his parents would tidy up their lives for his and Jack's sake and for the others who objected with varying degrees of insistence. But he had predicted wrong. They had fretted, but then not actually cared much what other people thought.

So what he said was, "She sounds great. Don't fuck it up. Whatever that means."

"Remember opposite days at school? Clothes on inside out. Last period first." Jack answered his own question. "I just have to do the opposite."

———⟶⦿⟵———

"I'm going to call Dylan about his birthday," Kate said to David, and then they both looked up at the ceiling. The cats were rampaging overhead; their thundering steps sounded more like small horses than eight-pound felines. David heard them slide across the tile floor of the bathroom. There was a thump so loud it sounded as if they both ran into a wall, then silence before they resumed the chase.

He remembered Dylan and Jack playing too wildly and then hiding all signs of pain from their collisions. They only wanted to continue the game, and he had admired their toughness. Some of the neighbor kids seemed to treasure every bruise and enjoyed the drama of comfort, but his boys always had something they wanted to get back to. Jack once finished a soccer game with a broken arm—a fact that still embarrasses Kate, the parent on duty and a nurse no less, but he knew he would have been just as taken in by Jack's stoicism.

Kate reached Dylan and, by her expression, it was happy news. He and Lily would take off work early and be home a week from Friday for Dylan's birthday the next day. Saturday birthdays always seemed lucky even though they came around regularly every seven years. Or did Leap Year change that? Who could ever recalculate Leap Year? David liked the whimsical phenomenon of it, though: things are coming out uneven. *I know, we'll add a day!*

"He said we should invite Jane if we want to. What do you make of that?"

"I don't know," he said. The boys seemed to be able to dislike the situation but not dislike Jane. Maybe they didn't even hate it any more but refused to go on record as anything but opposed. "I'm still baffled by them. About what's best."

"No," she said. "You don't always get to do that. You have to say something. In any direction that you want, but something."

David had avoided thinking about this very topic. He hadn't anticipated or welcomed Kate and Jane's emerging friendship, and he'd been surprised to discover nothing harmful about the two of them as friends, nor anything unpleasant about the three of them spending time together, but he had never arrived at any *policies*.

"All right, since you asked, I will tell you this: that during those times when we're together—whether it's just you and me and Jane, or whether there are others around—life to me seems just about perfect."

She looked surprised.

"I don't think about you getting sick again," he continued, "and I forget about my own imminent tumors—and whatever is waiting to strike Jane or the boys. I stop thinking about the press waiting to descend and ruin our lives. I don't even think about *William*." He had worried a lot about William until Kate pledged to tell him every detail about every contact she had with him. And he knew she *had* told him, and none of it was romantic or threatening. In fact, he was a little tired of hearing about William's blossoming post-divorce life. Kate had apparently been a big confidence booster. *Go William!*

"It feels *safe*. I know there's nothing the least bit safe about any of it, but I have the illusion of safety. It's..." his voice trailed away as he concluded, "lovely."

"Well, let's definitely invite Jane then," Kate said, and before he had a chance to laugh, she walked the few steps towards him and despite her much smaller frame, enveloped him in a strong, tight hug.

"Hurry up, guys," Jack called out from the living room. "We've got the film festival ready to roll." The three of them had arrived in time to cook dinner together. Dylan and Lily prepared the only impressive dish they'd mastered, chicken with a very long list of ingredients. "We have to invite different friends to dinner each time," Dylan explained. "And we never give out the recipe." Jack made Caesar salad, as well as brownies-from-a-mix, which was almost like cooking from scratch these days, his mother told him, sounding genuinely impressed.

Kate and David put the finishing touches on the kitchen cleanup and joined the others in front of the TV. While he was washing dishes, David had heard some distant hilarity, but still, he wasn't prepared for the first movie to be *My Favorite Wife*. "It's a 1940 British screwball comedy," Dylan announced. They watched as Irene Dunn, declared dead by the court following a shipwreck, and now rescued and in love with a fellow survivor, returned to her husband, Cary Grant. Kate began to snicker and then laugh, and David found himself joining in.

Dylan periodically fast-forwarded the film, summarizing the skipped plot because they had "a number of movies to get through." Simultaneously, David and Kate grasped the theme of the film festival and laughed harder. At the end of the movie, they applauded and Kate said, "I mean, why would anyone *not* choose Cary Grant?"

Lily said, "I get that now. I hadn't seen him young enough before to understand the fuss."

The next movie, *Too Many Husbands*, also 1940, featured Fred MacMurray, this time thought drowned in a boating accident, only to return to find that Jean Arthur had quickly married his business partner, Melvin Douglas. She discovered that having two formerly inattentive husbands competing for her love was very pleasant and a situation worth drawing out—though only for 81 minutes—and far less with Dylan and Jack's editing. Jack was masterful at summarizing twenty minutes of plot with one compound sentence.

David tried to say, "Is this supposed to be instructive some-how?" but could barely get the words out. They were all tired and silly from laughing.

"I noticed a few useful Cary Grant mannerisms." Jack said. "It's too bad Jane couldn't be here. Or is it?"

"Oh, she will be so annoyed that she missed this," David said emphatically. Jane was visiting her mother. She and Dylan had a surprisingly long phone conversation earlier that day. David thought Kate might not love this, but she seemed only pleased when Dylan passed on Jane's greetings and regrets.

"Now we have a remake of the previous film as a musical, *Three for the Show*," Dylan announced. They settled in to watch as Betty Grable found herself married to both her long lost husband and his replacement.

"Of course, you'll have to decide which one you want more," someone official told her, to which she said, "Why?"

David and Kate tried to sing along with the bits of lyrics they could remember to "I've Got a Crush on You," "Someone to Watch Over Me," and "Just One of Those Things," though the boys allowed them only the first few lines of each song.

"Now, this next one is amazing," Jack announced, as he studied the text on the box. "I doubt you've ever seen it. It's the unfinished footage from Marilyn's last movie. She died before it was completed and, from 1962 to 1990, it was buried in a vault and almost no one saw it."

David realized that he had seen a lot of the clips when they were finally broadcast as part of a documentary. He'd been mesmerized by her sexual power. Until then, he'd kind of wondered about the obsession, but after the swimming pool scene, he got it. They settled into *Something's Got To Give* and watched Dean Martin pretend he wouldn't have immediately sent his new wife packing and hauled his shipwrecked wife off to bed. The pool scene was everything he remembered.

"This would have been the first sound picture to feature a mainstream movie star in a nude scene," Jack read.

"Who had the honor instead?" Lily asked.

Jack consulted his printouts. "Jayne Mansfield, 1963. *Promises, Promises.*"

"Tacky," Dylan offered.

"Never heard of her," Lily said. "Or maybe I did—big blond?"

They ended with *Move Over, Darling*, a remake of Marilyn's aborted effort, with its now-familiar story of Doris Day's return from a lengthy stay on an island with a handsome survivor. James Garner had searched for her for years, but a man can only wait so long, and he had her declared dead just prior to leaving on his honeymoon. Dylan skipped the slow spots but showed all the Don Knotts scenes.

"Well, that was quite a montage," Kate said, over the final

credits. "When was the last time I laughed that much? Though I have to ask, were you boys even the least bit worried that we'd be offended?"

"No, Mom." Jack answered for them both. "We weren't."

Kate looked at Lily quizzically. "I trusted Dylan," Lily said. "Well, I trust him a lot more now that I see you both had fun."

"Did you notice that in every case, the spouse who had been left had to decide between the new spouse and the old one?" Kate said. David saw the boys exchange a micro-glance.

"Oh, well," she said, when it was clear no one else was going to answer. "Those kind of movies were always so puritanical. And punitive. They're lucky no one got killed off for real to teach them a lesson."

———⟡———

Later, in their dark bedroom, Kate whispered, "Are you thinking of Marilyn?" She was on top of him, something that hadn't happened in years, and in the light sneaking past the closed blinds, she looked like his bride. He was glad she was interested tonight. He was glad the kids went out to the bars. He rarely approached Kate. His policy remained the same, he had clarified for her: "If I don't have a fever of 103, then I'm available."

He didn't want her to have to regularly turn him down, or worse, force herself. Still, a few weeks ago, when she returned home from yoga—something about that always got to him—he told her that he *really* wanted to go upstairs with her. She laughed and said okay but he shouldn't expect anything snazzy and he said, "You need to believe me that I don't care—you can lie there and work on the grocery list." She laughed again at his vehemence and they went upstairs. She wasn't able to come and didn't want to keep trying. "It's fine, though, it's really fine—nostalgic, like when I was new at sex and the boys knew nothing, and I couldn't always, and the guy's enjoyment was my payoff. It's fine—altruistic but fine." She had seemed relaxed enough that he believed her.

Now she seemed to be waiting for his answer.

"It's always Marilyn for me," he said. He could just make out her smile. Both of them had stopped moving, and then, almost whispering, he half sang, *What do you see when you turn out the light?*

She took the question seriously. "I know the facts may not support it, but I still feel you're mine."

"I am yours." His voice caught on the words. He didn't care if he cried. He met her look head-on. "If this hurts you, I will find a way to live without her."

"I know you would. I know you would try."

She leaned towards him and they finished making love. It didn't feel exactly sexual. It felt like something else—something sacred—and he was certain that even Kate, for whom sex was becoming, at least sometimes, more like the light and easy thing it used to be, felt the same.

⸺⸱●⸱⸻

David was trying to remember if either he or Kate had asked the boys to call and check in when they reached their respective apartments. As if on cue, the landline rang, followed by Kate's cell and then his. Confused, he and Kate moved towards the home phone but not in time to answer it. They both froze when they heard Martha's message.

"Turn on the evening news," and then, "I'm so sorry. It's on ABC. Maybe the others too, but ABC for sure."

David was the first to find the remote and fiddled with

it, trying to switch from the DVR. Kate took it and located the evening news in time to see a middle-aged couple beaming fondly at an older woman. She looked embarrassed.

"Mrs. Stennick, can you tell us what it was like when the miracle drugs started to work?" The camera stayed on the anchor's falsely bright teeth a moment too long.

The older woman looked at her lap. Why, David wondered, was she doing this? It was so obviously painful.

She must have forgotten the instructions on where to look, so her gaze landed off to the side. "At first, I just thought that other people were being more clear. I thought it was nice that they were speaking up and making more sense. It felt normal. I didn't think much of it at first. I didn't remember that it was about me. That I was the one." Maybe someone motioned because now she looked at the camera. "But then one day I did. I understood I had been the problem."

'Yes," Kate said to the TV. "I remember that part. I get it. *I'm* the problem. I'm the one who was gone."

"Tune in tomorrow for the morning show. We'll have three experts on Alzheimer's and a gentleman from Dallas who was in the same clinical trial. Don't miss 'Back from the Dead.' And remember, we're here for you. And let us hear from you!" The young woman somehow widened her smile, and the camera returned again to Mrs. Stennick, who wasn't expecting it. She looked sad, and though her mic was off, they watched her mouth the word *dead*. David thought she said it as a question.

The phone rang again. "Let's wait," Kate said, and they listened to her father leave a message. "I'll call them while you get back to the boys. I think he was crying. Jesus, how can I put them through anything more?"

Fifteen minutes later, David found her still on the phone,

winding down her conversation. "Yes, Dad, I know I don't have to talk to anyone if I don't want to. And if I do, which I don't, I can set the terms. Got it." She nodded, like a child dutifully memorizing rules. "And I'll come stay with you if I need to. Except you can be found as easily as we can." Her father must have made either a joke or a threat because she laughed, and then they said goodbye. She looked at David quizzically.

"Dylan was driving so we were quick. He heard it from Jack. He basically said, 'This sucks. Tell me what to do.' Jack saw it online. He wonders if they'll find him. He wonders what to say. Then he said not to worry—he's expert at not saying more than he wants to. Did we know this about him?"

Kate looked as if she was trying to make up her mind.

"And Dylan says you can hide out with him and Lily if you need to, though Lily says nothing will stop them. Especially once they figure out the Jane part."

"She will never put up with this," Kate said, and David nodded miserably. He knew she meant Jane.

CHAPTER TWENTY

Kate clicked the remote start but left her car idling prominently in the driveway. She and David snuck out the back door to his car, which was parked one block over. Martha would come by in ten minutes with a spare key and shut Kate's car off. Later that day, Martha reenacted the scene for him.

"Hyenas. Shouting over each other like you see on TV. They'd quiet down any time I opened my mouth. So I asked *them* what time was it. I asked if they knew the chance of rain today. I asked if they had any good lottery numbers. They only followed me for two houses."

David could see that Martha enjoyed having a way to help. And maybe it helped her manage her outrage at the invasion and the fear of how the hounding would affect Kate. He was grateful. And nervous. After work, he and Kate would be on their own getting back into the house. Reporters, duped, are hungry animals.

"Mrs. Sanders, how are you feeling? Do you think you'll have a relapse? Is it true your husband remarried while you were ill? Is she living here? What's her name? Where does everyone sleep?"

David was glad he didn't own a gun. By the fourth day, he wished he did. That morning, the reporters were waiting at the back door, having figured out the ruse. He hoped they were embarrassed it had taken them so long to notice it wasn't really cold enough to warm up a car for ten minutes. Luckily, he hadn't locked the backdoor yet so he and Kate were able to quickly retreat and hide in the house with the shades drawn. After thirty minutes, he called for a taxi, and when it arrived, they ran out the front door. Unbelievably, the reporters were still camped out in the back yard.

"I'm glad the kids didn't major in journalism," Kate said, and they both laughed a little hysterically. The driver looked at them through his mirror, alarmed.

Just before lunch, an acquaintance from the Psychology Department stopped by David's office. This wasn't usual.

"Look, David, I came by to give you a quick lecture in learning theory and schedules of reinforcement. You may have had it in college, but you need a review course. It applies to dealing with the media. Trust me on this."

A few years ago, this well-respected psychologist had been involved with some controversial and misunderstood research that attracted unwanted national attention. David remembered feeling very sorry for the guy.

"If it's better than my fantasies involving automatic weapons, let's hear it."

"You just have to not reward the reporters in any way, and they'll move on. Don't give them any crumbs. Don't say something intelligent that you think they'll quote correctly. Just don't. But you have to remember this: at first they'll get worse."

Sometimes, people are kind in unusual ways.

———⟫●⟪———

David and Jane spoke by phone several times a day. They pretended things were normal, but when he offered to come to her house, he did it half-heartedly, and she didn't hesitate before rejecting the idea.

"I miss you too," she said. "But I can wait. I'm going to stay with Lucy and Tom for a while."

"You shouldn't have to deal with any of this. I feel terrible."

"You mean you and Kate *should* have to deal with it?"

"No," he tried to explain. "I mean that you especially shouldn't have to deal with it."

"I know you know that makes no sense," Jane said. "We're in this together. Some people might even think I was the one most deserving of...a bad outcome." Then she cheered him up by describing the plan to evade the reporters, a scheme in which Tom's sister would leave Jane's house in a memorably purple raincoat purchased at TJ Maxx.

The reporters only tried once to find David and Kate at the university. A bored security force was happy to have a project. Jane's downtown office was always well guarded, though so far no one seemed to have figured out where she worked. David thought that was surprising. The practice had a really good web site.

Tom and Lucy's back deck felt safe enough, surrounded as it was by a tall privacy fence. David and Jane decided to sit outside and share one of the oversized beers Tom stocked.

"This is nice," Jane said. "I was getting claustrophobic. And I missed you. I'm glad you insisted on coming over."

It was David's third time courting her here at her friends' house. Today was the first time the house was empty. He should send Lucy some great flowers for that one. It was nice to be outside without being accosted, but he hoped they'd go inside soon, before the five residents returned. He couldn't tell if that's what Jane was thinking.

"Hello?" a man called. "Hello, is anyone there?" He knocked on the gate and the hardware rattled. "Lucy! Tom! I thought I heard voices."

Whoever it was didn't try to unlatch the gate, so David was pretty sure he wasn't a reporter.

Comprehension crossed Jane's face. She didn't look pleased, but she did get up and walk over to the gate. Her hand shook as she lifted the bar. David went to stand behind her and got a look at the man waiting.

"Jane!"

"Charlie."

"I didn't know where you lived. By that, I mean I never paid any online company to give me your address." He smiled and David watched something uncanny happen to Charlie's face. He went from merely handsome to charismatic. *I want him to like me.* At first glance, David guessed Charlie was ten years younger. Then he remembered he was Jane's age, five years younger, but passing for ten. Or more.

"What are you doing here?" Jane asked.

"The news about you was so extraordinary..."

Charlie seemed at a loss for words. David guessed that didn't happen much.

Charlie tried again. "I manage some investment accounts for your university here. So I thought it was a good time to meet with them face-to-face. Hearing about you was so...unexpected."

This guy seemed totally unperturbed that David was there. He wasn't rude. He included David in his eye contact. He even directed a wry smile at him.

"You heard *about* me. You didn't hear *from* me. You can't think that's an invitation."

"Oh, Jane, of course not. I've gone about this all wrong, and I am very sorry for barging in." He seemed genuinely embarrassed. "It's just that we were married a long time, and it would be nice to catch up. Maybe coffee before I leave? Just coffee?"

She didn't say no.

"I'll have my phone call your phone," Charlie said. "I have your work number." He smiled again at David. "It was nice to meet you," he said, without using his name. In fact, no one had used David's name.

"Well, that was weird," Jane said, after a too-long silence.

He wondered if she would have said more if they hadn't heard Tom and Lucy's out-of-tune Subaru pull into the driveway. Tom got out first and moved to block the gate.

"Groceries," he said, motioning to the trunk, as the kids tried to get past him. They headed back to the car, muttering.

"Quick reflexes," Lucy said. "Was somebody just here? A really nice car just pulled away."

"I'll tell you in a minute," Jane said, and David made his good-byes before walking the six blocks to where he'd left his car, just in case.

———————

It was strange that it wasn't more strange to be talking about this with Kate. He wasn't totally un-self-conscious, but at least he could talk. And not hide anything.

"Tell me again," Kate said. "Surely you've left out something."

"Not really. It was all very fast, and then he was gone and then I was gone."

"And you've not heard anything from Jane in 24 hours. More,

I guess."

"I left her one message."

"I feel like I'm a person who usually knows what to say," said Kate, moving closer to him on the step, and he moved a little too so she could be in the shade. "But I have no idea what to say. Or what's going to happen. I had the impression that he was nothing but a bad memory. An embarrassment."

"Oh my God. First love is such an imprint. We're all sort of ducklings still fixed on the first love object we followed." David leaned in to kiss her. "Look at me. Am I not proof of the power of first love?" He missed Jane, but he didn't feel *amputated* this time. There wasn't anything more he could do, or rather there wasn't anything more he *would* do. He wasn't leaving Kate. And God knows, there wasn't one more thing Kate could do.

He felt pleased with this summation for a few more seconds until he thought of the last time, the time before the news frenzy, when he and Jane were together. When everything he wanted still felt possible. He wondered who had ruined things. Dr. Tsang said he didn't know, and David believed him. The data were still good, the doctor reassured them, but the attention, he agreed, was a miserable consequence.

"You make a good point," Kate said. "First love and new love: powerful drugs both." He saw her examine his face, but whatever she saw, she let it go.

***

Charlie suggested the restaurant of Jane and David's first proper date—the one where at least one of you knows you're going to have sex later—but she steered him across the street to a place she didn't like. He was very picky about food and wouldn't thank her for this. She didn't think she'd be eating anything. Her body felt entirely unreal, without any corporeal needs, as if she were navigating in a dream. They each ordered a glass of wine, and when it arrived, Charlie told the waiter he'd flag him down if they wanted anything more. She thought he looked as anxious as she'd ever seen him. It made him seem like a different person.

"I'm going to say something stupid, and you won't believe me, for which I do not blame you, but I still want to say that I am not the same person you knew."

Jane summoned up a neutral smile.

"I mean I am not full of shit any more." He sat back. Did he think he had explained himself?

"Look," Jane said, "you can tell me anything you want, but I am not asking you any questions." This came out harsher than she intended. He didn't seem to notice.

"I hurt somebody else after you, Jane. I didn't think I would, but I did, and she was a really good person too. She trusted me. I was so miserable, and I guess it seemed like a convincing amount of misery." He gave a half smile. She would have to say he looked embarrassed. Did she even know he was capable of such a thing?

"I did finally get some help then. I can't say that I figured out the whys of my behavior. It was as if I thought that if I *could* do it, I should do it. It was like *squandering* to say no."

Jane made a non-committal sound. She didn't think she would stay much longer.

"I understand the rest of it. I understand that I flirted and seduced. Women didn't just knock on my car door." He hadn't touched his wine. "I *groomed* them."

She had never heard him use this tone of voice before. It was disgust, she realized. Or at least that was a possibility.

"I could make it seem as if they made the first moves, and

sometimes they did, but usually it was me. New bodies, new people. That's powerful. I know you must understand some of what I'm talking about. The sex part. You know, it wasn't that I didn't know *how* other people could be faithful. I didn't know *why*."

She saw him look to his left and warn off the waiter. "Actually, I *don't* understand what you mean," she said. "I mean, the power of variety—yes, I get that. But I don't understand risking everything—ruining everything. That's addict stuff."

He gave a slight grimace. "Thank you for using that word. I feel pretty protective about the 'A' word. People don't like it. They think it's a shield. Did you know men have trouble finding good male therapists to work with? All too often, it turns out that their therapist envies them."

She nodded. She knew the next thing would be David and Kate. Charlie was about to carefully draw her out, and then find parallels between her and him, and then close the deal. Some deal. Something. Yes, she realized, he wants to find common ground between them—that his infidelities and her current situation were the same. Similar enough. Similar enough for him to be absolved.

"I'm glad you found someone good. I liked David. How he stepped back and trusted you. No macho stuff." Charlie swallowed hard a few times, and then took a sip of water. He set the glass down too hard and some spilled. "But I'm still going to be an idiot and say that if you wanted, if it would be better, if there's some part of what you have that isn't what you need…we could, we could get to know each other again."

Jane leaned back sharply and her back hit the wood of the booth. If she hadn't met Kate, if her life hadn't taken the turn it did, then this would be the most surprised she had ever been.

PART IV
AFTER

Jane went to the fridge and brought out two key lime pies. "Every last lime was squeezed by me," she said. "And since I missed Dylan's birthday, we have to consider one pie to be his.

"One of the best gifts on record," Jack declared, and Dylan said, "Better late pie than no pie."

Kate had cobbled together unused remnants of decades of birthday candles from their tiny boxes in the back of various drawers until the mismatched assortment totaled Dylan's age. "I think you'd better hurry," she said, as she and David finished lighting them.

"You all know what I'm wishing for," Dylan said, "but I think it will still come true." If his birthday were six months ago, he would have wished for Jane to disappear, but he no longer wanted a vote on their lives, except to wish that his mom stay healthy. He and his mother exchanged a look, and she blew him a kiss across the table.

He acquitted himself well, but as the candles shortened, he motioned for his brother to help.

"Thanks, dude, but you spit on my pie," said Dylan.

"Hey," Jack said, "I didn't have time to prepare myself."

Then no one spoke except for occasional inadvertent sounds of pleasure. The cats slept coiled and overlapping in the copy-paper box that had held the pies. They woke periodically to take in the lingering smell of fish tacos until Fred, resigned, left.

"Watch him go," Jane said, "looking for all the world as if he has somewhere to be."

With his mouth still full, Jack asked about her visit with her mother. "If it rained all the time, what did you end up doing?"

"Her new boyfriend came over so I could meet him," Jane said. "She's been doing online-dating for like twenty years, and she's finally met someone good. It's really promising." She smiled. "She wants me to try it too—I've never gotten around to telling her about this lot." She had picked up a few of Ian's lines. "She wrote up a profile for me. I'm quite a bit younger than I realized—and a triathlete."

"Well, she only wants the best for you." It was Dylan's joke, at which Jane loudly laughed, which caused him to blush.

Everyone reached for seconds of the pie and they were quiet again until they rose as a group to clear the dishes. David sorted out the chaos by making three people sit down. The dishes were left to soak, and they moved to the front porch to play Jack and Dylan's choice, "Trivial Pursuit."

"Dylan, you have to let us each skip one category," Kate wheedled. "Dad and I never get past sports. Once, we never even got a second turn." David spoke up to agree with her. He liked sports but found himself unable to memorize anything—like history was for some people.

"I don't know, Mom," Jack answered for Dylan. "What about geography? Don't you need to sit that one out also?"

"Okay, there's that, too."

Dylan quickly appraised everyone and paired his dad with Lily, Jane with Jack, and himself with his mom. "There," he told Kate. "We'll have everything covered. You do literature and culture of the baby boom and I'll do everything else."

Jane said, "Do I detect a little over-confidence? Pride goeth..."

David studied his family in the slant of the evening light. When the rays moved lower, they would need to lean and bend to protect their eyes but, for now, everyone was still as they watched Dylan set up the game. We look like a tableau, David realized, and then he told them this, though he had to explain it to the boys—one more odd thing that people did before electricity.

"That's a good book topic," Jack suggested. "Weird stuff people did before TV. Like singing for each other after dinner. Is it possible that men started wars out of boredom?" Jack had been thinking about Erica and how she would fit right in here. He could picture her on the remaining small wicker chair, the rickety one, and how she would insist it was fine even though everyone would see it wobble as she spoke.

They began to play, forgetting at first who their teammate was or sometimes remembering but impulsively volunteering a clue to the others. "Jeez," Dylan said, after David gave an answer to another team. "We know you're all evolved, wonderful people, but it's a game. Compete. Try to win. You don't have to share *everything*."

Kate picked up the small spray bottle they used to keep the cats off the table and Dylan pretended to flinch. They played a few more evenly matched rounds, though David had apologized to Lily in advance for all the answers he wouldn't know. He was distracted by a powerful sense of contentment—a contentment tinged with fear around the borders as if the tableau contained their abundance, but just beyond it lay distant worries: a small lapse of memory, an icy road, cells gone out of control. If he looked too hard, the future seemed frightening. If he just lived and waited, it was merely unknowable. He knew they weren't through with the press, and that if the good results continued, they'd be in and out of hiding. The press are like mosquitoes. Sometimes you just have to stay inside.

"It's your turn, Dad," Jack said. "Lily can't possibly know this one—and she must be tired of carrying your..." he paused and ended with, "hapless—your more-than-usual hapless game."

"Oh!" David said. "Was I driving?" The Sanders exploded in laughter. Jane and Lily looked mystified and the other four began to tell the joke, competing to give their version of two elderly ladies riding together, one unaware that she was the driver.

"Stop," Kate said. "If we're rolling out a dementia joke, I think I should be the one to tell it," and they laughed more and then quieted enough to let her.

One of the boys had left the living room TV on after checking a score. The sound of the promo for the eleven o'clock news traveled out to the porch, though reduced to a murmur, and none of them was close enough to hear: "My husband came back from Alzheimer's. The biggest wonder drug trial yet."

Oblivious, and free again to sit on the front porch, they sipped their beer, except Kate, who stopped at less than one, and Lily, who was pregnant with the baby she hadn't announced yet, even to Dylan, and who only pretended to drink. She knew he would remember the recent middle-of-the-night moment when they woke to find themselves having sex. Even when they woke more fully, neither pulled away. When Dylan asked if she was okay with what happened, she said she thought she was. *Good*, he said, as he pulled her on top of him. *I'm tired. You do the work this time.*

Lily was afraid. Not so much of the lottery of a healthy baby, and not so much of the juggling or finding the right daycare, or even of the nights to come worrying about a teenager driving stupidly, or drugs or binge drinking, things even she and Dylan, comparatively sensible as teenagers go, still had done too much of. She was afraid of her child having a middle-age illness in middle age or, like Kate, an old-age illness in middle age, or that by then maybe everyone would have some kind of cancer, having poisoned themselves and the planet with exhaust and plastic bits, like in a Margaret Atwood novel. She was afraid of an apocalypse, and that order would break down and their child would never know safety. And if not their child, she was afraid for their grandchildren, who will live in a foreign and unimproved version of an already brutal world. She was afraid of things she couldn't imagine, along with everything she could.

And yet she was extravagantly happy, as if she had waited her entire life for this child—even though she'd scarcely given children a conscious thought, and when she did, it was always *not yet, not convenient,* as if a child was a nuisance, a dentist appointment arrived too soon. She needed these last hours before she told Dylan because she knew he would be afraid too, and she wanted him to name his fears if he wanted to, and she would be calm and agree with him that everything he feared was possible. Her neutral acceptance of his disaster list would perversely disarm him, as agreement does, and they would set catastrophe aside. Then she could give in to the abundance of her delight, as if they had done something remarkable, as if they had invented something.

Lily looked up to see Kate watching her and she saw that Kate had guessed her secret. She was looking at Lily and at the prop of a beer bottle her hand, and they made eye contact. Kate smiled broadly. Lily smiled too, her finger to her lips. The two of them kept looking at each other, trying not to giggle.

David turned to Kate. "What are you so happy about?" he said. "You do realize you're not winning?"

Kate ignored him and mouthed the words "I love you" to Lily, and David turned again and said, "You love who?" and she said, "I love it all. I love the whole damn mess." She touched Jane's forearm. "I'm really glad you're here. We're going to have so much fun. There will be more birthdays. And then weddings and babies. Or babies and weddings."

She might not be there, but these things will take place. For the first time, Kate found herself counting on the idea that Jane could be there for the boys. Never before had she delegated to Jane—even mentally—any aspect of being their mother, but tonight the thought was a comfort, an odd insurance policy. And David. David would be sad again, but less alone. Anxiety was missing tonight, and her mind felt clear and deceptively young. It was as if she herself was savoring an unannounced pregnancy.

Dylan observed his mother and Lily communicating in some archetypal, female code. He tensed at first, but it didn't seem to be about him, so he returned his gaze to the game board, stopping first to watch his father, made whole by a change of fortune and somehow tolerating the perils of happiness.

"And dogs," Jane said. "Don't forget dogs." She didn't know if it was the celebration or the lighting or the perfection of the air— the ideal mixture of balm and warmth, with a breeze so slight it felt like breath—but she knew she'd never forget this evening. Perhaps she hadn't needed as much as she thought she did—or she needed something different than she had believed. The exposure by the press had resulted in a gift for her—the chance to know Charlie again and to hear him say what he was and what he had done. She believed everything he said, and she thought his good intentions were real. But she was loved by someone who didn't have to work hard to be good, and so after she and Charlie talked for three hours, she kissed him on both cheeks and left the restaurant that she had never liked.

David smiled at Jane. He had come to accept that he would soon be walking one or more dogs in the rain, though he did plan to propose that Jane and Kate consider sharing one animal. Or maybe not. Maybe he would learn what kind they wanted and buy each whatever she desired. No, they would want to choose for themselves. But he'd go along and he'd be enthusiastic. He didn't really mind walking in the rain. He was pretty sure he had a firm hold on gratitude, and he wasn't going to fuss about dogs. David didn't know what had happened to Jane after Charlie tracked her down. She was out of his life for a few long days and then she was back. One afternoon, he looked up and she was standing at the threshold of his office. "There's nothing to tell," she said.

Lily also watched the slant of the light on the porch. She wanted to look at Dylan and Jack and imagine them as boys. She wanted to listen to David and Jane and Kate try to sneak hints to help their competition, as if everyone could win. She had the thought—and it was a new one—that time goes by just slowly enough to trick you into thinking life is long. She wasn't quite ready to tell anyone about the future. She needed to watch them all a while longer. With love and amazement, she needed to study her strange new family before she stepped onto center stage.

In the deepening angle of the sun, the young looked radiant. The same light was kind even to the three aging faces. Though realistically there might not be many more easy years, the three of them looked forward, trained as they all were to think not of death but of love and work.

The young, still young enough to imagine their parents always with them (even Dylan and Jack had resumed this fantasy), looked up from the colored plastic wedges and the messy pile of spent trivia and saw the game abandoned for the beauty of the night. They smiled too as they looked all around and waited for the rest of it.

ACKNOWLEDGEMENTS

With thanks to:

Bruce Bortz and Bancroft Press,
for loving this book and taking a chance

Stanford Creative Writing Workshops,
where the first chapter was finally written

Sandy Linabury, a first reader, and
Ann Speltz, a final reader

Elizabeth King for kindness

My parents, who let me read anything,
at any age, from their jammed bookshelves

My sons, who taught me what smart and
funny young men might think and say

My husband, who said, "I think
we can get along on only my income"

Andy, who seemed to think I could do this--
before it even occurred to me to try

Every scientist working to cure the loss of memory
and every family that has lost someone

ABOUT THE AUTHOR

Deborah Carol Gang's beautifully written and ultimately uplifting debut novel will remind readers of Anne Tyler's lyrical and slightly off-kilter novels. And Tyler, who steadfastly continues an anti-blurb campaign she began in 1986, wrote the author to "tell you directly how much I enjoyed *The Half-Life of Everything.*"

Gang's short fiction has been published in *Literarymama*, *Bluestem Journal* and *The Driftless Review*. Her poetry has appeared in *JJournal/CUNY*, *New Verse News*, *The Michigan Poet*, *Arsenic Lobster*, and *The Liberal Media Made Me Do It*. Her research as a clinical psychologist has been published in *Education and Treatment of Children*.

Originally from Washington, D.C., she moved to St. Paul, Minnesota to attend Macalester College and then attended graduate school in Kalamazoo, Michigan, where she remained for her work as a psychotherapist and because of her love of Lake Michigan. She now writes full-time.